# MY BABY MAMA IS A LOSER

## QUAN MILLZ

# CHAPTER ONE

**BUZZ. BUZZ. BUZZ.**

My hazy eyes slowly lifted opened to the sound of my iPhone buzzing away at the side of my bed. "Man, who the fuck is this?" I grumbled smacking my teeth, slowly moving my hand close to where my phone was at.

It was a hot ass summer afternoon, I could feel the sun piercing the side of my face through my bedroom window. Hours deep into a nap, I was trying my best to get as much sleep as I could before I had to head to my second job. A nigga worked a double last night at my security job, so you already know I was tired as fuck. Damn crackas at the night club I worked at on the North Side were actin' a muhfuckin' fool last night. Shit, I almost had to put my hands one of them Jimmy John's sandwich eatin' peckerwoods.

Anyways...Whoever the fuck this was calling me had better be calling me with some important ass shit. Shit, it better be this lil thick yella bitch I met last night.

I grabbed my phone off my nightstand and took a quick

glance at the screen. I didn't recognize the 773 number. I was hesitant to answer, but something told me this wasn't no telemarketer or a bill collector. Shit, I was staying with my mama still, so I knew I didn't really owe nobody no money. My Charger was paid off, too. And I didn't have any credit cards. Anyways, I went ahead and answered, "Hello?"

"Dre..."

The voice sounded familiar but since I was still in a daze from my nap, I couldn't quite register who it was. "Wassup? Who dis?" I asked cracking my neck.

"This Neicy..."

"Neicy?" Suddenly my eyes widened a bit. I didn't expect my baby mama's sister to be calling me. Why in the fuck was she calling me?!? I didn't even know how this ugly ass bitch even got my number. "Wassup? Why you calling me? How you even get my number?!?"

"Bruh...Listen, don't worry about any of that right now. But look, I don't wanna start no shit or nothin' like that, but you need to come check up on ya triflin' ass baby mama."

"What's going on?" I asked as I sat up in the bed, wiping slight crust out of my eyes.

"Bruh, she on some straight reckless shit, fa real, G. She in the car with some nigga who look like a dope boy. And she got Ariyanna in the back. I think she suckin' this nigga's dick or somethin'. Probably smokin' loud, too."

My head flew back in confusion. "Fuck is you talm'bout?!?"

"Yeah! You heard exactly what I said! Trish in her muhfuckin' car with some nigga I ain't never seen before! He look dangerous, too! And I think she fuckin' this dude while my niece in the backseat!"

"I know you mothafuckin' lyin'! Stop playin' games with me!" I responded smacking my teeth.

"Bruh! I'm not playing games with you! I'm watching her ass out the window of my house right now as we speak!"

"And you said Ariyanna in the backseat?!?"

"Hell yeah!"

"Oh okay! Bet! I'mma be there in five!"

"Yeah! Come handle ya, business partner. And don't tell her I told I told you."

I still couldn't believe what the fuck I was hearing right now. Was I in a dream or some shit?!?! Shaking my head, I realized this was very much real and if Neicy was telling the truth, I was about to put my foot so far up Trish's ass! She knew she was straight disrespecting me by having another nigga around my kid! She knew I didn't like that shit! "Man, bruh, you playin' fucking games with me! Is you for real right now?!?"

"Bruh, I wouldn't be calling you over no mess. I don't like yo fuckin' ass but what Trish doin' is straight wrong. Look, just come handle ya shit, bruh!"

This definitely wasn't the way I had imagined I'd start my Friday afternoon. I was still confused on exactly how Neicy even got my number 'cuz I never really talked to her like that. However, with her calling me with this bullshit about Trish being on some super-hoe shit around my daughter, I had no time to waste. I had to hop in my whip and pull the fuck up to see what the fuck was really going on.

Boyyyyy! I swear to God! Let me tell you something right fuckin' now! If I pulled up on that bitch and saw Trish in the car with some nigga and my daughter was in the back, I swear on my granny's grave I was gon' kill her and that fuck ass nigga!

Bro, I swear it was so strange how intuition worked. From the first moment I met Trish, my mothafuckin' spidey senses kept telling me that her ass wasn't on shit and wouldn't be on shit for the rest of her raggedy ass life.

But like every typical nigga, my stupid ass fell and fell mothafuckin' hard for the pussy. Yeah, I couldn't lie. Trish was a beast in the bed. Bitch had some bomb ass head and pussy. But the bomb ass head and pussy didn't compare to the migraine this bitch had been steady giving me from the moment I slipped up and got her ass pregnant.

Now don't get it twisted...I loved my daughter, Ariyanna. She was my everything. I'd do any and everything for her. In fact, truth be told, at this point, I was doing everything for her. Why? Because my mothafuckin' baby mama was a straight-up loser. Out of all the women I've dated before in my life, none compared to Trish. Bitch ain't have no job. Didn't have her own crib. Wasn't in school. She stayed wearing the same raggedy ass Rainbow shit. My mama told me she wasn't on shit the day she met her.

"Son, I can smell trouble brewing a mile away from that pissy pussy tramp!" I could hear my mama's voice going off in my throbbing head, warning me about this reckless ass hoe as I popped up from my bed. With my outfit still on from last night, I hopped in my Jordans then zipped to my dresser where I kept my .45 and a clip. I loaded that mothafucka up and then dashed out of the house and hopped into my Charger.

Trish lived north from me over in Chatham. I was currently staying with my mama out in Roseland, so I knew I could hop on the e-way and be at her spot in a less than seven minutes if traffic was a breeze.

Once I chucked the engine up and sped off, I had nothing but murder on my mind. Calm down, Dre. Calm down. Don't do nothin' stupid. The voice of common sense was trying to reason with a nigga, but I wasn't trying to hear any of that. Not when a bitch was fuckin' trying me by doing some rank ass shit with my baby in the backseat. I swear to God I was 'bout to get locked the fuck up today! All over this stupid ass bitch! I had to have someone to calm me down. The only person I could think of who would talk some sense into me was my mama. She was at work but I needed to hit her up ASAP to let her know what the fuck was going on.

Mama was a supervisor at a Boost Mobile store up in Bronzeville. My cell phone connected to my Bluetooth system in my car, I dialed her cell. Within seconds she picked up.

"Boy, why you calling me when you know I got customers and shit?"

"Mama! I swear ta God I'm about to kill this bitch!" I screamed as I swerved in and out of traffic on the Dan Ryan.

"What you talkin' about, Dre?!?"

"Man, Trish's ugly ass sister just called me some moments ago talkin' about Trish in the car with some nigga and got Ariyanna in the backseat. She said she givin' this nigga ass!"

"WHAT?!?! You going over there now?!?"

"Hell yeah! I'mma kill her, mama! She tryin' the fuck out of me!"

"DRE! Do not do nothin' stupid! You know you a hothead!"

"Mama! I can't let her disrespect me like that!"

"DRE! SON! STOP AND THINK FOR A MOMENT! It ain't worth it!"

"Mama! I can't! I gotta go!" I said, immediately hanging up the phone. Guess that didn't work in trying to stop me from going ape shit crazy on Trish.

I got off the 87th street ramp and within a few minutes, I was barreling down Trish's block. I immediately spotted her raggedy ass Altima parked on the curb. I wanted to catch this bitch off guard, so I slowed the fuck down and then crept slowly until I was about a good fifty feet away from the car.

My gun had been resting on the front passenger seat, but I picked it up with my right hand and then slowly drove down the block until I was about a good ten feet away from the car. I hopped out and dashed toward the driver's side window. Her windows were tinted, but I could see right through that mothafucka. And lo and mothafuckin' behold, this nasty ass bitch was straight sucking off this dreadhead nigga as he laid back with his eyes closed, pushing her head up and down in his lap.

I suddenly lost it. Yeah, I was going to jail today.

"BITCH YOU GOT ME FUCKED UP!"

## CHAPTER TWO

**MOMENTS EARLIER...**

"Aiight, sis, I'mma head out now. We'll be back around seven or somethin' like that," I said strolling toward the front door of my big sister Neicy's apartment.

Although I was going on a date or something like that, I wasn't dressed in my usual bad bitch attire. I just had on some basic ass jeggings, a t-shirt and some sneakers. Ariyanna, my 11-month-old daughter, was fast asleep in her car seat. Thank the fuck God. Eye Roll. Ughh! I just wished her fuck ass, triflin' ass daddy had her for the weekend. I should've called his ass up and asked him if he could watch her but I already knew he was gonna trip and make up some sob story like he'd always do. He always ran me the same ass sorry excuse. "Oh, I gotta work. I can't do it."

Bleh. Bleh. Bleh.

I ain't never met a nigga who worked that much in his life. And if you working like that, then you need a new job, pussy nigga! Shit, that clown was probably lying and just wanted to spend his weekend messing with some other hoe. Let me find out and I was gonna for sure run down to the judge and try to get full custody. Shit, a part of me also wanted to text his baldheaded, no-edges having mammy to see if she could watch Ariyanna. I knew if I ran her the right story she'd take Ariyanna off my hands for the weekend but she and I weren't on the best of terms as of late.

"So, where ya'll goin? And who is that nigga, Trish?" Neicy asked as she approached me with her arms folded. She turned her attention toward the living room window and gawked at my date standing outside next to his box Chevy. UGHH! Here she go again with her little judgmental ass. Always had some shit to say, especially when it didn't really concern her.

At first, I didn't want to answer her. Shit, I felt like I didn't need to. "Damn, bitch! You always up in my shit! He's just some dude I been talkin' to for a minute now," I replied with a scrunched up face.

Twisting her face back at me, she scanned me up and down, her arms still folded. "Damn, sis! I was just asking! Shit, I can't ask where you going with my niece? Plus, from the looks of it, that nigga look shady as fuck! You don't think I have the right to know?!? All these women out here getting kidnapped and shit?!? Don't yo ignant ass read the fuckin' newspaper?!?"

For a split second I turned around and looked out the window, staring at Dayveon, the nigga who I was about to go out with. Yeah, so the fuck what he was a dope boy. Not all dope boys were dangerous. Most dope boys I knew were just tryin' to hustle. Dassit!

I didn't like the little attitude my big sister was giving. Yeah, she might be older than me but she wasn't that much older. Besides, she ain't have kids herself and she didn't know all I had to go through being a single mother. Shit, I needed to live a little. "Damn, girl! If you all that worried, then you need to watch her!"

Neicy rolled her eyes. "I would but you waited til the last minute and I had already made plans. Besides, I don't know if you got the memo, but when you become a parent, sometimes you can't be going here and there. Sometimes you gotta stay home, you know..."

"Man, bruh, like for real, I don't have time for any of this shit right now. Especially, if you not gonna be any damn help! And what the hell you know about kids?!? Bitch, you work at a daycare. That is far different from being a parent!" I replied. Damn, she was really trying it.

"Help? Girl, I'm letting you stay with me rent-free! That is help! Fuck you talkin' 'bout?!?"

"Okay and?!? I'm thankful for all that but still, I gotta live some fucking times! Shit!"

"Fine! Whatever! I just don't like the vibe I'm getting from the dude outside. And you know Dre wouldn't like this shit! No nigga would actually..."

"Man, fuck Dre! He get to do whatever the fuck he wanna do! Why can't I?!?! Besides, you don't know nothing about buddy outside! Just mind your business for once in your life, please?"

"You can mind your own damn business when you have your own place to stay at!"

I couldn't say shit in response because truth be told she was right. It was her place and she did kind of have a right to know my whereabouts, especially since I had my baby with me. I just lowered my head and looked away, tapping my right foot rapidly against the unpolished oak wood floor of the foyer. "His name Dayveon! Damn! You happy now?!?"

"And what does he do? How you know him?"

"Girl, I didn't ask all that yet! That's the reason for a date!"

"Girl, bye...," she said as she walked off shaking her head.

"Whatever," I mumbled as I opened the door and proceeded to make my way out toward Dayveon with the car seat in my hand.

Soon as he saw me approaching him his smile turned a bit flat. "You bringin' yo baby with you??!? You couldn't find a sitter?!?"

"Sorry," I apologized looking a tad embarrassed. "I would've texted you but I was just too busy. You don't mind, do you?"

"Nah, it's cool."

"Oh, okay!"

Dayveon reached in and gave me a hug. "Damn, you smell good as fuck," he commented as he rubbed his hand down my ass.

"Uh-ughhh! It's too early for that! And don't do that shit now! My sister probably watching us from the window. I don't want her seeing us!"

"Sorry," he said as he released me.

"So, you still gon' hook a nigga up, right?"

I froze for a moment knowing exactly what he meant. "Yeah...I guess...You got my money, right?"

He smacked his teeth with a huge grin. "Haha, girl, you tweakin'. Anyways, let's do it in your car 'cuz I just got my shit cleaned out and detailed...If you don't mind..."

I fell silent again and pursed my lips. "Okay," I said as I quickly spun on my heels and looked back at the apartment living room window hoping Neicy wasn't staring at us. "My car right there," I said. "The green Altima..."

Damn, this nigga had the thickest, longest dick I'd ever seen before in my life. As I slurped up and down his shit, my pussy was getting so damn wet. Too bad 'cuz I definitely wasn't gonna give this nigga no pussy. What I was doing right now was just a simple transaction.

Dayveon was this nigga I met some weeks ago at North Riverside Mall in the 'burbs. We had been talking off and on but I told him straight up that I didn't want no damn relationship right now and that if he wanted something out of me, he was gonna have to pay.

And that he was willing to do. Not surprising. When niggas really wanted something, they were willing to do any and everything to get it.

Don't judge me but I had no shame in my game. A bitch had to do what a bitch had to do. I wasn't currently working 'cuz I had got fired from my job at Wal-Mart a few months back and I didn't feel like going back into retail or customer service. I was trying to get into this nursing program, so I figured in the meantime in between time, I could just stay with my sister and collect public assistance until I get some loans to pay for school and shit.

Anyways…Just to give this nigga some quick head he was willing to knock me off $400. Afterward, he said he was gonna take me and baby out to eat at Pappadeaux's. A bitch loved her some seafood and they had some decent ass crab cakes and drinks!

Ariyanna was in the backseat in her car seat, still knocked the fuck out! That was that mothafuckin' Benadryl! Boy, that shit did that job every time! Thank God, 'cuz this was a bit embarrassing for me to be giving a nigga some head while my baby girl was in the backseat, but I had no other choice. I would've just handled my business back in the house but I didn't want my nosey ass, judgmental ass sister all up in my shit. Ughh, sometimes I couldn't stand her ass. From the moment she let me stay with her, she was always poking and prying, acting like she was our mama or some shit. With that being said, I had to do what I had to do and keep it moving.

"Damn, shorty, you suckin' the shit out of that shit," Dayveon moaned as he kept pushing my head up and down in his lap. Thick weed smoke filled the car, giving me a slight contact high. I needed to hurry up so Ariyanna wouldn't get any of that shit in her system. Damn, girl, you so fuckin' reckless. *What the fuck is you doin'?* avoice kept repeating in my head but I had to dead that shit. Now wasn't the time to have morals and shit 'cuz I really needed them coins.

As my tongue glided down his veiny shaft, I put one of his balls in my mouth and sucked softly on it. Niggas loved getting their balls sucked and played with, so hopefully, he'd throw me a few extra bucks on top of that $400 if I showed him how a real bitch is supposed to suck on a dick.

"You like that, huh?" I moaned seductively, sounding like a straight-up porn star.

"Hell yeah! Fuck! You suckin' that shit better than my wife!" he responded, pushing my head deeper into his lap.

WIFE?!?! See, I knew it! But I wasn't gonna trip 'cuz half these niggas out here be lying anyways. And like I said, I didn't want to be in a relationship with this nigga. Just pay me and I'd be on my merry mothafuckin' way.

"Bitch sound wack as fuck," I replied with a chuckle. "You need to link up with a real bitch," I mumbled as I slurped on his pretty dick. I couldn't lie-his dick indeed was pretty. It was the most gorgeous dick I'd ever seen my life! And I have seen plenty!

He didn't respond. He just kept moaning, his tongue draped down the side of his mouth. Yeah, I was putting that magic on this nigga. A part of me wanted to go ahead and risk it all and hop on the dick to show him the power of this pussy but he probably didn't even have any condoms. And, of course, I wasn't walking around with any because I just don't randomly fuck dudes like that.

Some Lil Baby song boomed from the car's stereo speakers as I carried on, hoping this nigga was seconds away from cumming. I had been straight murdering his shit now for nearly five minutes and I was thoroughly surprised this sloppy ass head didn't have him busting a nut already.

"I would hop on that dick, but you probably ain't got a condom," I said.

"I think I got one in the glove compartment...," he mumbled wiping his face. "Shit, we can slide up to the store and get some. Shit, I can even pull out. Fuck all that condom shit."

"Boy, bye! How I know you ain't got some shit?!?"

"Man, I'm married. If I had some shit, my bitch would've killed me..."

"Hrrrm," I replied holding his still-hard dick that was covered in my spit. "I guess...," I smiled, ready to go ahead and just hop on the dick. Truth be told, I needed to get some guts dug out 'cuz I was so horny right now.

Without hesitation, Dayveon grabbed my head and shoved me back down to continue sucking his dick, which I gladly didn't mind. Something about sucking dick just turned me on even more. Not gonna lie though...Although Dayveon was ugly as fuck, his dick could be a GQ model. I was just so mesmerized by his dark brown meat.

I closed my eyes and began to ramp up my head.

"BITCH YOU GOT ME FUCKED UP!"

PLOW!

"AHHHHHHHH!" I screamed at the sound of my car window being busted out, millions of pieces of glass exploding everywhere! "What the fuck?!?!?"

## CHAPTER THREE

Turning the butt of my .45 into a hammer, I exploded the fuck out of Trish's car window. I didn't give a fuck! This bitch was on some other shit if she thought this was okay to be sucking off nigga with my daughter in the back! What in the fuck was wrong with her! Who does some shit like this?!? No fucking morals!

"BITCH! GET OUT THE MOTHAFUCKIN' CAR!" I yelled, flying my hand into the window that now had a gaping hole in it. I quickly reached down and opened the door from the inside.

"NIGGA! WHAT THE FUCK IS YOU DOIN'?!?" she squealed, thoroughly surprised to see me! Yeah, bitch! Didn't see any of this comin', huh?!? I thought as I didn't even hesitate in dragging Trish out of the seat of the car.

"OH SHIT!" the dreadhead nigga screamed once he realized what was happening. His eyes widened in fear, he tried to quickly pull his pants up and then he dashed out of the car.

"FUCK IS WRONG WITH YOU, HOE?!? YOU SUCKIN' THIS NIGGA OFF WITH MY DAUGHTER IN THE BACK?!? BITCH, I'M GONNA KILL YOU!"

I was seconds away from really putting a bullet in this bitch's head but I was trying my best to control my temper. Hell-like fury burned through my core as I really had to fight off thoughts of murder.

Grabbing Trish by her hair, I dragged her out of the driver's side of the car and onto the street curb.

"LET ME GO! WHAT THE FUCK?!?!? WHY THE FUCK ARE YOU EVEN OVER HERE?!?!" she screamed as I yanked her up and cocked my fist back.

"BITCH, SHUT UP! FUCK IS YOU DOIN'?!?!? I SHOULD KILL YOU AND THIS NIGGA!" I screamed, leaning into her, ready to punch the fuck out of her. *Don't do it, Dre! DON'T HIT HER!* That thought flashed across my mind as I let her go and threw her down to the the curb.

I could hear Ariyanna screaming and crying from the backseat of the car. Although it was tearing me up on the inside hearing my baby girl scream uncontrollably, my rage was consuming me, damn near having me on the verge from straight slaughtering this hoe. I mean, who the fuck got the gall to be doing some foul ass shit in front their child like this?!?! Trish got up and dashed to the lawn, afraid I was about to really pull the trigger.

"MY BAD, BROSKI! I DIDN'T KNOW SHE WAS YO BITCH!" buddy screamed as he tried to make a dash toward his candy painted box Chevy I presumed belonged to him.

"MAN, FUCK YOU! GET THE FUCK OUT OF HERE!" I screamed back, pointing the barrel of the gun up in the air. I pulled the trigger, letting a shot out.

*POW!*

"OH SHIT!" the dreadhead nigga said falling to the concrete. The second he realized I hadn't shot him, he quickly got up, flew into his car, chucked up his car engine and sped off.

"WHAT THE FUCK IS WRONG WITH YOU,

HOE?!?!? You fucked up! LIKE YOU REALLY FUCKED UP!" I said as I made my way back over to Trish.

I hadn't noticed but a crowd of neighbors began to form into a makeshift group outside a house on the sidewalk across the street.

"NO! Don't do that young man! Don't hurt her! Don't do it unless you wanna go to jail!" some old, frail nigga wearing a Kangol barked. I quickly threw him a glance but then threw my murderous gaze back onto Trish. "GET THE FUCK UP, BITCH! I SWEAR TA GOD I'M GONNA FUCKING KILL YOU!" I yelled grabbing her, dragging her across the lawn of the apartment building.

Neicy suddenly dashed outside and lunged up to me and Trish. "Let her go, Dre! DAMN! Let her go!"

I glanced up at Neicy and flashed the gun at her! "Man, FUCK YOU! You the one who called me over here!" I growled, letting Trish go as I dashed back over to the Altima. My goal now as just to get Ariyanna safely out of her. I made my way toward the backseat of the Altima and flew the car door open.

"WHERE YOU GOIN' WITH MY BABY?!?" Ariyanna screamed. Then I guess it hit her that I said Neicy was the one who called me over here. All I heard was, WAIT??? You called him over here, bitch?!?! I should FUCK YOU UP! NOSEY ASS, FAT ASS BITCH!" Trish suddenly got up from the lawn and lunged at Neicy.

Trish was a bit on the petite side, weighing no more than 120 pounds but she was throwing her hands and fighting Neicy like she was a welterweight Mexican nigga in a Golden Gloves boxing competition.

Neicy was much bigger than Trish. She was definitely a bit on the BBW side but she was ducking, trying to avoid Trish's fists from landing on her chest and face. "STOP IT, TRISH!" was all I heard coming out of Neicy's mouth.

# MY BABY MAMA IS A LOSER

While I let those two birds go at, I ran to the backseat of Trish's Altima, grabbed Ariyanna and her entire car seat and then dashed back to my Charger. "Sorry about all of this, baby doll," I said as I quickly attempted to strap Ariyanna into my backseat.

"Ya'll stop that now! CUT IT OUT! The police on they way!" I heard an older woman say as a few neighbors dashed across the street and tried to break up the fight between Neicy and Trish. But it seemed like their intervention only made matters worse. Neicy was able to muster up some strength and she began beating her way through one of her older female neighbors trying to hold her back. Next thing you knew, an entire brawl broke onto the lawn of the apartment building.

Once I had Ariyanna secured in her car seat, I hopped in the driver's side of my car. All I could hear was, "HE TOOK MY BABY! STOP HIM! HE TAKING MY BABY!" But no neighbor dared tried stop me. Guess they saw I was with the shits and had my pole on me.

Once I chucked up the engine, I sped off down the street and made my way back onto the expressway and headed to my mama's job up in Bronzeville.

About fifteen minutes later, I was on 35$^{th}$ street, pulling into the parking lot of the shopping plaza where my mama's Boost Mobile store was at. Once I parked in front of the store, I quickly got out, grabbed Ariyanna, and made my way inside the store.

Mama was tending to the sole customer inside the store. She stopped everything she was doing when she heard the doorbell go off as I opened the door and walked inside.

"DRE!" she squealed turning her attention away from the

customer and toward me. She looked back at the older nigga and said, "Excuse me, sir! This my son! I need to talk to him for a minute if you don't mind!"

"No worries," the chubby, older nigga with a baldhead mumbled as he walked off and looked at other phones on display.

Mama quickly sauntered up to me, her eyes widened with anticipation about what happened.

"So you took yo dumb ass over there!" she exclaimed, her hands gripped to her waist. "WHAT DID YOU DO?!?!"

"Man...," I replied smacking my teeth. "I got my kid, that's what the hell I did!"

"DID YOU PUT YOUR HANDS ON HER?!?"

I didn't respond. I lowered my head as I held onto Ariyanna. "Like I said, I had to do what I had to do. I didn't punch her or anything! I just busted out her car window."

"DRE! What the hell is wrong with you?!?! You tryna catch a case?!?!"

"I know, mama! But when I got up there, she was literally in the car sucking that nigga's dick!"

The moment I said that, mama turned her head and saw that her customer was staring dead at us. "I'mma just come back," he said.

"I'm sorry, sir. Just come back and I'll give you a $10 credit on yo bill," she apologized. Soon as the man marched out of the front door of the store, mama looked at me and said, "Nigga! You doin' the most right now! You and that nasty ass baby mama of yours! Goddamnit! You and your damn generation! I thought I raised you better than this son! Give me my damn, grandbaby! Comin' up to my job like this 'bout to have people complaining on me and shit!"

"I'm sorry, mama! But it was just dead wrong what Trish was doing!"

"I TOLD YO DUMBASS THAT BITCH WAS SKANK! BUT NOOOO! You didn't wanna listen to me!"

"I know…"

"Don't tell me you *know!* Boy, you don't know shit! You just like yo hardheaded ass daddy!"

"Man, whatever. Look, at least I got Ariyanna. Got my baby smelling like weed and whatnot."

As mama rocked Ariyanna, I stood back shaking my head in disgust. I couldn't believe this was my life right now. Never would've imagined in a thousand years that the first woman I'd have a child with would turn out to be such a reckless ass bitch. But, mama was right. From the moment I laid my eyes on Trish I knew she was trouble. I should've known better, too, 'cuz she let me hit the first night I met her.

"First thing yo crazy ass is gonna do is run down to the police station and tell them EXACTLY what happened!"

"Man, I ain't doin' all of that!"

"NO! You need to go now! In fact, I know one of the detectives down at the precinct. I'mma call him and have him to talk to you and you give them a statement. You tell them you were defending yourself! DO IT NOW before that nasty bitch make some shit up and have you arrested!"

"What I'm gon do about Ariyanna? Who gon watch her?"

"I'll watch her for now! Don't wait either! GO NOW!" mama said as she walked back over to her register. "Take yo stupid ass right down to the precinct near the house and talk to Detective Greggs."

"How you know him?!?" I asked mama, shaking my head with doubt.

"He's one of my customers…Now, GO NOW!" she said.

"Fine!"

Doing as mama instructed, I left Ariyanna with her and headed back down to Roseland to go talk to this detective. Mama called me while I was in the car and told me she called

Detective Greggs and he was waiting for me at the station to get a statement about what happened. And, of course, mama knew best. Detective Greggs and I talked for about a good thirty minutes. I told him exactly everything that happened... My side of the story, of course. He said that if my story checked out to be true, more than likely charges wouldn't get pressed because Trish would likely face child endangerment charges.

## CHAPTER FOUR

"HE TOOK MY BABY! STOP HIM! HE TAKIN' MY BABY!" I kept screaming at the top of my lungs as I watched that fuck ass nigga go into the back of my car and steal Ariyanna right in front of my eyes! I couldn't believe Dre would do this! What the fuck was he thinking?!?!?

"COME ON YA'LL! YA"LL NEED TO STOP!" Ms. Andrews, one of my older neighbors cried as she tried to pull me away from Neicy.

"I'mma fuck this bitch up! GET OFF ME! GET THE FUCK OFF ME!" Neicy roared as another neighbor tried to hold her back.

A few other bystanders were around but only a few were trying to break up the fight between me and my sister.

"COME ON, BITCH! DO IT THEN! SNITCH ASS HOE! ALWAYS UP IN MY SHIT! I HATE YO MOTHA-FUCKIN' ASS!" I bawled as I tried to get out the grip of Ms. Andrews and storm up to Neicy. Ms. Andrews was at least sixty-years-old, but she had some size to her, so I really couldn't fight her off. If it was any other bitch, I would've fought them off and went straight for Neicy's chubby ass throat.

I was so blown right now though! I honestly couldn't believe this bitch would have the audacity to do me like this! Fat ass had the nerve to go and call up Dre and tell her what I was doing. Her fat ass needed to worry about her own shit and why she wasn't getting no dick. I couldn't stand a bitch that was always worried about the next bitch. Stop worrying about the dicks I put up in me!

"Bitch! GET CHO SHIT AND GET OUT OF MY MOTHAFUCKIN' HOUSE, YOU LOW LIFE ASS BITCH!" Neicy yelled as Mr. Garrett as he held her back. He was another neighbor of ours from the third floor.

Within seconds, I saw Dre take off down the street and disappear with my baby! Soon as I got away from these people and got back inside the crib, I was gonna call the police and press charges against Dre for kidnapping my kid!

Tears and sweat streamed down my face as I stood there wracked with pain, confusion, and numbness all at the same damn mothafuckin' time. Here I was, just tryna do me and live my life, and I had my own blood call up my baby daddy so he could start some fuck shit with me!

"BITCH! I'LL BE GONE ASAP! Don't worry about calling me up again!" I spat back to Neicy.

"Bitch! Fuck you! Don't you worry about calling me up again! You're a fucking pathetic ass low life! If mama was still alive right now she'd be so fucking disgusted with you!"

The second Neicy mentioned my mother and how she would've seen me as a disappointment, I lost it! "BITCH, I'MMA KILL YOU!" I screamed as I fought off Ms. Andrews and stormed Niecy to deck her fat ass in her swollen ass, Debbie cake eating face! "FAT ASS BITCH! SAY SOME-THIN' ELSE!" I screamed as I managed to land a punch in her face. But within seconds, a few other men, presumably neighbors I'd never seen before, pulled me away before I was able to really dig in and beat that hoe's ass.

Out of nowhere, I heard police sirens fill the block. With one of the neighbors holding me back, I turned my head and saw twelve hop out of two squad cars and run up to the crowd.

"What's going on?!?" one of the officers, this thick ass yellow nigga with tattoos all up and down his arm, said as he approached us.

"My baby daddy took my baby!" I cried.

"HE NEEDED TO, OFFICER! DON'T BELIEVE HER! SHE WAS ENDANGERING HER CHILD!" Neicy interrupted.

"BITCH! MIND YOUR OWN DAMN BUSINESS!" I barked back.

"Wait! WAIT! WAIT ONE MOTHAFUCKIN' MINUTE!" the other officer, an older, dark-skinned black lady with cornrows, growled as she injected herself in between Neicy and I. "Everyone SHUT the fuck up! Jason, take this young lady over there and get her story," the female officer said pointing to Neicy. Then the female officer glanced at me with a serious face and said, "You...Come with me."

The butch-looking officer took me over near her cruiser and then asked, "So what happened?"

"I was in the car with one of my friends! I had my baby in the back and then out of nowhere, my daughter's father pulled up in his car, hopped out and busted my window out with a gun! He hit me and threw me to the curb! I didn't do nothin'!"

"Where is this friend you are with?"

"He left already...," I replied, wiping my face free of tears.

"What's his name?"

"Dayveon..."

"Ok, and what's the name of your child's father?"

"DeAndre Williams, but everybody call him Dre..."

"And where does he live?"

"Wit his mama down in Roseland..."

As the officer continued to ask me a few more questions, the other sexy ass officer strolled over shaking his head. "Put some damn handcuffs on her," he said.

"THE FUCK FOR WHAT?!?!?" I bawled. "What the fuck did I do?!?"

"Because I just spoke to your sister and a few other neighbors. They said you and your child's father started everything!"

"Oh really?!? I knew yo ass was a liar!" the female officer said as she grabbed my shoulders, twisted me around and then slammed onto the car. "Put your hands behind your back, young lady!" she said.

"I didn't do nothing! I SWEAR TA GOD!" I cried as the officer squeezed tight a pair of handcuffs around my wrists, damn near cutting through my skin. She then opened the back door of the squad car and threw me inside.

Once she hopped inside the front of the car, we sped off. I tried to ask a million questions about why she was arresting me, but the bitch ignored me all the way to the police station.

"Ms. Latrisha Johnson," an older, cracking voice echoed into the holding pen of the police station. A few hours had passed since I was arrested and taken down to the police station. These mothafuckas wouldn't let me call nobody! Not even my lawyer! They said I had to wait until I spoke to a detective.

My head lowered, I raised and gawked up at this Carl Winslow-lookin' ass nigga in a suit and tie.

"Yes...," I replied as I got up from the corner of the holding cell. I was the only person in here at the moment.

"I'm Detective Greggs. I hear you, your sister and your child's father got into an altercation earlier. I'm gonna need a statement from you before we let you go home...," he replied.

"Ok," I said standing up from the bench inside the holding cell and made my way over to the pen's opening. He escorted me upstairs and took me to his desk where he asked me a number of questions. I did my best to tell them everything that happened. Of course, I wasn't going to tell him the whole truth about what me and Dayveon was doing. That was none of his mothafuckin' business! Besides, it wasn't like I was selling drugs or selling my food stamps or anything. Everything I did in that car was strictly legal!

"So, just to confirm to get your story straight, you said you were just talking to one of your guy friends and out of nowhere your child's father just busted out your window."

"Yes, I said that a million times already! I didn't do nothing!"

"And your child was in the back?"

"Yes!"

"Okay, cool. Cool beans...Well, unfortunately, I'll be referring child endangerment charges over to the prosecutor. Before you came down here I had a chance to actually speak with your child's father. He came on his own volition and told me everything that happened. His story somewhat corroborates what your sister told the responding police officers. He said he caught you performing oral sex on a gentleman while your child was in the backseat. He also said once he caught you, you hit him and the other gentleman started to attack him." Detective Greggs said.

"WHAT?!?! That's a fucking lie! I wouldn't dare do nothin' around my kid like that! AND DRE HAD A GUN!" I obviously lied but I wasn't gonna sit up there and admit the truth.

"Ma'am, DeAndre is a legal gun owner. He showed me his FOID card," Detective Greggs said.

"Fuck this! I wanna speak to a lawyer," I bawled

"Umm, lower your voice, and second of all, I'm gonna go ahead and read you your Miranda rights right now before you have a chance to speak with your lawyer," he said shaking his head.

"THIS SOME FUCK SHIT!"

## CHAPTER FIVE

It was close to midnight when I suddenly woke up to the sound of Ariyanna crying in her crib. A few days had passed since I went over to Trish's spot and took my baby from out of that fucked up situation. I was still so floored that she would stoop that mothafuckin' low by suckin' another nigga's dick while our baby was in the back seat.

"Here I come, Princess," I mumbled as I wiped my eyes and got out of my bed and strolled over to Ariyanna's crib. More than likely she just wanted a bottle. I picked her up, left my bedroom and went into the kitchen. I thought Mama would've been sleep but she was in the living room, adjacent to the kitchen, watching television and smoking a square.

"Hey, mama," I said as I opened the fridge with one hand and held Ariyanna with the other.

"Damn, she woke up?" Mama asked.

"Yeah…I'm about to fix her a bottle."

"Damn, my bad. Let me put my cigarette out because I don't wanna be smoking around my grandbaby," Mama said as she put the square out and got up from the couch. She made her way over to me and grabbed Ariyanna out of my hands while I prepared her bottle.

"So, I assume based on everything that happened you are gonna be filing for full custody, right?"

I stood there frozen for a second trying to process what Mama just said. Damn, I had been thinking about that shit off and on now for a few days but I was definitely going to do that shit. Trish was unfit to be a mother and now I had to step up and get full custody over my child. That bitch was just nasty and reckless. God knows what else she had been doing around my daughter.

"Yeah, most definitely. I ain't got no choice now. Who knows what else she was doing around Ariyanna," I said.

"Exactly! And on that note, I had already been doing research on a family lawyer you need to contact. I found him on the Google. I already spoke to him and everything. You need to come up with a $1,000 retainer. You got a stack saved up, right?"

"Damn, ma! But yeah, I got a g saved up."

"Good…," Mama said as she slipped her free hand in her back pocket and pulled out a small piece of paper and handed it to me. While she rocked Ariyanna, I pulled the bottle out of microwave and handed it to her. I looked down at the piece of paper and saw Mama had wrote down the contact information for this attorney, "SHERMAN HARRINGTON, ESQUIRE". I'd give him a call tomorrow in the morning.

"Well, I need to take my behind to bed," Mama said as she handed Ariyanna back to me.

"Me, too," I replied. "Good night, mama," I said and walked back to my room and put Ariyanna to sleep some minutes later.

My alarm clock went off the following morning. It was seven AM on this seemingly sunny Thursday morning, and as usual, I had to get up and get ready to take my ass to my other job – I was working part-time at Home Depot all the way out in the 'burbs. Shit, I ain't even gonna lie, a nigga was still tired as fuck from dealing with all of these shenanigans. Truth be told, I truly didn't want to deal with those mothafuckas today, but I needed every dollar I could get my hands on. But then again, it hit me, I needed someone to watch Ariyanna and I also needed to run down to this attorney's office to go ahead and see what I can do to get full custody over Ariyanna.

After I got done showering and putting on my outfit, I quickly hit up my cousin Tanisha to see if she could watch Ariyanna. She agreed and then I also hit up my job to see if I could have the day off. Tony, my boss, didn't mind. So, I was good to go. Once I got Ariyanna ready and gathered a few of her belongings, I headed into the kitchen where my mama was standing guard near the kitchen, stirring up a pot of grits and frying up some bacon.

"Good morning, son, you up bright and early this morning!" Mama greeted as I stood off to the side holding Ariyanna.

"Yeah, I'mma have Tanisha babysit Ariyanna while I go talk to this dude."

"You called the attorney already?" Mama asked as she made her way over to me and smiled in Ariyanna's face. "Hey cutie! You up now! You want some grits?" she playfully asked baby girl.

"Nah, I ain't call him yet. But I'mma call him first thing when his office open up and see if I can get an appointment today."

"Ok, well, handle ya business. What about your job?"

"I called them and told them I wasn't coming in," I said as

I opened the fridge and pulled out a carton of some orange juice.

"I see you ain't wasting no time," she said walked back over to the stove and glued her eyes onto the big pot of grits. With her right hand stirring away, she used her other to sip out of a coffee mug.

I walked over near her and pulled a glass down from a shelf and poured some juice. Once I got done drinking some, I put everything back and then went back into my room and get all of me and Ariyanna's shit.

"Aiight, mama. I'm headed to Tanisha's house now," I said as I made my way to the front door.

"Aiight, give me a call when you get done talking to the lawyer," she responded.

"Aiight, bet."

After I dropped off Ariyanna at Tanisha's place, I immediately hit this lawyer up to see if I could come in pronto to talk to him about this situation. Money wasn't going to be an issue in paying this dude and I wanted to get this shit over with ASAP so I can begin to plan out how I was going to make some life adjustments knowing I was about to become a full-time parent.

It was truly a shame Trish and I had to come to this place. When she first got pregnant, although by that point we were broken up and barely talking, we made an informal arrangement that she would watch Ariyanna during the week while I worked and then I would let her have the weekends. Ever since I got that damn nightclub security guard gig some months ago, it seemed like Trish wasn't willing compromise and watch Ariyanna during certain weekends when I had to work. The other thing that was really pissing me the fuck off was that although the bitch ain't have me on papers paying child support, I was steady giving that hoe at least $600 a month ON TOP of the fact that I was still buying shit for our daughter every week. There should've been no reason at all why Trish wasn't able to do her part and fully take care of Ariyanna during the weekends when I needed to work.

But now that she showed her true colors and proved she was unfit to be a mother, I was definitely going to get full custody of my child. Yeah, I was gonna have to make some adjustments to my work schedule and figure out some other workarounds but I was gonna make this happen. I wasn't going to be that type of nigga to not give a fuck about his child. I knew what it was like to have a sperm donor daddy who didn't give a flying about their child, so I wasn't going to let my baby girl have that same type of upbringing.

Anyways, I was cruising down $47^{th}$ street, making my way to Downtown Hyde Park where this lawyer's office was at. Once I got onto $53^{rd}$ street, I found some street parking and made my way into this big ass building.

After I got off the elevator on the fifth floor, I found his office and strolled right in. Some weird-looking white girl was working the front desk.

"Hey, Good Morning, I'm here to talk to Mr. Harrington. I called earlier and he said I could come right in," I explained to the twentyish-looking girl.

"What's your name?"

"DeAndre Williams..."

"Yup! He's expecting you! You can just go down the hallway and he's the last office."

"Thanks," I said as I quickly made my way down the hallway and toward the office. I knocked twice.

"Come in," I heard a baritone voice rumble through the door.

I opened the door and this old nigga with a bald head and

a bright gray beard stood up and walked up to me. "DeAndre?" he asked with a grin.

"Yeah," I replied as we shook hands.

"Have a seat...," he said as he pulled a chair out in front of his desk. He sat back down and then pulled out a yellow legal pad and a pen.

"So, like you were telling me on the phone...You're looking to get full custody over your daughter, right?"

"Yeah..."

"What's wrong with the mother?"

"Well, I caught her having sex with some random dude while my daughter was in her carseat in the back of her car."

Mr. Harrington's eyes lit up with curiosity. "Really? Damn! Like you saw everything?!?"

"Hell yeah!"

"And what happened afterwards? You called the police..."

I paused for a moment. Damn, I had to get my story straight because I did technically lie to Detective Greggs about all that happened. "Well, she got out of the car and started to fight me along with the dude. I had my gun on me and then I had to defend myself," I said. "I got my FOID card though so I didn't get arrested. I did immediately go down to the police station and filed a police report. The detective hit my line a day ago and said that he was gonna be pressing charges against her for child endangerment," I explained.

"Good! This should be an easy case. Ain't no way in hell a Cook County family judge would let that woman have custody over a child."

I instantly felt elated hearing that. "So, how much I owe you for all for this?" I asked. "Well, this case would be simple, so all I'd need is the $1,000 retainer. That includes court filing costs and other administrative fees. Pay today and I'll get started on everything ASAP."

"Cool, I got the cash on me right now!" I said as I pulled out my wallet.

Once I handled that transaction with buddy, I headed out of his office, excited yet still a bit nervous. Truth be told, this should've been something I did some time back but I was really trying to give Trish the benefit of the doubt. But now this shit definitely had to be done and I had no qualms. In fact, I was going to even ask the judge that Trish have no visitation rights either. That bitch just needed to get gone and try again with another nigga. Maybe then she'd learn her lesson and be a more responsible person.

I hopped back into my car and pulled off, headed back South to go pick up Ariyanna. I wasn't even three minutes on the road when I got a call from a 708 number.

"Who is this?" I said to myself, hesitant to answer. But I went ahead and answered. "Hello?"

"Dre…I'm pregnant," the female voice replied.

"WHAT?!? Yo, who the fuck is this?!?"

"Nigga, don't act like you don't know who the fuck this is! And yes, this ain't no mothafuckin' game! I'm pregnant, nigga! And it's yours!"

## CHAPTER SIX

I had been crying nonstop since the day Dre took Ariyanna away from me and had me arrested on them false ass charges. Child endangerment my ass! It wasn't like I was hitting my baby or getting my baby high! And Dre and Niecy had absolutely zero evidence that I was in the car with Dayveon sucking his dick. Granted, I knew I was wrong and I should've just did the shit inside of my bedroom, but all of this right here was just some straight-up, complete bullshit. I was not a bad mother! I did everything in my power to take care of my kid to the best of my abilities. I would never put Ariyanna in harm's way. I bet you Dre and Neicy had been plotting this for quite some time so she'd have a good excuse to kick me out. And Dre's wack ass, baldheaded mammy probably put him up to this just so she could have Ariyanna all to herself.

That Saturday I got arrested, I had spent the night in jail but luckily I didn't have to stay in there for too long 'cuz my best friend, Monique, came and bailed me out. Luckily, my bail was only set at $2,000, so I had to come up with $200 to get out ASAP. I had the cash on me but Monique told me to hold onto to it so I could use it for other things. She was my life saver. Shit, truth be told, she was more of a sister to me than Neicy's fat ass. From the day I was born, that bitch never liked me. I didn't know why but it is what it is. I was completely done with her. After I got out of jail, I did have to go back over Niecy's place where she already had most of my shit packed up for me to leave. Her and I didn't say anything when I went over there. Ironically, she had a neighbor there for protection in case some shit popped off. Scary ass. ANYWAYS!

Monique was such a sweetheart though. I told her what happened and she never judged me. *"Girl, we all been there, done that,"* she said when she picked me up. That was what a real sister and friend was supposed to do. Don't judge. Just offer help any way you can 'cuz if the tables were turned you'd expect someone to do the same. On that note, since I didn't have anywhere to go, she definitely didn't want to see me out on the streets or in a shelter. So, she convinced her boyfriend, Chadwick, to let me stay with them until I got back on my feet.

Monique and Chadwick stayed all the way up on the North Side in Rogers Park in this big ass three-bedroom apartment. Monique was an LPN for some old folks' home in Glenview and Chadwick worked as a technician supervisor for Comcast. Apparently, he was making some big bank 'cuz he drove a Lexus and the nigga always had had the latest Jordans. I was proud of my best friend for finding a man who could truly take care of her. Shit, I wish I could say the same for Dre when we were together. That nigga wasn't on shit when I met him. Now that he had him two jobs, this nigga was acting like he was like Mr. Responsible. Fuck him! I got his ass alright! He fucked with the wrong bitch.

It was Tuesday afternoon and I was in the spare room of their apartment just crying my heart out nonstop. I was crying tears of sadness and rage. I was thinking up of so many things to do to get back at Dre. I couldn't believe that nigga would go to the police station and lie on me like this.

From the day I got to Monique's place, unfortunately, I had been sleeping on an air mattress, so you already know my back was so damn sore. A brutal migraine throbbing inside of my head almost had my shit ready to explode. Monique said she was planning on getting new furniture in the house so soon I wouldn't need to sleep on the air mattress. Thank God!

Anyways...I was going through my phone, flipping through pictures of Ariyanna. I was already missing her so much. Dre was fucked up for putting me through all of this. I was having separation anxiety to the point where I felt like I was seconds away from having a panic attack.

Suddenly, my crying came to a halt when I heard Monique and Chadwick arguing in their bedroom across the hallway. Then I heard loud footsteps thundering down the hallway and the front door slamming. I couldn't quite make out what they had been arguing over but whatever it was it had to be fucking serious.

Then I heard two knocks at my door.

"It's open," I said as I quickly wiped my face. I didn't want Monique to see that I had been crying.

"Hey, girl, I'm about to head out to work. You need anything?" Monique asked as she walked in, decked out in her nursing scrubs. Monique and I favored each other except she was a tad darker than me. She had long microbraids running down her back.

"I'm good, girl. Thank you for checking up on me though," I replied as I somewhat sniffled and wiped my nose.

"You were in here crying?" she asked as she made her way over to me.

I didn't say anything in response. I just looked at her and burst into tears.

"Yeah," I cried lowering my head. "I miss my baby so much! Dre is such a clown for doing this to me!"

"Shhh! Shhh! Girl, it's gonna be alright! Just be calm and work on getting your shit together," Monique consoled.

"I know his ass is gonna try to get full custody! I just know it! Nigga think he know it all and he think he better than people. Ever since I got fired, I've been trying to get my life right and this nigga will not let me catch a break! All of this because I wanted to be done with his ass...," I explained.

"Damn...But I thought Dre broke up with you though?" Monique asked.

"Man, nah! I killed that shit! He was so emotionally abusive to me! Nigga was so controlling," I explained. Yeah, maybe Dre did technically break up with me first, but by that point our relationship was already on the rocks and I had told him for months that I was done with his mothafuckin' ass. All of this started simply because I didn't want to get an abortion. Yup! You heard me right! Dre wanted me to get rid of Ariyanna and I refused. Ever since then this nigga had been giving me all types of grief."

"Oh, well, girl, you're just gonna have to do what you gotta do and make sure you still can see your child," Monique said as she got down next to me and rubbed my back.

"I know. He don't know who he fuckin' with! This nigga must think I'm some stupid ass, simple bitch that don't know shit! I'mma show him some shit!"

"Come on, Trish...Now ain't the time to be trying to get back at him. Just focus on trying to get a job and getting your own place. Hell, if anything, if ya'll end up in court, you wanna be able to prove to a judge that you got yo shit together," Monique explained.

"Yeah, yeah, yeah. I hear you, but it's gonna take me some

time before I even get all of that. Besides, my credit jacked up! How am I even gonna get an apartment that quick?!?"

"Girl, me and Chad's credit was messed up, too! But we talked to a landlord who was willing to work with us. Besides, one of Chad's homeboys does credit repair. I can see if he can help you out."

"Nah, girl, you ain't gotta do that," I said shaking my head. I didn't want any of Chad's homeboys all up in my shit. And truth be told, Chad was kind of sheisty to me. Fine as fuck but sheisty.

"Well, what about a job? What you gonna do about that?"

"Girl, if I go out and get a job now I may not be able to get into that nursing program and besides, they gon' reduce my public assistance. I might as well not get a job," I explained.

"Girl, umm, no. You gonna have to get a job! Besides, why would you wanna be on public assistance for a long ass time?!?!?"

I had to stop for a moment and think about what Monique was saying. Was she really sitting up here judging me? Like, damn, bitch! You, too!

"I know, girl, but all I am saying is it's gonna take time!"

"Well, please, girl, do what you gotta do ASAP because Chad is already a bit upset that you are staying here," Monique said.

"Why?"

"Because..."

"Because what?"

Monique pursed her lips. "He thinks you're a bum."

"Oh," I replied lowering my head. I didn't know what to say to that. That was kind of fucked up though. That nigga really didn't know me like that to have that type of assessment on me. "He can think whatever but I know that's not true."

"Right, and I know it's not true either, which is why you gotta get your shit together. I can't just let you stay with us forever. Besides, Chad the one paying all the bills. I can only do so much," Monique explained as she got up and made her way over to the door. "Anyways, there is some leftover pizza in the fridge and we also got some wings in there still from Shark's."

"Thanks," I replied nonchalantly.

Monique left the room and then I heard her leave out the apartment to head to work. I guess Chad must've left, too.

My bladder felt like it was about to explode, so I quickly shot up from the air mattress and made my way into the hallway to the bathroom. I sat on the toilet and began peeing when I got a phone call. It was from a number I didn't recognize, so I didn't answer it. Opening up my Facebook app, I wanted to see what was happening on social media. However, the person who just called me left a voicemail.

"Hrrrm" I mumbled when I dialed my voicemail to see who had left me a message.

*"You have one new message..."* "Hey, LaTrisha! This is Mrs. Whitaker, the nurse from Near North Health Corporation calling you back with your test results! Please call me back ASAP because this is extremely important."

My eyes widened with fear. I wonder what this was about. Hesitant at first, I dialed the clinic back ASAP. I had forgot I did my annual check-up not too long ago and wanted to get tested to see if I was carrying anything...Damn, I hope I ain't have some shit...

## CHAPTER SEVEN

"Nigga, don't act like you don't know who the fuck this is! And yes, this ain't no mothafuckin' game! I'm pregnant, nigga! And it's yours!"

"YO! Who is this?!?!" I was so thoroughly confused as to who this was fucking playing games with me.

"DIS SHELLY!"

"SHELLY???!?! I don't know no fuckin' Shelly! Man, whoever this is stop playing fucking games with me!"

"DRE! You gon' really act like you don't know who the fuck I am?!? That's some bitch nigga shit for real!"

Shaking my damn head out of confusion, I had to think for a second. *Shelly. Shelly. Shelly.*

OH SHIT!

I remember exactly who the fuck this was. Shelly was this sexy ass, dark-skinned, Asian-looking slim-thick situation I had a drunken one-night stand with some months back. Me and my boys went to this club out in the south suburbs some months ago. That was where I met this Shelly bitch. Make a long story short, me and shorty popped it off in the back of the Charger but I swear on my Granddaddy's grave I had a rubber on when I dicked her down.

Now don't judge me. Shit, a nigga gotta live sometimes. She was goin', I was goin'. And let me tell you something right fucking now, I definitely wouldn't put my dick in no random ass broad without wearing a condom. After dealing with Trish's crazy, gutter ass, I learned a valuable lesson to always wrap my dick the fuck up.

"Man, ay, look, I don't know what the fuck you got goin' on but I damn sure was wearing a rubber that night!" I shouted. Given that this bitch fucked me after only talking to her for a few hours, I knew she was fucking other niggas left and right.

"Nigga, I only fucked one dude over the last three months and THAT was you! And yeah, I remember you wearing a condom but guess what! Accidents fucking happened! So what the fuck you gonna do?"

Still shaking my head, I just knew this hoe was playing fucking games with me. "What the fuck you mean what I'm gonna do? And if you really pregnant, why the fuck you came at me this way?"

"'Cuz I don't like the way you fucking disrespected me! I thought you and I had something going but you just fucked me and dipped out on me!"

"AND?!?!" I replied back, my face twisted. "You knew what the fuck we was on that night! Yeah, we exchanged numbers and shit, but that wasn't for us to link up or nothin' like that! I was just being nice! Bitch, you the one who wanted more than what I was willing to give you and I told you that shit from the get go! Besides, why the fuck would you want a relationship and shit out of me when I fucked you in the backseat of my car?!? Bitch, don't you got some sense of decency?!?"

"Look! I don't wana hear all of that right now! I just wanna know what your game plan is!"

"What do you mean what my *game plan* is? Bitch, I don't even know if that's my fucking baby! And how do I know you even really pregnant?!?"

"Look, dude! Just CashApp me $300 and I'll take care of this mistake for you, okay?"

"Bitch! Fuck you! That's extortion! Look, get the fuck off my line!" I suddenly hung up.

"Man, what the fuck!" I yelled punching my steering wheel as I swerved in and out of traffic. I was on level ten now, ready to fuck someone but I had to calm myself down. Quickly opening up my glove compartment, I pulled out my vape pen and took a few tokes. I needed a quick blast of some Kush to simmer my mothafuckin' nerves. Bitches, man! I swear to fuckin' God sometimes these hoes be doin' the most!

About a minute later, as the weed set in, my mama hit my line. Just that quick I forgot that she did want me to call her once I left this lawyer's office.

"Wassup, ma?" I answered, trying my best to conceal the anger in my tone.

"Why you sound angry?" she asked.

"Nah, nothin'. Just the job calling me with some BS," I lied.

"Oh, okay...Well, how'd it go with the lawyer?" she asked.

"Good, actually. Dude said he finne start working on my case ASAP. He said since Trish got arrested and got a current charge against her, a judge would immediately grant me full custody. He also told me he was gonna file something in court tomorrow to grant me temporary custody."

"Good! YES! God is good! Thank God!" Mama happily shouted, her voice echoing through my car.

"I'm on my way to pick up Ariyanna now from Tanisha's place," I said as I took another toke from my vape pen.

"Aiight, boy! Stay safe! Tell my niece I said hi!" mama said.

"Aiight, Mama. I'll see you soon," I said and then hung up.

About twenty minutes later I made it down to Tanisha's apartment. Tanisha was my mama's sister's youngest daughter. We were both 27. Tanisha was a part-time hairdresser but also sold weed on the low. She was my connect, getting all of my vape carts and shit straight from Cali. Crazy thing was none of my family members suspected her selling. Anyways...She was staying in her own crib out in South Shore. In fact, she was supposed to hook me up with trying to get me my own place in her building. Rent was cheap in her building. Tanisha was only paying I think like $500 a month for a two-bedroom. Then again, she was living right on 79$^{th}$ and Essex, which was one of the worst blocks in the city. All types of niggas hung around on her block.

I pulled up to her building, parked and went straight inside her building to her floor. I rang her bell and within seconds she opened the door.

"Damn, that was quick as hell, cuzzo! Everything went well?" she asked as she held Ariyanna with one hand and patted her big ass black bonnet with the other.

"Yeah, and I'm finne get full custody, too."

"Good," Tanisha said as I walked in. She closed the door then trailed me. The two of us then sat down in the living room.

"Baby girl give you any problems?" I asked as I reached my hands out to grab Ariyanna.

"Of course not!" she said as she rocked Ariyanna, playfully teasing her. Baby girl started smiling and giggling. "Ohhh, you such a cutie! You such a cutie, aren't you?!?" Tanisha smiled and held Ariyanna in the air. Then she handed me Ariyanna.

"I'm finne head out," I heard a female voice from behind me say.

I had no idea who it was, so I spun my head around. And

oh my mothafuckin' goodness – this yellowbone with this straight, devil red hair and a fat ass came around the corner and sat next to Tanisha. She had on a tanktop, exposing both of her tatted up arms. Shorty reminded me of Lauren London. Goddamn my dick was getting harder than a math exam thinking about that lil pussy.

I didn't say anything. I just sat there amazed. This was probably Tanisha's new girlfriend. Yeah, Tanisha was a dyke but not like a stud or nothin' like that. From the looks of it, you would've never thought Tanisha was into pussy.

"Candreka, this is my cousin, Dre. Dre, meet Candreka," Tanisha said.

"Sup," Candreka responded with a slight smile.

"This you, cuz?" I jokingly asked.

"Yeah, she my new boo," Tanisha responded.

"Well, anyways, I know you got some clients and shit coming, so I'mma head out, too," I responded as I sat up and made my way over to the door.

Candreka got up as well and followed me.

"You not gon give me a kiss before you go?" Tanisha joked as she grabbed Candreka's arm and pulled her into her embrace. Then the two of them made out like two high-schoolers getting ready to fuck on the night of prom. Damn, if Tanisha wasn't blood, I'd definitely try to figure out a way how to slide in. I always wanted a threesome with two bitches.

Candreka pulled away from Tanisha as I headed out the door. "Aiight, cuzzo, I'll holla. I might need to get another cart from you later on this week."

"Aiight, nigga," she said.

Once I was out into the apartment hallway, Candreka was a few steps behind me. I turned around and asked, "Why I ain't never seen you before? How you and my fam link up?"

"Excuse me?" she asked with a scrunched up face.

"What?"

"Dude, you don't think it's rude as fuck to be asking me those types of questions? I don't know you like that...," she replied rolling her eyes.

"My bad...," I responded.

"Anyways...I was in the military. I just came back from overseas. I was in Germany," she explained.

"Cool," I said.

"Well, nice to meet you. Guess I'll see you around from time to time," I said.

"Yeah," she said... "We'll be seeing each other around," she said with this slight seductive smirk and then scanned me up and down.

Hrrrrm. That look. I already knew what that meant but I wasn't going to go there with her.

## CHAPTER EIGHT

RING. RING. RING.

"Damn, how a bitch just call me and now they not even pickin' the fuck up!" I grumbled. I hated this fucking raggedy ass clinic. Them bitches were so fucking unprofessional! I should've just taken my ass to Northwestern or Rush to do my shit. Many seconds later, someone finally answered the phone at the damn clinic. "Near North Side Health Corporation, this is DeShaunta."

"Hey, umm, someone just called me about giving me my test results."

"And what's your name?" the receptionist asked rudely. Bitch...

"LaTrisha Johnson," I replied, giving the lil hoe some attitude. These bitches thought they were somethin' special just because they were CNAs or LPNs.

"Do you know who called you?" she asked, her tone still a bit snippy.

"Shoot, I think it was this lady....Umm, I don't know, some nurse..."

"Baby, we got plenty of nurses here. I need to know who you spoke to," the bitch responded.

I rolled my eyes. "I think her name was Mrs. Whitaker."

"Hold on for a second," the receptionist said without even allowing me to respond, immediately putting me on hold. Some corny ass music came on while I waited for the nurse to pick up. Ughh! I was definitely going to change doctors after this shit.

"Hoe ass bitch," I grumbled.

A minute or two had passed as I still sat on the toilet. "Damn, what's taking this old bitch so long!" I complained as my legs felt like they were about to go numb by sitting on the toilet for so long. Then a second call came into my phone.

It was Dayveon.

"Shit...FUCK!" I grunted, debating whether or not I should just hang up and see what the fuck Dayveon wanted. Truth be told, I had been meaning to hit him up and cuss him the fuck out. I couldn't believe that fuck nigga would just dip off like that while he watched me damn near get my ass beat by my baby daddy. Fucking loser.

I could always call the clinic back. So, I immediately switched over and didn't hold the fuck back. "What the fuck you want, nigga?!?"

"Damn, shorty! I was just calling to check up on you! That was crazy as fuck what happened!"

"Yeah, yeah, yeah! Now you calling to see about me?!? That was some hoe ass nigga shit you pulled. You know that, right?!? I mean, what kind of nigga gon sit there and watch a female almost get their ass beat by another dude?!? Man, fuck you! Get off my line, bruh!"

Dayveon smacked his teeth and said, "Girl, you tweakin' for real. Ya mans had a blickie on him. I wasn't poled the fuck up! Otherwise, I would've went to bussin' too!"

"Yeah, okay nigga. So what the fuck you want?"

"I miss you..."

"Miss me? Nigga, what?!?"

"Like for real. I've been thinking about you. Look, where you at? I can come by and pick you up. My wife took the kids to Wisconsin Dells for a field trip. I got the house all to myself."

"Uh-uhh, nigga! No the fuck I won't! Besides, you still didn't even pay me for what I did the last time!"

"Well, I got you and then some. Like for real, I'll give you two stacks if you just spend the week with me. I'm lonely like a mothafucka!"

"Damn, Dayveon! You doin' all of this just to have someone keep you company?!? It's so many bitches out there that would do that shit for a $5 box at Popeye's! Why the fuck you wanna waste that amount of money on me?!?"

"'Cuz...There's just something special about you. Now stop playing and let me come pick you up."

I sat there thinking for a second whether or not I should take him up on his proposition. The more I thought about it, the more I realized I needed that money. Two stacks was sounding fucking awesome right now. Besides, I did wanna get some dick. And some weed, too.

"Fine...I'm staying with my friend all the way up in Rogers Park. So, if you willing to make that ride, come and get me. I'm not CTA-riding bitch. Or you can get me a Uber."

"Okay, cool. I can be there in an hour. I'm gettin' in the car now. Just text me the address," he said and then hung up.

"Okay," I replied as I sent him a text with Monique's address. I got up from the toilet, flushed and washed my hands. Seconds later, I saw that same number calling me back. This was probably the clinic. I grabbed my phone of the sink's ledge and quickly answered. "Hello?"

"LaTrisha Johnson?" the female voice asked. This sounded like the nurse who left me a voice mail.

"Yes, this is she...," I replied.

"Hey! This is Mrs. Whitaker down at the clinic. I was just giving you a call to about your—"

Suddenly the phone hung up.

"The fuck??!? Hello? HELLO??!?" I pulled my phone away and realized our call got disconnected. I quickly dialed the clinic back but that was when I got hit with a message from T-Mobile telling me my phone service was disconnected!

"FUCK!!!!" I screamed. I did forget to pay my damn bill. With no time to lose and Dayveon on his way, I needed to pay my shit with the last few dollars I had on my debit card. I think I had about a good $100 left, which should've been enough to cover my bill. I called the 311 phone number, talk to a representative and paid my bill. Within minutes, my phone service was reconnected. That shit wasted a good fifteen minutes and I still needed to shower and whatnot. So, I quickly hopped in the shower, got ready and then waited for Dayveon to hit my line to tell me he was downstairs.

❦

*A few hours later...*

"SHIT! I'm cumming! FUCKKKK!" Dayveon roared as I clenched my tight ass pussy muscles around his dick, squeezing every last drop of nut out of him. That was that fire ass pussy for you. I knew how to make a nigga cum. Surprisingly, Dayveon made me cum back to back! I ain't never had so many damn orgasms before in my muhfuckin' life, G!

"Goddamn! Fuck!" I moaned aloud, thoroughly enjoying this third dick down session. Ever since he picked me up and took me back to his spot, we fucked back to back like rabbits.

Thank God I wasn't a super-bitch and didn't tell Dayveon to fuck off. I truly needed that thick nigga dick up in me.

Truth be told, I had been thirsting for some good ass dick for quite some time and Dayveon really showed the fuck out on this lil pussy of mines.

Saddled on top of him, I hopped off the dick and rolled over to his side. He grabbed me and cuddled me as we made out. Damn, it was a bit weird fucking a nigga in a bed that his wife was just in probably some hours ago. Oh well! Bitch should've been doing her job and poppin' her pussy the right way. If she as a good ass wife, she wouldn't have a nigga all up on another bitch. Yeah, yeah, yeah, judge me if you want to, but I obviously didn't give a fuck about fucking a married man. It is what it is.

"Damn, man, you really blew my mothafuckin' brains out," Dayveon commented as he squeezed my sweaty titties and planted wet, succulent kisses all up and down my face and neck.

"I know I did," I laughed as I played with his semi-hard dick. Damn, we didn't even wear a condom but I didn't care 'cuz I faithfully tracked my period on this period tracker app. I wasn't gonna be ovulating for a few more days.

"You wanna grab something to eat?" Dayveon asked with a big smile on his face, twirling his finger around my still hard right nipple.

"Yeah, we still ain't get no seafood. I want some crab legs," I said.

"Cool. Well, we can check out this crab leg spot out on 47th street. They just opened up, too," he said.

"Aiight, let's go!"

After kissing and cuddling some more, Dayveon and I finally got out of bed, took quick showers and then threw our clothes back on. Since Dayveon's wife and kids were out of town for a few days, I decided I was gonna spend the night. Before I left, I shot Monique a text telling her that I was gonna chill somewhere else for the next few days just to clear my head. Besides, I wasn't feeling the idea of staying with Monique no more since her nigga clearly had problems with me. Fuck him anyways. Nigga wasn't even all that.

Once Dayveon and I were ready, we headed out and hopped on 290. Dayveon actually stayed in Maywood, a west suburb right outside the city. Sitting back, coolin' in the passenger seat, I was on my phone scrolling through Facebook while Dayveon zoomed through traffic trying to get down south. Cardi B's *Press* blasted on the car stereo.

"So, what kind of seafood you like?"

"I'm a King Crab-type of bitch," I said. "Dem snow crabs so damn small!"

"Damn! For real? I'm the opposite. King Crab too fuckin' salty for my taste buds," he said. "I'mma get some shrimps though."

"Yeah, well, I like shrimps but—"

***POW! POW! POW! POW!***

"AHHHHHHHH!"

## CHAPTER NINE

Before I got back to the crib, I had stopped by CVS and some other places to go pick up some diapers, formula and some other things that Ariyanna needed. I damn near dropped $200 in an hour. Shit was a bit irritating given that if I had a responsible ass, working baby mama, some of this financial burden would've been off my shoulders.

Anyways, that was what my mothafuckin' ass get for messing with these simple ass, Chicago THOTs. Although I'd spend a million dollars to get any and everything my daughter needed, shit was just a bit annoying that I didn't have a spouse who could help a nigga out from time to time. Oh well. That's life, right?

All I knew was once I got with the next chick, if we became a serious item, I was definitely going to make sure she had the right head on her shoulders. She needed to have no kids, a job, a degree, and at least her own place.

Truth be told, I shouldn't even be thinking about all of that right now. In fact, now that I was focused on getting full custody of Ariyanna, I needed to ensure I got all of my shit together. Soon as I got home and fed baby girl, the first thing I was going to do was start looking into how I could finish my degree. I had dropped out of UIC in my junior year because back then I wasn't taking school seriously. I was studying political science but I had no idea what I really wanted to do. Now that I was going through this legal shit with Trish, all of this had me thinking I should just go ahead and finish my degree and possibly think about going to law school. I knew I could make one hell of a lawyer. In fact, when I was in high school, I was on the school's debate team.

Also, another thing I needed to start working on ASAP was finding a new job. Working these multiple jobs with this crazy schedule just wasn't going to work. I needed to get a regular, full-time 9-5 pronto. I should probably hit up my guy, Myron, to see if he could get me a gig working down at ComED. Apparently, their customer service department started paying people $20 an hour. My guy said with my experience, I could probably get as much as $25 an hour. Shit would be gravy if I could get in. I could probably still work security here and there on the weekends, too. All I needed right now was to at least bring in a good $60,000 a year and I'd be straight.

The more I thought about it, the more I also realized I needed to get out of my mama's crib. I was on the verge of turning 28 and it didn't make any damn sense for me to still be living at home with her. Although mama was cool and she liked my company, I needed to finally be independent and stop relying on her. I did pay her rent and helped out the with the utilities, but if I was gonna be paying all of that, shit, I might as well get my own place.

Anyways...

It was damn near seven PM once I finally got done running errands and shit. I pulled up to the crib, grabbed Ariyanna and her car seat and made my way inside. As usual, mama was on the couch smoking a square while a rerun of the Steve Harvey Show blared on the living room television.

"Hey, mama," I announced as I made my way into the kitchen.

"Hey, Dre...," she responded not giving me any eye contact. Cigarette smoke wafted in the air. Thought she said she wasn't gonna smoke in the house when Ariyanna was around but oh well. This was her place. This was another reason why I needed to leave 'cuz I hated the smell of them funky ass squares.

"You cooked dinner already?" I asked.

"Hell nah! Shit, I'm about to order something for Door-Dash. I got a taste for some rib tips. You think I-57 deliver over here?"

"Shoot, I don't even know. Check GrubHub, too. They tend to have better options."

"True," mama responded. "Anyways, I've been thinking...I think once you get full custody over Ariyanna, I think you should really try to find your own place. I mean, I'm not saying I wanna kick you out or nothing like that, but you gonna be thirty soon. Don't you wanna eventually stop wasting giving me money and get your own crib? All this money you payin' in rent can go to a mortgage and you could build up some equity in your own place..."

"Damn, that's crazy you bringing this up 'cuz I was just thinking the same."

"Oh, and I don't want your ass staying over there on 79th street either. Them niggas over there are crazy and dangerous. It's always somebody getting killed over there. I don't even know why Tanisha stay her ass around there. She too smart and pretty to be around them crazy niggas," mama said.

"I know right...But yeah, while I was driving back, I was thinking about getting a crib. Maybe somewhere in the 'burbs like Orlando Park. They got some decent condos out that way. I've been working on trying to get my credit together," I explained.

"Oh, okay! I'm glad to hear that!"

"I'm also thinking about starting back at school."

"That's good, too! Finally! Boy, it's crazy as hell that you gotta go through some bullshit drama to put a pep in ya step. But I'm glad you starting to make some serious life decisions," Mama said as she got up from the couch.

"Anyways, I think I'm gonna just order some Harold's. Now I'm pining some gizzards."

"Eww," I said scrunching my face.

"Ewww?!?!? Boy, please! You used to eat them all the time when you was a toddler. Don't act special now. You used to eat those and chitlins, too!"

"Really?!? You's a damn lie!" I couldn't believe it! Mama was fucking with me. Ain't no way in damn hell I would put them chewy ass shits in my mouth. And I couldn't stand the smell of chitlins. My granddaddy used to make them nasty shits all the time.

*Buzz. Buzz. Buzz. Buzz.*

Suddenly me and Mama's conversation was interrupted by the sound of my phone buzzing in my pocket. "Somebody calling me. Can you hold Ariyanna for a sec?" I asked Mama as I handed her baby girl. Mama took her out of my hands while I quickly reached inside of my pocket and pulled out my cell phone.

It was a number I didn't recognize. Hesitant once again, I thought it was that crazy ass Shelly. Bitch better go on somewhere like FA REAL! I didn't accept the call.

Then within seconds, I got a text message.

"DRE! IT'S NEICY! TRISH IS IN THE HOSPITAL! SHE GOT SHOT!"

"WHAT THE HELL?!?" I screamed.

"What's wrong?" Mama asked.

"I just got a text message from Neicy! She just said Trisha got shot! What the fuck?!?"

"CALL HER BACK, DRE!"

I didn't hesitate in hitting Neicy back. Within seconds, she answered.

"DRE! Trish got shot! OH MY GOD! SOMEONE TRIED TO KILL MY BABY SISTER!" she kept screaming and crying through the phone.

"Wait! Wait! Wait! Calm down! What happened?!? Who called you?!?"

"I just got a call from the police department! They said she got shot on the expressway. She was in the car with that same dude again!"

"OH MY GOD! YO! ARE YOU PLAYING GAMES WITH ME?!?"

"NO, DRE! I'm on my way to the hospital right now!"

"Is she okay?!?"

"I don't know!"

"What's hospital is she at?!?"

"Rush University!"

"Ok! I'm coming right now!" I roared, instantly hanging up the phone. "Goddamnit! Man, this shit is crazy!"

"What happened, Dre?!?"

"I don't know! Neicy just told me that Trish got shot on the expressway. She said she was in the car with that same dude who I caught her with! I gotta go, mama!"

"I'm coming, too! Oh my God! This is too much!"

Mama and I didn't hesitate rushing out the front door and jumping into my car. Once I chucked up the engine, we sped off and headed north to Rush University Hospital, which was about a good thirty minutes away.

Look...As much as I despised Trish for all of the shit she put me through, the last thing I expected was for all of this to happen. I almost wanted to cry on the inside because I definitely didn't want to see my baby mama get shot and killed. Especially over another nigga's bullshit. Something told me from the day I caught her with buddy that something bad was going to happen. I should've never went too ham on her. Shit, for all I know, that nigga probably could've had her set up and tried to get her killed. Probably because he thought I shot at him. As we got closer and closer to the hospital, a sense of dread overcame me. I felt so guilty. None of this probably would've never happened had I just controlled my temper and confronted her in a different way. If Trish died, I didn't know how in the fuck I was going to explain this to Ariyanna once she got older. I would've been the one to blame for all of this. Damn it, man. This was not how I wanted this shit to go. Please, God. Don't let her die. She didn't deserve this. She was fucked up in the head but she didn't deserve to go out this way.

## CHAPTER TEN

**A WEEK LATER...**

Beep. Beep. Beep. Beep.
I slowly awakened to the beeping sound of multiple machines chirping inside of a chilly hospital room. Hazy, I had absolutely no idea what happened or why I was even here. I was surrounded by my sister, a few doctors, police officers, Dre, his mama, Monique and Chad.

My vision blurry, I felt like I was cast into a deep dream but I knew this was reality when I went to move my hands and quickly realized I was cuffed to the rails of the bed.

"Latrisha...I'm Dr. Shakir. I'm the surgeon who operated on you. How do you feel?" some short Indian-looking man with a head full of jet-black hair asked me as he waved a small flash light across my eyes.

"I'm..I'm fine," I responded, confused as to why I was railed to the bed.

"Oh my God, Trish! I'm so sorry, baby sis!" Neicy cried as she cupped her mouth and tried to hold back her tears. Monique, standing to her side, consoled her.

Dre just stood there, holding Ariyanna, as he threw me this slightly weird gawk. He didn't seem sad nor did he seem happy that I was alive.

"What happened?" I asked the doctor. "And why am I in handcuffs??!?"

The doctor looked over at the two police officers and then they walked to the side of the bed. "I'll let them tell you what happened," he explained. "But in the meantime, I am glad to see that you are conscious and doing okay. You were in a coma for a week. You were shot in your chest and stomach and we had to put you into a medically-induced coma."

"Who shot me?"

"We'll discuss that later, ma'am," one of the police officers, some burly white guy with red hair, said. He pulled out a cell phone, quickly dialed a number and then said, "She's awake if you wanna come ask your questions, Detective," the officer said.

"What did you do, Trish?!?" Neicy asked, still crying.

"I don't know! All I remember is was that I was in the front seat of Dayveon's car...We were talking and chilling, listening to music, and then suddenly gunshots let out... That's all I can remember," I said.

"I'm gonna have to ask everyone to leave while the Detectives come in and question LaTrisha," the officer said.

Following the officer's instructions, everyone followed suit and marched out of the hospital room. Confused, I was ready to explode into tears trying to figure out why I was handcuffed to these rails.

"What did I do?" I asked the officer but he didn't say anything. Both of the officers then walked out of the hospital room, leaving me to myself.

A minute later, a young white police officer looking like Elvis Presley walked into the room. "Ms. Johnson, I see you are awake and doing well...," he greeted me. "I'm Detective O'Mara with the Chicago Police Department."

"What did I do?!?" I responded, sounding slurry as hell. A throbbing migraine began to pulse on the side of my head.

"We'll get to that in a second, but what's your relationship to Mr. Dayveon Parker?" he asked, pulling out a small notepad from the inside pocket of his brown suit jacket.

"I'm...I'm his friend," I responded. "His business associate...," I lied. I'd be damned if I was going to tell this pig about what me and Dayveon were doing.

"Business associate...What kind of business..."

"We do...umm...we do online marketing and whatnot," I lied once more. Damn, was that even a believable lie? Let me stop before I dug myself deeper into a hole I knew I couldn't get out of. These pigs always asked questions in such a way to trap you. But I knew I didn't do anything wrong. All Dayveon and I did was just fuck and we were on our way to get something to eat.

"Where's Dayveon at?" I asked.

"He's dead."

My eyes widened with fear. "Dead?"

"Yes...Dead. He was killed that same evening. You all were shot at by gang rivals. Did you know that Mr. Parker was affiliated with a notorious street gang?"

"Umm, no, not really..."

"Are you sure about that? You know lying to the police is a crime," he said. "Obstruction of justice is very much a real thing."

"I mean, I knew he possibly sold drugs but I ain't ask him all of them questions. We had a legit business going on

"Hrrrm, okay, well, your story isn't adding up. Unfortunately, you've been placed under arrest for conspiracy to traffic narcotics. That night you two were shot at, we discovered a kilo of cocaine in the trunk of his car. Also, there was a quarter kilo of heroin in your purse. How did that get inside of your purse?"

"What are you talking about?!? I ain't sold no drugs! And whatever was in my purse, Dayveon probably tried to put it in there!"

"When would we have done that?" the detective asked with a doubtful raised brow.

"Shit! I don't know! Maybe as he was dying?!? Look! I swear on my mama's grave I wasn't helping Dayveon push no weight or nothin' like that! All we did is have sex and we were about to go eat!"

"But you just told me you were his business associate. So now you were his girlfriend? Mr. Parker was married with kids..."

"And?!? And yes, I was his girlfriend..."

"Hrrrm, ok. Well, this still doesn't discount the fact that a good amount of narcotics were found in your purse."

"I wanna speak to my lawyer!" I yelled! This was crazy as fuck! First child endangerment now this shit?!? This couldn't be real! This was completely fucked up! I wouldn't dare be selling no damn dope, especially for no nigga!

"You'll have that opportunity but, in the meantime, I'm going to go ahead and read you your Miranda rights now that you are conscious."

"BRUH! This is so unbelievable! I didn't do nothin'!" I cried.

After this jake got done reading my rights and shit, he said I'd be allowed to have a few more visitors until the end of visiting hours. The first person to walk into the room was Dre and his mama. He was holding Ariyanna. Seeing her made me almost want to burst into tears. I missed my baby so much! But as I turned my gaze toward Dre, I realized all of this was partly his fault! I probably would've never linked back up with Dayveon had I just went out on that little date with him and got my $400! Now I was being accused of being an unfit mother and a fucking dope smuggler!

"Hey, baby girl! You miss mommy?" I asked as tears streamed down the side of my face.

"Hey, Trish," Dre said nonchalantly as he lowered Ariyanna close enough so I could get a good look at her. Ariyanna just looked the other way and held tightly to Dre. Damn, my baby didn't even miss me.

"Sup," I responded to Dre. I couldn't even give him eye contact.

"Hey, Trish," Dre's mama said as she looked over at me. "How you feelin', baby doll?"

"How you think?" I responded back with a slight attitude.

"Whatever," she whispered and rolled her eyes.

"Man, bruh, what happened? What did you do?" Dre asked.

"Man, I ain't did nothin'! And I wouldn't be here right now if you didn't pull that bitch ass shit."

"Come on, Trish! You tweakin' right now! How you gon blame me for all of this?!?" Dre responded, his face twisted with disgust.

"Because! If you were just to mind your business I would've gotten what I needed. Instead, one thing lead to another and now here I am shot the fuck up and also being accused of helping a dead nigga run dope in the city!"

Dre lowered and shook his head. "That's why you got them cuffs on you?"

"Yeah! That's the reason why?!?"

"Just tell me the truth, Trish. How you know that dude?!? I ain't gon' say nothin'. I swear," Dre said.

"Man, bruh, it ain't none of your business. Can ya'll just leave me alone, please?"

Dre stood there silent for a second. His eyes turned to venomous slits. "Leave, huh? That's the shit you on? Man, I've been coming down here everyday checking up on you to make sure you pulled through. I prayed by your bedside, asking God to let you live so you can have a second chance at life. But you know what, I also prayed about what I was gonna do next and I'm glad the Lord spoke to me 'cuz he's telling me to get full custody. Good luck, Trish, but you'll never see Ariyanna again. By the way, I already got temporary custody of her. We got a court date coming up at the end of the month. Hope you can make it," Dre said as he and his mama walked out of the door.

"NO! You can't do that, Dre! You just gon' take Ariyanna away from me?!? You can't do that! DON'T TAKE MY BABY! I SWEAR TO GOD?!?"

"Or what you gon' do? Kill me? Kill me behind jail bars? Have a good life, Trish. Also, I'll be asking the judge to revoke your visitation rights."

"NOOO! DON'T TAKE MY BABY!" I cried!

Without feeling any sympathy or remorse, Dre and his mama just walked coolly out of the hospital room. Wow. This was so unbelievable. This dude was going to take away the sole reason I had to live at this point in my fucked up life.

## CHAPTER ELEVEN

**TWO YEARS LATER...**

Abruptly waking up to the sound of my alarm clock bleeping from my phone, it was time to get my mothafuckin' day started. It was around five am and I had to get up ASAP to get Ariyanna ready for daycare and then head to work.

Ya boy had made some serious life changes since I was able to get full custody of Ariyanna. Crazy thing was it seemed like these past two years zoomed by quickly. After Trish was shot up on the e-way and got arrested, she was charged with being a co-conspirator to traffic narcotics. However, because she was a first-time offender and she didn't have any priors, the judge gave her a year in jail and then five years of probation. Now that I had full custody over my daughter, I also made sure that Trish didn't have any visitation rights. Bitch had me all the way fucked up if she thought she was going to try to see my daughter. Hell no. Thankfully Ariyanna was really too young to have any impression or memory of Trish. Once I finally got my shit together and settled down, hopefully, the right woman I needed in my life would be a better mother for Ariyanna.

I shot up out of bed, stretched and yawned. Although baby girl had her own room now, she was still sleeping in the bed with me. Yup, I had my own place now. After getting full custody, I worked my ass off to fix my credit and save up down payment and I ended up buying a nice lil townhouse over in Hyde Park. Shit cost me a grip, but it was worth every damn penny. And luckily, my boy, Myron, did pull through and helped me land a gig at ComEd. Since I had prior work experience and some college credits, I was able to transition into a management trainee program and now I was making $80,000 a year as a call center manager.

As for my love life, well, Ariyanna kept my ass very busy, so I didn't have a lot of time to be messing with no new bitches. Truth be told, I was very cautious about dating anyone new at the moment. I was just too focused on trying to finish school and work my ass off at ComEd. Now that I was back in school, shit was kicking my butt without a doubt, but I knew, in the end, it would be all worth it. My academic advisor told me that if I managed to keep up a 3.5 GPA and get a decent LSAT score, I'd be able to enroll in law school part-time and I'd still be able to get a decent gig working for a law firm in Downtown Chicago. I had my eyes set on DePaul University. They had a very good part-time law program.

Anyways, I strolled back over to the bed and slightly shook Ariyanna awake. "Hey, baby girl, time to wake up. Gotta go to school now and Daddy gotta go to work."

She slowly opened her innocent hazel eyes and began pouting. "I tired still," she mumbled in her cute voice. "I know, baby girl, but you gotta wake up! Time for school!" I smiled.

"Okay," my smart baby girl replied. She was so talkative and advanced for her age.

Once I got Ariyanna up and ready, I sat her up in front of the TV to watch some cartoons while I took a quick shower. After I threw my outfit on, I fixed her and me a quick breakfast. Then we hopped in the Charger and headed to her daycare. Her daycare was all the way over in Woodlawn. Mama got me a connect to get baby girl into the University of Chicago's daycare program. They were one of the best daycares in the city and had some strict ass admissions requirements. On top of that, I would've had to chuck up like $20,000 a year. However, Mama's connect, one of her church members, was able to get me in on a neighborhood scholarship program where I only had to pay like $4,000 a year! What a blessing!

We got to the daycare and quickly strolled inside. Her teacher was there greeting parents and kids. One of the things that I liked about this particular daycare was just how diverse it was. There was a mix of kids streaming into the classroom. Black. White. Asian. Arab. I wanted my baby to be exposed to the greatness and diversity the world had to offer. I'd be damned if she was gonna be the victim to some hood ass education.

"Aiight, baby girl, daddy's gonna pick you up around five! Be on your best behavior and learn a lot! I got a surprise for you when we get back home!" I said, planting a kiss on the side of baby girl's cheek then gave her a tight hug.

"Okay, daddy!" she replied with a big smile, exposing her tiny teeth.

"Love you!" I said as she waved goodbye to me as Mrs. Porter, her daycare teacher, grabbed her hand and led her into the classroom.

It was now close to 7:30 AM and I was making my way back to my car to jet to work. It was a Tuesday morning, so I already knew traffic was gonna be on some bullshit. My job was located up in the north burbs, so it was gonna take me at least an hour to get there. About thirty minutes later, I was sitting on the expressway, bumping some 21Savage when suddenly a call came into my phone. It was a number I hadn't recognized. Some 847 number. That area code was for the north suburbs, so it probably was the job calling me.

"Hello? This is DeAndre," I answered in my fake ass white boy professional voice.

"Dre, Dre, Dre...," a female voice answered.

My face twisting in surprise, I had to pause for a moment to figure out who this was. And then it hit me, this was Shelly! *WHAT THE FUCK?!?*

"Shelly?!?"

"YUHP!!! Didn't have to think hard this time, huh?"

My eyes widened with rage. "Yo! What is your problem!?!? Why in the fuck are you stalking me?!?"

"'Cuz, nigga! A bitch gotta stalk a nigga to get her child support! That's the fuck why!"

"Yo! What the fuck are you talking about?!? You still on that shit?!!?" I screamed.

"Yup! And I'mma going to court right now as we speak to get them to force you to take a paternity test, fuck nigga! So drink some muhfuckin' water and get ya weak ass bladder ready, pussy nigga!"

Yo, I swear to God after I hung up with this bitch, I was gonna file a police report on this crazy ass hoe! Ever since that day she called me with that bullshit talkin' about she was pregnant, crazy thing was the bitch didn't even call me back! If she was for real about this baby belonging to me, she should've been hitting me up left and right. Now I was about to cuss the fuck out of this bitch and then block her ass for real!

"Man, look, bitch! This is the last mothafuckin' time I'm gonna tell you this shit! You're a fucking liar and a manipulative ass bitch! If you were a real ass woman about your shit, you would've been tried to hit me up to prove that baby was mine! Why the fuck would you wait two years?!? Like, nigga what?!? You went through the rolodex of niggas you were fucking and they all came up short? Bitch, I'm not some nigga that is about to play some Maury Povich Who The Daddy fuck ass game with you! Get the fuck off my line and if you call me back, I'm gonna file a police report against your crazy ass for stalking me!"

"WATCH YO BACK, NIGGA! I GOT PEOPLES! I KNOW SOME REAL HITTAS THAT'LL DO YOU!"

"BITCH, BYE!" I screamed, instantly hanging up the call.

"Man, what the fuck!" I yelled, punching the steering wheel. I would've popped my vape pen out and took a few tokes but my job had a serious drug policy and I wasn't finne risk my $80,000 over some bullshit.

I turned the music up in my car, trying to fade the anxiety away from my mind. I just kept thinking to myself, damn, what if this baby truly was mine? I would've felt extremely fucked up knowing that I was neglecting my own blood. There was a part of me wanted to call her back and just go ahead and take the damn paternity test just to see if the child really belonged to me. Don't judge me but I had a weak spot for kids. Like I said before, I knew what it was like to live without a father figure. I couldn't fathom the idea of having a seed of mine go without having a father in their life. Every child deserved to have both parents in their lives. That was so long as both of them were stable and didn't have a bunch of bullshit going on.

Still sitting in traffic, I had to think for a moment about what I needed to do. Probably the best person to give me advice was my mama, so I immediately hit her line.

A few rings later, mama quickly picked up. "Hey, son! You still bringing my grandbaby over here?" mama asked.

"Hey, ma! Yeah, I'mma still bring her by. Did the toys and stuff come from Amazon?"

"Yup! I ordered some more stuff for her, too! She's gonna be so surprised."

"Spoiling her as usual, I see," I nervously laughed.

"Shit, it's the least thing I can do since her mama ain't nothing but a trifling guttersnipe. To this day I still don't know how and why you linked up with that no good ass heffa. But that's water under the bridge. What's up? Why you callin' me this early?"

"Well, listen, mama, I don't want you to judge me but I got a little crazy situation going on," I replied then tightened my lips. I didn't know how exactly I was going to frame this revelation to my mother. I just knew she was about to go the fuck off.

"Wassup, Dre? What did you do this time? Oh God! Here we go again! I'm ready!"

"Mama, please. Just listen..."

"I'm listening..."

"Well, about two years ago, I went out with the guys and ended up sleeping with this chick I met at the club. Her name is Shelly."

"You got her pregnant! GODDAMNIT, DRE! WHAT THE FUCK?!?"

"Ma, please! Listen! It's more complicated than that!"

"Please explain all of this shit to me! You got too much good going for yourself now! The last thing you need is for another kid in your life to fuck it all up for you right now!"

"I know, mama! Just listen though..."

"Tell me, Dre!"

"Well, this girl, Shelly, claims that I got her pregnant. That night, I swear to God, I wore a condom. Like, for real. But she claims something must've happened to the condom."

"Wait, so this woman called years ago about this mess?!?"

"Yeah, and she never called me back! And now she's popping back up!"

"Well, she sounds crazy as hell!"

"Right!"

"So what you gonna do?"

"I'm asking you! What do you think I should do?"

"I think you just need to go ahead and man the fuck up, call this crazy bitch back, take the test and see what happened to shut her up. If the child is yours, then you need to take care of him or her. If it's not, well, you proved to this scalawag that the kid ain't yours, and then you move the hell on with life. Simple as that! But I hope this is a wakeup call for you!"

"Mama, I know! Trust me! That's why I ain't been dating."

"Just beatin' ya meat, huh?!? That's what the hell you should've been doing in the first place until you met the right woman!"

"Eww, mama! TMI!"

"Boy, whatever. Get off my line! I gotta get to work. Call that woman back and tell her you gonna do the test," Mama said.

"Aiight, Mama. Love you."

"Love you, too, son," Mama said and then hung up.

Shaking my head, I quickly called back the 847 number and within seconds Shelly picked up.

"WASSUP, BITCH NIGGA??!?" Shelly screamed.

"Man, look, calm the fuck down. I'll go ahead and take the damn test, Shelly. If the kid is mine, I'll do the right thing and take care of it. But if it ain't, you need to get the fuck on and lose my number. Where the fuck I gotta take this test?!?"

"Good! I'm glad you came to your mothafuckin' senses. And your son's name is Junior! DeAndre, Jr! Named him right after his punk ass daddy!"

Slapping my forehead, I exhaled. This bitch was looney

toons like for real FOR REAL! Who the fuck does that? Name a child after a nigga she didn't even have proof belonged to him. This bitch not only was crazy as fuck but wack as fuck.

"Man, whatever. Just tell me where I gotta go," I said.

"We can do a walk-in appointment at LabCorp in Downtown! We can handle this shit right now!"

"Bet! I'mma call my job and take off!"

"Aiight, fuck nigga! See ya soon!" she said and hung up. I immediately hit my job up and ran some bullshit sick excuse to my supervisor. Thankfully I never used my PTO or sick time, so my supervisor, Bill, gave me the day off. I was one of the top management trainees anyways and Bill told me I needed to take some time off.

Once I got off the phone with the job, I got off the expressway and made a U-turn to head back Downtown. Shelly texted me the address to this LabCorp location, which was located right off State Street, not too far away from DePaul. Within thirty minutes I got there, parked and headed inside the building's lobby. And boom, there Shelly was, sitting there, holding this boy who looked no older than two.

"Damn, you got here quick," I said rolling my eyes to the ceiling.

"Hey, Dre...," she said softly, her tone no longer vicious. Bitch was now putting on a front in front of all of these people inside the lobby.

"Sup...," I replied and rolled my eyes again. "Let's just go and get this over with," I replied as I walked up to the receptionist's desk.

Shelly got up, holding the kid in her arms. I took a quick glance at him to see if any of his features resembled mine. And damn, there was a part of him that somewhat resembled me. We both had the same texture of hair. His eyes were a bit similar. But then again, the kid also resembled Shelly.

I couldn't lie though, having this kid really put some meat on Shelly...This bitch was looking really thick in all the right places. Maybe I did kind of fuck up by not trying to cultivate something serious with her. As she got a foot away from me, I could smell her perfume wafting in the air. Man, she kind of reminded me of a young ass Nia Long. She had these Asian-esque eyes that could pull any nigga in.

*Man, wake the fuck up! Stop thinkin' with your dick!* I suddenly snapped out of the daze and turned my attention toward the receptionist.

"You guys have an appointment?" the young Latina receptionist asked. This Latina bitch was looking spicy and sexy as fuck, too. Man, I didn't know what the fuck was going on, but suddenly I was finding myself super-horny being around all of these broads. But with too much stress and anxiety on my mind, my dick couldn't even get hard thinking that this kid might belong to me. I started to add up all the numbers in my head, thinking just how much I would now have to muster up to take care of this kid on top of Ariyanna.

"Yes, we do," Shelly smiled and then looked at me. "We're doing a paternity test," she explained.

"Okay, cool beans...," the receptionist said. "I'm gonna need the both of you to fill out this paperwork and then someone will come and get you," she said as she handed the both of us clipboards. We both sat back down and immediately began to fill out the mound of paperwork attached to the clipboard.

Out the corner of my eye, it seemed like Shelly zoomed through the paperwork as if she'd been through this a million times. Probably did. Hoe ass.

I took my time, however. Within seconds, she turned her attention to me and said, "You know...I'm sorry if I came across as aggressive and mean, DeAndre, but I just didn't know how else to handle this situation. I do apologize," she whispered sympathetically.

"It's whatever. Like I said, if the child is mine, I'll take care of my son. But if it's not, I wish you the best of luck in finding the father...Okay?"

"Okay," she replied as she rocked lil man.

Five minutes later, some fat ass old white lady with alopecia came into the lobby. "DeAndre Williams...," she said in a raspy voice.

"That's me," I said as I stood up, brushing lint off my shirt.

"Good luck," Shelly replied. *Good luck?* Bitch, this ain't the SAT, I thought to myself.

Rolling my eyes and shaking my head out of slight disgust, I didn't respond. *Good luck?!?* Nah, bitch! Good luck to you! Because if this kid wasn't mine, yo ass was gonna leave me the fuck alone! I knew that for sure!

As I followed the white lady down the hallway, she led me into a room and then handed me a cup. "We do a triple-proof test just make sure we don't have any false positives or false negatives. First, we are gonna take a saliva test. Then I'm gonna draw blood. Afterwards, I'm gonna have you to urinate in a cup, okay?"

"Sounds good to me," I nervously replied.

After the nurse, or whatever the fuck she was, took a saliva sample and drew blood from me, I went into a bathroom across the hall and began peeing in the cup she gave me. Before I headed out, I looked in the mirror and said a tiny prayer.

"Please, God...Please...I don't wish harm or ill on Shelly or lil man, but I can't afford to have another kid right now. Please..."

I made my way out into the hallway where the nurse was

standing guard, patiently waiting for my urine sample. "Alrighty! We'll have the results ready in about thirty minutes. You can go back out to the lobby!" she said. Marching slowly down the hallway, I could feel dread coming over me.

About a good thirty minutes passed. I was sitting in the lobby, and Shelly sat beside me, side, rapidly tapping her foot against the floor.

"Alright! We have the results ready!" the same fat ass white nurse announced as she walked into the lobby of the testing center with two manila envelopes in her hands. She handed one to me and another to Shelly. "These are certifiable results, so you can use these in court if you like," she explained.

"Thank you," I replied, hesitant to open the folder.

"Well...," Shelly said, turning her attention toward me. "Like you said, if he's yours, then you're gonna take full responsibility, right?"

"Yes, and if not, then I wish you the best of luck, Shelly. Sorry things had to go this way but it is what it is. Hopefully, you'll find the father so lil man can have a dad in his life. I know what it's like to live life without one," I said.

She didn't say anything back. Holding lil man in one hand, she hastily opened the envelope to read the results. I did the same.

"OH MY GOD!" Shelly suddenly cried, cupping her mouth to contain her shrieking.

My eyes widened with surprise, my mouth flung wide open. "WOOOOOOOOOOOOOOOOOW!"

# CHAPTER TWELVE

"... And I want you to hold onto God's unchanging hand! Be a finger of love, Dear Holy God! Lord, heal LaTrisha's body from this demon, Lord. Wipe it away, God! We ask all of these things in your name! In Jesus' name, we pray! AMEN!"

Pastor Shirley held me tight as she held her hands over me and prayed over me. With other women surrounding me, a few were crying and chanting, some were even speaking in tongues.

"AMEN!" everyone in the room responded in unison at the end of the prayer.

I opened my eyes, wiping my face free of tears. These last two years had been filled with so much tribulation for me. I couldn't believe this would end up being my life. Since the day I got shot and subsequently arrested, I was given a year-long jail sentence for trafficking drugs plus five years of probation. To this day, I was still thoroughly confused as how Dayveon's drugs ended up in my purse. I knew I was completely innocent in that situation, but because I couldn't afford an attorney, I ended up with a crappy public defender who pretty much made me sign a plea deal. He told me if I didn't take the plea deal, Cook County and the Feds were gonna slap me with ten years in prison.

Although Neicy and I weren't getting along before everything happened, she had a sudden change of heart and tried to start a GoFundMe to raise money for an attorney but all she could do was raise $2,000. That wasn't even enough to hire a top-notch criminal defense attorney. She told me she would've needed at least $20,000 to get someone working on the case ASAP but she didn't even have that type of money saved up. Not even Monique could help me. But truth be told, I couldn't expect them too. I had to realize all of this was my fault.

Anyways...

While I was still in the hospital, I also learned some devastating news. The day the nurse, Mrs. Whitaker, tried to call me about my results, she was also trying to call me to tell me that I had stage 2 cervical cancer. Soon as I got to prison, I was put on a combination of chemo and radiation treatments and spent the good part of my prison sentence inside of a hospital. You would think being in a hospital was better than being in the general population with a bunch of evil women who were ready to tear you apart and kill you. But it was quite the opposite. Being inside of a prison hospital, receiving poor care, and then watching others around you die left and right was the worse experience on Earth. Not to mention, the rounds of chemo and radiation absolutely tore my body into shreds. With my hair falling out and my frame becoming frail, there were times where I just knew I was going to die. And die a horrible, painful death. But while in the hospital, I decided to change my life around. I did what I thought I'd never do and that was give myself over to Christ. I became a born-again Christian.

After I got released from prison, I was immediately sent

to a halfway house. I ended up at this place on the West Side of the city called House Of Hope and Deliverance, which was operated by Evangelist Dr. Shirley Jenkins. She was a former crack and heroin addict who served ten years in prison for drug trafficking, prostitution and a range of other things. After she got out, she got her PhD in ministry and theology and started a reentry program for women who were formerly incarcerated.

I had been living at Hope, as we called it, now for some months and life was starting to get back to normal. At least I thought it was...Today, I was scheduled to go to the doctor to go check to see if my cancer was in remission. That was why Pastor Shirley and others were praying over me. We had just completed a weekend of intense fasting and praying, hoping today I would get positive results back. I just knew the Lord would come through and make this cancer go away.

"Reach out and touch somebody's hand! Make this world a better place, if you can! REACH OUT AND TOUCH SOMEBODY'S HAND! MAKE THIS WORLD A BETTER PLACE IF YOU CAN!" Pastor Shirley, a voluptuous dark-skinned woman with a big soul, started to sing as we all joined in.

We formed a circle, holding each other's hand. About nine of us were inside of this conference room, singing our hearts away. After we got done and hugged each other, I made my way back to my room and began to get ready for my doctor's appointment.

*Knock! Knock!*

Two loud knocks thumped on my room's door. "It's open," I mumbled as I scurried looking for my purse and cell phone.

"Hey, Ms. Trisha...The van is ready to take you to the doctor," Ms. Geraldine, one of the home's caseworkers said as she made her way into my room. She took was a former crackhead who turned her life around.

"Thank you, Ms. Geraldine," I replied, grabbing my bible and then limped my way to the door. I was now walking with a cane since I had surgery on my right leg. The cancer spread to a part of my hip, so I had a hip replacement not too long ago. I was slowly recovering.

"You got everything you need, child?" Ms. Geraldine asked.

"Yes, ma'am," I responded.

"Oooh, I forgot my prayer cloth," I said, quickly forgetting one last thing. Spinning too quickly on my heels, I almost lost my balance and I dropped my bible and phone on the floor.

"Don't worry! I got it!" Ms. Geraldine said as she leaned down to pick up my stuff. I limped back over to my dresser, grabbed my red blood of Jesus prayer cloth and then limped back to the door where Ms. Geraldine handed me my bible, my phone...and a picture of Ariyanna. My sweet Ariyanna...

A sole photo I had of my baby girl was tucked away in the back of the bible. From time to time, when things seemed to get dark and dreary, I looked at the picture and thought about my baby girl, hoping she'd beam me some inspiration to keep carrying on this life's journey.

God knew I missed her so much. I hadn't seen her since that day in the hospital. DeAndre hated me so much for everything I did that he not only stripped me of custody and visitation rights, but he even absolutely refused to bring her to the prison to at least let me see her once. I tried to write him so many times, telling him how sorry I was for everything, but he never called me or wrote me back. I even tried to have Neicy talk to him, but he refused and said that our family was completely cut off from ever having ties with Ariyanna.

"Who is that?" Ms. Geraldine asked.

"My baby girl," I said.

"Oh, I didn't know you had a child! Why you didn't say anything?"

"Well...'Cuz...Well, my child's father took custody away from me and I don't have visitation rights."

"Wow. I'm so sorry to hear that."

"Yeah," I replied. "It's cool though."

Ms. Geraldine froze and gave me this melancholic gawk. "Sister LaTrisha...It's not cool. I know you miss her. Don't be ashamed. We've all been through what you're going through. God will make a way. You just gotta pray that one day your child's father will see the necessity of having you in your daughter's life."

"Yeah...I know," I said, somewhat trying to fight back tears. "I'm fine though, Ms. Geraldine. I don't wanna be late for my appointment. I first need to find out if I'm gonna live to even hope one day I'm gonna see my daughter again," I explained, a tear trickled down the side of my face.

"Understandable...Well, let's get going. I'm pretty sure the doctor has some good news to give you," she said.

"Hopefully..."

Once we got outside to the entrance of Hope, a van was parked ready to take me to the oncologist.

❦

*Knock! Knock! Knock!*

The door to examination room I was patiently waiting in slowly opened. Dr. Pirtle, my oncologist, sauntered in and quickly closed the door.

"Hey, LaTrisha! How you feelin', sweetheart?" she asked, a smile flexed across her golden honey face.

"I'm fine, Dr. Pirtle. Too blessed to be stressed," I said, smiling back to her although anxiety was roaring inside of me.

She opened up a manila folder and scanned a few sheets

of paper. Probably my test results. I quickly said a prayer, hoping the Lord will show me through this trial.

Dr. Pirtle pursed her lips and then stared up at me. "Well...LaTrisha...We've run a battery of tests on you. Unfortunately, your cancer has come back. And it's come back aggressively. It's now spread to your kidneys and liver..."

My face twisted with bewilderment. My eyes flung open with panic. "Huh? But, I...I, umm, I feel fine, Doctor. What do you mean?"

Dr. Pirtle lowered her head. She yanked a seat from the desk inside the examination room and pulled it up to me and sat down. She glanced up at me and said, "Sometimes aggressive cancers can be asymptomatic. We can try some other treatment options, but Trisha, I have to be completely honest and upfront with you. It's not looking too good..."

Closing my eyes and lowering my head out of perplexity and dismay, I couldn't wrap my head around what I was hearing. "So, you're pretty much saying that I'm gonna die?"

Dr. Pirtle didn't say anything immediately. "I didn't say all of that, LaTrisha. I'm just saying right now your prognosis doesn't look too good. We can try some other experimental therapies. I'll come up with a list of things we can possibly try. But in the meantime, just try your best to continue taking your medicine, stick the diet I gave you and also do a lot of praying and meditating. Right now, you don't need your immune system to go into overdrive by being stressed out."

"I can't believe this, Dr. Pirtle. I'm just so confused right now. None of this is making sense to me," I cried, wiping my face free of fears. All of the praying and fasting I had been doing over the last few weeks seemed to be pointless.

"I know, sweetie, but please, just don't stress yourself out. We're gonna hopefully find a solution but I don't want you to stress yourself out, okay?"

"Okay," I replied.

After Dr. Pirtle told about me about some other treatment options, I left the office and made my way outside to the halfway house's van. I got in and Cyril, the driver, looked back at me asking, "I hope you got some good news. I know the Lord showed out! Tell me my God did??!?"

"Yes...I'm claiming recovery in the name of Jesus," I lied. "He's gonna see me through this. I know he will..."

"That's good to hear!"

I knew I was going to die. I felt it now. It was just a matter of months, if not weeks. And if that was the case, I needed to see my baby. I needed to see Ariyanna to let her know her mother never forgot about her and that I loved her. The first thing I was going to do when I got back to Hope was try to call DeAndre.

## CHAPTER THIRTEEN

"WELP! He's your kid," Shelly exclaimed. She quickly looked at lil man and happily said, "Say hi to your daddy, Junior!"

"Hiii!" he replied back, waving at me, smiling hard.

I looked over at lil man and stared at him so hard...*Damn.* This was *my* son. My mothafuckin' son.

I couldn't believe this shit. *This had to be a fuckin' dream or some shit. No it ain't nigga. No fuckin' dream. Wake the fuck up. You got a son now,* my mind roared.

My head dropped damn near in my lap. I couldn't say I was surprised, but something just kept telling me this entire time the kid was mine. *But how? HOW?!?!? I used a condom!* My thoughts about this situation weren't mitigating the confusion swarming my mothafuckin' mind. Wow. I was now batting two for fuckin' two. Two kids now had my last name. *Un-fucking-believable.*

"Well, my word is my bond. He's mine, so without a doubt, I gotta do what I gotta do. Sorry for all of this, Shelly. Truth be told, I wish you would've come at me the right way from the beginning and I would've been better prepared for all of this, but hey, I can't blame you. If I was in your shoes, I would've done the same. So, truth be told, I guess you did the right thing," I said. "Can I hold him?"

"Well...I'm glad you and I have a common understanding...And yeah, I do apologize for coming at you that way. But like you, I, too, know what it's like to not have a father so my anxiety was through the roof. And I'm not a liar, Dre. Sure, I may have been on some super-hoe shit that night, but trust me, I don't mess with dudes like that. I wasn't even prepared for all of this but at the same time, I just don't believe in abortions."

"Understandable," I said.

She handed me my son and then I began to joke and play with him. "You look just like yo daddy," I laughed, while a tear escaped the corner of my right eye. Although I was caught by disbelief by all of this, I wasn't upset. If anything, looking my son in my eyes made me realize how innocent this kid was and thank God Shelly and I were mature enough to come to a quick understanding to resolve all of this.

"So, what's next?" I asked. "We going to court?"

"Look, Dre...I'm an attorney. We don't have to do all of that because I know what that family court system is all about. We can come up with some sort of arrangement. Maybe we can swap weeks."

My eye brown raised out of curiosity. "You're an attorney? I was thinking about going to law school myself!"

"Really?"

"Yeah..DePaul..."

"That's where I went!" she commented with a smile.

"Anyways, that can work...And he'll have a chance to play with his half-sister, I guess."

"Oh, you have another kid?"

"Yeah...A daughter. I take care of her full-time."

"If you don't mind me asking, what happened to the mother?"

"Make a long story short, she ended up going to jail for selling drugs. But I got full custody and stripped her of her visitation rights."

"Wow...I guess you had to do what you had to do, right?"

"Yeah..."

"Well, I don't wanna suddenly push Junior onto you right now...Let's set a play date maybe for this weekend if you don't mind. You want to come over to my place?"

I froze for a moment. Man...This seemed so weird. She and I literally went from damn near killing each other to the point now we were acting as if we were best friends. "Sure... Or you can come to my crib. It's whatever," I explained.

"Where do you live?"

"I live in Hyde Park...I just got a townhouse and everything," I said.

"Cool! I live in the West Loop."

"Well, I'll just swing by, since it'll probably be easier for me to get to your place," I said.

"Okay, well, I guess you have my number now," she smiled.

"Quick question for you...You really know some hittas?" I jokingly asked but I was a tad serious.

"No, boy. I was just saying that shit to scare you."

"You're funny as hell," I laughed. "Anyways, Shelly, I'll hit you up this weekend."

"Ok, cool..."

Shelly and I chatted for a few more minutes before I headed out and made my way to my car.

Once I hopped in the Charger and chucked up the muhfuckin' engine, I needed to immediately hit my mama up. Boy, I just knew my old lady was going to be pissed. But, oh well. This was my life. Not hers.

Now on the e-way, headed back home, I dialed her up.

Within seconds, she picked up. "Hold on, Dre. Let me go outside. I don't want these customers all up in ma business."

"Okay," I said, weaving in and out of slightly thick Lake Shore Drive traffic. I was actually shocked to see that there was traffic at this time of the day.

Some seconds later, mama said, "Okay, so tell me what happened?"

"You have a grandson. DeAndre, Jr...," I replied.

"WHAT?!?! You have GOT to be mothafuckin' kidding me, Dre!?!? OH MY GOD!"

"Mama, please...Just calm down!"

"What you mean by calm down! No, you need to calm the fuck down!?!? So what in the hell are you gonna do now?!?"

"Ma, please! I already talked to Shelly. We worked it out. I'm going to chill with her this weekend and bring Ariyanna over there. We're gonna hash out some details about everything. She's actually an attorney," I said.

"Ughh!" Mama exhaled. I could hear the anger in her voice. She was definitely pissed as fuck with me.

"Whatever, Dre. Just handle your shit. Listen, when you come over tonight, we'll talk about this more. I can't handle all of this right now."

"Okay...Well, I took off for the day. I'm about to head over to Tanisha's."

"Aiight, boy...," Mama said.

"Love you, mama," I replied and then hung up.

Lord knew I needed to get fucking high. Yeah, yeah, yeah. The job had a strict drug policy but I needed something strong to simmer my mothafuckin' nerves right now. Tanisha, in fact, hit me up telling me she had some bomb ass Billy Kimber OG Kush straight from Las Vegas. I hadn't smoked some flower in a minute. But like I said, although I was a bit paranoid of smoking 'cuz of my job, I figured if they did do some random drug test, I could just take some Niacin and pass that shit. Besides, I hadn't smoked in a minute. You gotta smoke a lot of weed for that shit to stay in your system for a long time anyway...

Some thirty minutes later, I ended up on 79th street, seconds away from pulling down Tanisha's block. I found a spot, parked and made my way up to her floor.

Once I got to her door, I knocked twice and to my surprise, Tanisha didn't answer. Candreka did. These two were still an item.

"Sup...Tanisha ain't here? She just texted me and told me she'd be home."

"Bleh! Her ass all the way out in fuckin' Skokie. She had to do a drop. But she told me she texted you and said that she was running behind," Candreka said.

"Nah! I ain't get a text from her!"

"Well, sorry, don't know what to tell you. What were you looking for?"

"Man, she told me she had some new Kush straight from Vegas."

"Well, I can go through the stash and see if she still got some leftover..."

"What? You're helping her push now?"

"Nigga, I've been helping her push. Besides, who you think is the one doing all the accounting and logistics? Tanisha just gets the clients, I organize all the shipments," she laughed.

"Oh, really?" I smiled. Damn, Candreka was so damn thick and sexy. I hope Tanisha was treating that lil pussy right.

"Well, come in. Don't stand out here in the hallway," she said, inviting me into the apartment.

"Bet," I said as I walked in and closed the door behind me. Trailing Candreka, I was so floored by the sight of seeing her in these tight ass jean shorts. Her ass cheeks were damn near falling out of those muhfuckas. She had on a tank top as usual, exposing her tatted arms. As she took each step, each ass cheek moved side to side in a melody. Damn, I eat that ass, too. Thick ass red bitch. Booty hole probably taste like birthday cake.

"Damn, Tanisha just let you walk around and interact with muhfuckas like that?"

"Like what?" she asked with a scrunched up face.

I looked down at her shorts and then back up at her. "Like that..."

"Oh, boy please! Come get this shit...," she said as she made her way into the kitchen. She opened up a big cardboard box, the smell of fresh west coast weed instantly hit my nostrils. "Damn, that shit loud as fuck!" I chuckled, cupping my nose. "That shit fire as fuck, too," she commented shaking her head. "You wanna try some before you leave?"

I hesitated for a moment. Damn, I didn't know how I felt about smoking with cuzzo's bitch while she wasn't home. But then I thought about it, I had nothing to lose. Besides, I still had a few hours to burn before I had to go pick up Ariyanna from daycare. And besides, Candreka was a dyke. Wasn't like she was gonna try some shit.

"Sure, why not?" I said, moving closer into the kitchen. Other cardboard boxes, presumably filled with vape carts, flower, and edibles, littered the kitchen floor. "Damn, how much ya'll making selling this shit?" I asked, my curiosity burning my brain cells. These bitches looked like they were making serious guwap!

"Man, bruh, you nosey as fuck," Candreka laughed shaking her head. "But since you family, I'll let you in on the secret. About thirty stacks a month...One time we almost made a hunned grand in a month!"

"WHAT THE FUCK?!?! Are you fucking kidding me?!? Why the fuck ya'll ain't put me on?!? You know how many people I know?!?! Man, ya'll made more than my salary in a month!"

"Yeah, well, Tanisha likes to keep her shit on the low-low…"

"Yeah, I feel you," I said as she handed me a 3.5. "How much I owe you?"

"Nothing…At least, not right now. You good," she laughed, sticking her tongue out. *What the fuck did that mean?* I was confused.

"You sure?"

"Yeah…I'm sure…"

"Okay! Cool then! Well, I'mma holla at ya'll later!" I said but before I could spin on my feet and make my way to the door, Candreka blurted out, "Damn, nigga! We was supposed to smoke together! You forgot that quickly?"

"Oh shit! My bad! You right!"

"How you usually smoke flower? Papers? Blunts?"

"Man, I'm a blunt-type of nigga," I said. "You got Swishers."

"Hell fuck no! Them nasty shits! Boy, we smoke nothin' but Backwoods around here."

"Damn, ya'll some muhfuckin' vets!"

"Boy, you goofy as hell! I got my shit out in the living room," she said as she walked past me and threw me this look, scanning me up and down. Man, this bitch was acting really different. Any other time we interacted, she kept her distance. Now today she was acting like she was feeling me. What the fuck was that about?

We both sat down on the sole couch in the living next to each other, smack dab right in front of this big ass, 5k hi-def television glued to the wall. CNN was playing on the TV. "You can change the channel if you want to," she said. "I ain't watching that shit. Tanisha always watching the news. I don't like that shit. Shit be too negative," Candreka said, pulling out a fresh baggie of Kush from the coffee table in front of us. She then grabbed a pack of Backwoods and began breaking down the 'gar.

"Cool," I uttered, quickly grabbing the remote. I flipped through channels while Candreka rolled up.

Some minutes later, the blunt was rolled up. That shit was fat ass fuck, almost looked like a damn dick!

"You wanna spark up first?" she asked.

Terrified, my eyes grew big at just how the big the blunt was. "Man, girl, that shit is big as hell! How much weed you stuffed in that muhfucka?"

"Man, I usually roll up with a quarter. We get high as fuck around here," she giggled, sticking her tongue out.

"Yeah, I can tell..." She extended her rose and skull-tatted up hand out to me and passed me the freshly rolled blunt. Bitch used honey to seal everything together. "Damn, you use honey to roll up your blunts?"

"Yeah, make that shit burn slow, too..."

Candreka handed me a red BIC lighter and I lit that bad boy up. I took two tokes, but I couldn't handle the thick smoke that suddenly filled my lungs. I started coughing left and right like I had the fucking flu or some shit.

"Damn! SHIT!" I growled, punching the right side of my chest, trying to get the plume of smoke out of my lungs! "Shit is strong as fuck! What the fuck is the THC percentage on that shit?!?"

"Shit, that OG right there close to forty percent! That's some special lab created shit! That's why we be havin' so many damn customers. Niggas in Chicago be selling that wack ass reggie."

It didn't even take a full minute before the high began to set in and take over every damn square inch of my body. "Damn...I already feel that shit," I said as I sat back and held onto my chest. Within seconds, it felt like my entire body was vibrating. "Man, I'm high as FUCK!"

"Told you, boy!" she laughed, taking toke after toke from the blunt.

By now, I was so mothafuckin' zooted, I felt like I was on an entirely different planet. However, as I glanced over at Candreka, it seemed like her tolerance was high as fuck. She just kept puffing left and right on the blunt.

Minutes later, I closed my eyes and began to drift off... Shit. I hope I'd wake up in time to go pick up baby girl.

Sometime later, I didn't know exactly how long, my eyelids slowly lifted open. But I was caught by surprise by the sight of Candreka snuggled up on me. "Damn, we both passed the fuck out," I said.

"I didn't...," she commented as she moved her hand closer to my chest and began to twirl my right nipple.

Confused, I looked over her and said, "Damn, what is you doin'?"

"Man, don't act like you ain't been feelin' me all this time...," she moaned as she lifted up my shirt and ran her hand over my abs.

"From the day I laid my eyes on you I was destined to get some of this dick. I know you want this pussy," she said.

"Man, folks, you tweakin', for real! I can't do that! You almost like blood to me now,"

"Man, boy, what the fuck ever. Tanisha be doing all types of shit with other bitches from time to time. Shit, I wanna get some dick. Plus, she ain't gonna be back for a few more hours. She texted me and said she wasn't gonna be back home until eight. Now stop playing with me and let me suck that dick," she commanded as she unbuttoned and unzipped my pants. She stuck her hand down my boxers and began to play with my semi-erect dick. I couldn't help it.

"FUCKKK!" I groaned. "Man, I don't know…"

"You about to know. Now stop playing with me. You know you want this pussy," she said.

## CHAPTER FOURTEEN

After I got back from my doctor's appointment, I went straight to my room and went into deep prayer. Hours had passed and I was ready to call it the night. But then, the thought of everything that transpired today came back to me so I had to go back into prayer. There was just so much I was thinking about and I needed the Lord's light to shine upon me right now.

So, after saying a quick prayer, I sat the edge of my bed, shivering with anxiety. The real dilemma I was now facing was whether or not I should try to call DeAndre. A part of me was like, *No, Trish, don't do it. He will get mad at you and hang up. He will make your life even worse.* But then another part of me was like, *No, that's your daughter, too. You have every right to see her.*

Not knowing the right next step to take, I closed my eyes once again then I began to say another prayer—

"Dear Lord, please give me the guidance and courage to press forward. Please give me a sign that I need to call DeAndre and get into contact with him to see my baby girl. In your name, I pray...Amen..."

My eyes opened, God's hope cloaked me. And now I felt in my spirit that the Lord would manifest some sort of sign letting me know what to do next.

A few seconds later, my phone began to vibrate. My phone was attached to my charger on my nightstand. I quickly reached over, grabbed it and saw that it was my bestie, Monique, calling me. I quickly answered the phone call. "Hey, Monique!" I exclaimed. I was so grateful that my friend was calling me.

You know, through it all, Monique had been there for me, no questions asked. I was thoroughly shocked that she was still my friend despite being put through this nonstop blazing fire of tremendous difficulty.

"Hey, sis! How are you feeling? Did you get some good news from the doctor, today?" she asked.

"Well..." Closing my eyes, I exhaled trying to fight back tears...I clasped my chest trying to formulate the right words. I didn't want to tell her the truth but I couldn't be a liar no more. That was my past.

"Well, what?" she asked.

"No...," I responded. "I didn't. In fact, the cancer has spread. The doctor told me things ain't lookin' too good..."

"Oh, noooo! I'm so sorry to hear that, Trish! Nooo!" Suddenly I could hear her burst into tears. Her crying instantly triggered me into doing the same. I could no longer hold back all the grief I had from hearing that devastating news earlier. This was just all too much. But the little morsel of faith I had inside of me kept me somewhat strong.

"I know, sweetie. I know...But I'm hanging in there. Don't cry, best friend. It'll be alright. I'm just hoping the Lord will come through and bless me with a miracle," I consoled her although right now I was the one truly needing all the consolation in the world.

"You've been through so much, Trish. I just hate that all

of this is happening to you. You don't deserve any of this. You really don't. And I think it's so messed up that you still can't even see Ariyanna. It ain't right. It just ain't right," she replied in between her crying and sniffling.

Then and there, once she dropped Ariyanna's name, I became promptly tempted to ask for her advice as to whether or not I should try to get into contact with DeAndre again. I paused for a moment, closed my eyes and then asked, "Do you think I should try to reach back out to DeAndre? I've been debating about this ever since I got back from the doctor's office. Like, I really need to see my baby girl. It just ain't right...I miss her so much. I feel so terrible on the inside."

"I think you should! But maybe trying to contact him ain't the right thing to do. Maybe you should try to call his mother. You know, at the end of the day, his mama might be a lot more forgiving and lenient than him. Any mother should sympathize with the situation you got going on. I know I would do the same even if we weren't necessarily getting along..."

Dang. She was right. That was such a good idea. Something I hadn't considered. DeAndre's mother should be a lot more forgiving and try to talk some sense into DeAndre's head. He was being way too harsh on me. I truly didn't deserve this type of treatment. Granted, I knew I made my fair share of mistakes. Yeah, I had a horrible past. But who didn't? And in this present moment, I was trying my hardest to overcome that past. But you know what – Ariyanna was my daughter, too! I deserved to be in her life, and she deserved to be in mine!

"Thank you so much, Monique. This is exactly what I needed to hear! Before you called, I had prayed for a sign to let me know whether or not it would be the right thing to do to try to get into contact with DeAndre. See, I know my God is going to pull me through all of this!"

"Yes, girl! I'm praying for you, too!"

"Thank you. I really appreciate it!" I exclaimed, feeling overcome with joy. I was ready to bust out in a praise dance.

"When can I come and see you?" Monique then asked.

"Well, I'll have visitation hours this weekend."

"Okay, I'll come and bring some cupcakes. You still like red velvet cupcakes?"

I smiled. Bestie still remembered those little small details about me. "Girl, I wish I could eat those but my doctor told me I can't eat any processed sugar. She said sugar will feed the cancer cells. I really appreciate it though."

"Okay, well, I'mma still come. Chadwick supposed to be going out of town this weekend. He's going to Florida with some of his friends for a bachelor party. Maybe you can ask your probation officer if you could spend the weekend with me?"

"I could see...I don't know. I'd have to call her."

"Do it! I miss you so much, Trish. I need to see my friend. I've been thinking about you so much."

"I miss you, too, sis. I'll give the probation officer a call tomorrow and see what she say."

"Okay, girl. Well, go ahead and call DeAndre's mama and see what she say."

"Okay...Love you, girl. Enjoy the rest of your night," I said.

We hung up and I quickly went through my contacts and found Dre's mother's phone number. I hoped she still had the phone number. Shoot. People be changing phone numbers nowadays like they change their drawers. And it had been quite some time since we last spoke. And that last time was in the hospital, which obviously didn't end on good terms.

I glanced down at her contact info and then immediately called her. Some seconds later, she picked up.

"Hello?" she answered, her tone flat.

"Ms. Williams..." I paused for a moment and then clasped my mouth. I was so nervous. "Hey...How you doin'?" I nervously asked, biting the tips of my fingers. My eyes grew wide with anxiety. Something told me in my soul she was about to hang up on me.

"Who is this?" she responded, her slight curiosity mixed with agitation oozed through the phone.

"This is...This is LaTrisha...How you doin'?"

"Trish...Hey...," she responded nonchalantly. "Why in the hell are you calling me?"

"I, ummm, I just wanted to give you a call 'cuz..." I lowered my head and closed my eyes, fighting back tears. "I just wanted to say and say that I'm sorry for everything I caused ya'll. I've been trying to write Dre and get into contact with him but he ain't been responding to any of my letters or phone calls."

"Shit, well, understandably so. You put him through a lot of hell, Trish. Wouldn't you agree?"

"Yes...," I confessed.

"So what the hell you want?"

"Well, Ms. Williams...I'm calling because I ain't been doing so good lately. I, umm, I've been diagnosed with cervical cancer. I just found out today that I might have terminal cancer now."

Silence engulfed the phone for some seconds. I guess that revelation took her by surprise.

"I'm sorry to hear that, Trish. I really am."

"You don't have to be sorry for me. It's life, I guess...But, ughh, the other reason though I'm calling is 'cuz now that I'm possibly dying, I was wanting to see if you could talk to Dre and see if I could come over for some time and see Ariyanna."

Ms. Williams exhaled. "Uhhh…Hrrrm, I don't know about that, Trish. I don't wanna get in between any mess you and Dre got going on. And besides, Dre is doing so good right now and the last thing he needs is for some more drama in his life. Especially coming from you…"

"I understand but Ms. Williams, I really don't know how long I got left to live. I could be dead within weeks or months. I just wanna see Ariyanna and let her know I love her. I think about her every day. I know I wasn't the best mother when I first had her, but I'm trying to make things right now before I possibly pass away," I explained, wiping tears free from my face.

"Trish…Look…I'm so sorry about all of this. I really am. But I cannot do this. I'm sorry. I gotta go now," Ms. Williams said and then abruptly hung up.

"Really?" I grumbled, still sitting at the edge of my bed frozen and shocked. I couldn't fathom that she would just hang up like that! That was so rude! And she had no sympathy for me. Like, wow! She was so ruthless. It was like everything I just told her went in one ear and out the other!

So much emotion began to flood me, I didn't know if I could take it anymore. Quickly shooting up from my bed, I scurried over to my dresser and found a bottle of my Vicodins. I needed to end it all right now! This was just too much! What was the point of living if I couldn't even see my own daughter anymore?!? She was truly the only thing I had left to live for. With trickles of sweat and tears running down my face, I tried to pop open the bottle with the little strength I had left. Once I had the bottle open, I saw I had about a good fourteen pills left. That should do the job! To hell with everything!

*No, Trish! Don't do it! Be encouraged no matter what's going on! God is with you, even in this midnight hour.* I heard a voice pop up in my head, and instantly I dropped the bottle, pills splattered all over the maroon carpeted floor. I fell to my knees and began to cry out loud! "WHY GOD?!?!? WHY!?!? Why am I going through all of this?!?!?"

Rocking back and forth on the ground, I was fighting the urge to kill myself but I knew God was speaking to me, telling me not to succumb to Satan's desire to see me go.

*You're already dead. Just go ahead and finish the job. You are worthless. Look at you. You suck. You are worth nothing!* Suddenly suicidal ideations swarmed my mind again. Why is the devil doing this to me? Tempting me to take my own life! Then this energy overtook my hand and inched me closer to the pills on the ground. "Sorry about this, Lord. I can't do this anymore," I cried softly. I cupped as many pills as I could into my hand and threw them in my mouth.

## CHAPTER FIFTEEN

"You know you want this pussy," Candreka said as she played with my dick. My shit was getting so damn hard as she stroked me.

"Come on, breh, don't do this. I can't. I can't do this," I begged as I quickly clasped my face with hands, not wanting to give into the delectable temptation in front of me. I couldn't believe this sexy ass bitch was doing this to me. This shit just seemed like a set-up. I should've known better. She was giving me all the fucking signals and my dumb ass was barely registering them. But goddamn, man! I swear from the moment I met her sexy ass some years ago, it was like she knew all along I wanted to muhfuckin' tag that shit, write my goddamn name all over her lil pussy.

"Just sit back, Dre. Stop actin' like you don't want this," Candreka seductively said as she pulled down my pants along with my boxers and went to devouring my shit.

"Oh, shit! Oh, fuck! FUCK! FUCK! FUCK! FUCK!" I groaned as shorty stuffed the whole entire dino down her throat. Using her tonsils, she gargled on my dickhead, making that muhfucka swell up like my shit was some old lady's ankle after she ate too much salt. I could feel my precum oozing from my tip, probably now dripping in the back of her throat. With all eight inches planted in her throat, I could feel the bed of her tongue dancing on my shaft. "FUCK!" I screamed as I looked up toward the apartment ceiling clenching my fists tightly. This bitch was putting a spell on me! I HAD TO RESIST!

"NOOOO!" I yelled as I grabbed her head and pulled her off my dick.

"DRE! SHUT UP AND SIT BACK! YOU DOIN' THE MOST! From the day I met you I knew I was gonna get that dick! So stop playin' fuckin' games with me!" Candreka shouted as she still held onto my rock-hard meat.

"FUCK!" I growled. "Man, fuck it!"

"That's what I thought!" she growled, instantly going back to devouring my shit. Candreka was a vet when it came to her dick sucking skills. This was perhaps the best head I'd ever had before in my life. On God, I swear with the way she was sucking my shit, my balls were gonna be emptier than a broke nigga's wallet when she got done draining me.

She went up and down, lathering up my dick with her thick saliva, getting that muhfucka so nasty and sloppy. Yuhp! Just the way I liked it, too. "Damn, you's a lil nasty lil bitch, you know that," I groaned. God knew I loved it when a lil THOT got real gutta with the dick sucking. That shit was a turn on! She kept going up and down my shaft, making sure every square inch of my meat was satisfied. Eventually, she made her way down to my balls and gently sucked on the muhfuckas just the way I liked it, too!

"Damn, 'Dreka, man, fuck! What is you doin'?!?!? I swear ta God I'm 'bout to buss a nut all over you!" I cried, feeling like I was on the seventh level of heaven. Then she did the unimaginable, she took my left ball out of her mouth and then trekked down to my taint and began to lick it! I suddenly had the urge to fight that shit! "YO! What the fuck?!? Nah! I don't get down like that!" I'd be damned if I was gonna have a bitch play with my ass like that. That was some gay ass shit!

"Boy! Relax! Besides, you don't know what the fuck you missing out on!" she said, trying her best to convince me that I was gonna enjoy possibly getting my ass played with.

"I don't know," I said, doubtful like a muhfucka.

"Dre...Just sit back and relax...It's not gay," she said.

I didn't say anything. I just sat back. She pulled my pants further down and then lifted my legs up. Then she didn't even hesitate in eating my ass. Now, I ain't gonna sit up here and tell a lie. That shit felt so fucking good. I was thoroughly amazed at the feeling of getting my ass licked. That shit was an unthinkable feeling. She stuck her tongue down in my shit as she tickled my balls and stroked my still-hard dick. Now I understood why sometimes them porno niggas be letting them bitches eat their ass. Every time I watched a flick and saw a nigga letting a broad do that to them, I just knew those niggas were gay or bisexual. But fuck all of that. Them niggas was onto something though, like for real, G! This shit felt good as hell, dude. Shorty had me experiencing a new level of my sexuality.

"FUCK! Goddamn!" I moaned, my mouth hung wide open.

Seconds later, I lowered my legs. Now I was ready to see what this pussy was all about. "Get up!" I commanded her. I stood up, quickly taking my clothes off. She did the same. And Oh. My. Mothafuckin'. Goodness! Shorty was built like an Amazon goddess. Her curves were like none other.

"Damn, you thick in all the right places," I said as I grabbed her and began to ferociously make out with her. I didn't even give a fuck that just seconds ago she had her tongue deep up in my ass.

We stood there making out for a minute or two before I shoved her down into the couch. I got down on my knees and spread her legs wide open. I was instantly hit with the sight of her soppy ass pussy. Her juices were glistening all up and down her clit and fat ass pussy lips. "Damn, you wet as fuck already," I commented. She had the prettiest lil fat pussy. I know that's kind of oxymoronic but that was the only best way I could describe the heavenly sight in front of me. I threw my head in between her legs just to get sniff of that pussy and ass. I loved the smell of vaj. Especially day-old pussy. Yeah, I was kind of nasty like that. Sometimes, ladies, doin' all that washing can rid the pussy of your natural scent. Let them juices marinate for a day or two, you feel me? Anyways...I didn't even hesitate in eating the fuck out of her pussy. I wrapped my lips around her clit and began to suck away like a fat ass young nigga sucking on a lollipop. She grabbed my head and pushed me deeper into her pussy, damn near suffocating me. But I didn't give a fuck. My upper lip and nose danced across her lightly shaven pussy hair. Them pussy hairs were so straight, too. Thank God. I couldn't stand a bitch with nappy ass pussy hair. That taco meat will cut your lip the fuck up like a brillo pad. Anyways...you already know a nigga had to reciprocate the ass eating, so I didn't even hesitate in getting a taste of that tight pinky booty hole of hers. I hoisted her legs up and ran my tongue down from her pussy to her taint and then straight to her ass. Candreka was so damn wet, her cream was dripping down into her booty hole. I sucked that juice out and went to work on that mothafucka.

"Fuck! Eat that shit, nigga! Get all up in there," Candreka moaned, once again pushing my head deeper. She wrapped her legs around my neck and locked in. As I continued to suck on her booty hole, I used my thumb to play with her clit, making her cum back to back.

A minute later, I pulled her legs from around my neck and then leaned up, ready to pipe her down with all eight inches. I looked down at my dick. Buddy was jumping up and down in full excitement. Although Dreka's pussy was wet as fuck, I wanted that shit to be more slippery and sloppier. So, I drooled down on my shaft to lubricate it, then I slipped my dick straight inside of her.

"Goddamn! Fuck!" I moaned as I could feel her warm, tight walls wrap around my dick. Taking some test strokes, I had to make sure I didn't bust too early. Now don't judge me…Yeah, I should've been wearing a condom, but I didn't give a fuck. If she got pregnant, she was probably smart enough to run her ass down to Walgreen's and get a Plan B. If not, I was definitely gonna show the fuck out and force her ass to get an abortion. I was tired of playing reckless with these hoes.

"How that pussy feel? You like that?" she asked as I kept going in and out of that shit.

"Shit feels amazing, girl…Fuck!" I said as I dug deeper and picked up the speed. I began to fuck the shit out of her.

🐚

"Shit, that was some bomb ass sex," Candreka moaned as we stood side by side in the hallway bathroom. We just got done fucking some fifteen minutes ago and we were now in the bathroom, tidying as much as we could, making sure that we didn't leave a trace of evidence that we had been fucking. An hour had passed and I still had a good hour to go before I had to head up to Ariyanna's daycare to pick her up.

"Yeah, it was…Damn…It just sucks we won't be able to continue this," I said as I pulled my pants up and then stepped over to the faucet and ran my hands in steaming hot water.

"Who says we can't?" she replied, pulling her hair up into a bun. She threw me this gawk as if I said something disrespectful.

My right eyebrow raised out of curiosity. "Really? Girl, you tweakin'," I said. Yo, lil mama was crazy as fuck if she thought us fucking around with each other on the low was a good idea. Besides, the more I thought about, the more ill I became at the thought knowing that I was fucking with my cousin's bitch. That was some low-life ass shit and a part of me was regretting that I even let myself take it this far. Damn. I had absolutely zero self-control but I was so damn horny. Truth be told, I hadn't busted a nut in over a year. It was almost inevitable that I was going to end up letting loose on someone.

"Boy, you so damn scary. Tanisha ain't gon' do shit even if she caught us..."

"Nah...That's what you say. Besides, that's family. It's just something kind of foul about what we did..."

"But you liked it, right?"

"Yeah, I did..."

"Well, it is what it is. You do you. But all I know is if you come back over here and we are alone, don't be surprised if I hop on that dick."

I began to chuckle. This bitch was doin' the most. "Yeah, well, we'll see about that," I said as I dried my hands with some paper towel and made my way out of the bathroom. She followed me and then we made our way into the kitchen. "Ya'll got anything to drink like some water? I'm thirsty as shit," I groaned as I clenched my throat.

"Yeah, look in the fridge," she said. I walked over and opened the fridge and my eyes instantly grew in terror at the sight of three big white bricks sitting in the fridge. "What the fuck is this??!?"

"Boy, mind ya business and get ya damn bottle of water! Damn, you so nosey!" Candreka growled.

Frozen, I couldn't believe what I was seeing. Was cuzzo also pushing coke?!? Damn! What the fuck was she really getting herself into?!?

"Yeah, aiight...Well, let me go ahead and get the fuck out of here. Anyways, thanks for the weed...and the umm...You know what I mean...," I smiled as I grabbed a bottle of water and closed the fridge. I then made my way toward the front door.

"Yeah...Thank you, too," she devilishly smiled.

I scanned her up and down, a bit remorseful I fucked her. But, damn. There was a part of me that should've at least asked her if she was clean or if she was worried about getting pregnant. Oh the fuck well. She seemed like she had a good head on her shoulders and besides cuzzo wouldn't be messing with no woman if she was burned, you feel me? Anyways, I strolled out the door and headed downstairs.

Walking up to my Charger, I pulled out my keys. All of a sudden, I heard some footsteps creep up from behind me. "Wassup, nigga!!!" I heard a voice yell. But before I could turn around, I felt something hard come across the back my head and I blacked out, instantly slumping to the ground.

## CHAPTER SIXTEEN

"Sorry about this, Lord. I can't do this anymore," I cried softly. Cupping as many pills as I could into my hand, I shoved them into my mouth and was ready to swallow this deep pain away.

*Buzz. Buzz. Buzz.*

All of a sudden, my phone began to vibrate on my bed. I didn't swallow the pills just yet. I paused for a moment, having to quickly think about what I was about to do. *Trish, what are you doing?!?! Spit them out! You're about to kill yourself! Stop, girl! STOP IT!* My mind raced as I could still hear my phone vibrating in the distance.

Without hesitation, I spit the pills out of my mouth, all of them landing back onto the floor. Exhausted and weeping, I dashed over to my phone, hoping it was Monique or Neicy calling me. The Lord knew I needed to hear one of their voices right now. He had to stop me from doing the unthinkable. I reached down, grabbed my phone and my eyes instantly exploded with surprise. It was Ms. Williams calling me. I wasn't expecting her to call me back that quickly after what she just told me. Did she have a change of heart? I wondered.

I answered and muttered, "Ms. Williams?"

"LaTrisha...Look, I'm so sorry about that. I don't know what came over me. I really don't. I just...I'm just still so mad and upset about everything that transpired between you and Dre. I'm so sorry, LaTrisha. I know deep down inside you're probably a good girl just trying to get things together. It's just so messed up that you just made some unfortunate decisions. But I can't hold this type of grudge against you for so long. I can't have that type of hate in my heart," she consoled.

Lowering and shaking my head out of relief, I was so thankful to hear that she was calling me back to offer me at least some sympathy. "I understand, Ms. Williams. I'm sorry about everything I put you all through. I truly mean it. I'm so glad you called me back. Lord knows I'm truly grateful," I cried.

"I don't even know why I said what I said. That was just so mean and harsh of me. Look, I've been thinking too, about this entire situation. And truth be told, I'd been meaning to talk to Dre about this too. Lord knows I've been thinking about you. I truly have. I really do think at the end of the day, if you are trying to get your life right, you do deserve to see Ariyanna," she confessed.

Hearing those words instantly filled me with hope once again. "Really?" I asked, my reddened, teary eyes amplifying with joy.

"Yes...," she responded. "Look now...Dre is supposed to be coming over here soon with Ariyanna. This might piss Dre the hell off but you should come over here. I had bought her a bunch of toys and what not as a surprise," she explained. "And I think it would also be a good gift for her to see your mother..."

"Ms. Williams! Really? Like now?"

"Yes, girl! Come over now. He should be over here within two hours or so. Can you get here?"

"Well, I could leave but I gotta be checked back into my room by nine PM."

"Okay, well, order up an Uber or a Lyft and come over. Where are you currently staying?"

"I'm over at a halfway house. I could probably get there in an hour," I said, a waterfall of tears still running down my cheeks.

"Okay, well, get here as fast as you can," she said.

"Okay!" I replied. "Thank you so much, Ms. Williams! I really appreciate it! I really do!" I said.

"No problem. Just please, I'm asking you to be on your best behavior."

"Okay, I will! I promise," I replied.

"Okay, see you soon!" she said and then hung up.

Not wanting to waste a second, I didn't even hesitate in trying to quickly clean up my room. Pills were still splattered all over the place and if someone had walked in right now they would've known I tried to kill myself. Getting down on the floor, I scooped up all of my pain pills and threw them back into the bottle. I made up my bed and then grabbed my cane, purse, Bible and cell phone. Since I was working part-time as an office assistant at the group home, I was getting a small stipend, so I had enough money to order an Uber to get to the South Side. I didn't have the app on my phone, so I had to download it so I could quickly get a ride.

As I made my way out into the hallway of the halfway house, still fumbling with my phone to download the app, I ran into one of the other girls who was currently staying here. Her name was Donna.

"Hey, girl!" she greeted me, this somewhat devious grin flashed across her face.

"Hey, sister! How you doin'?!?" I asked as I kept walking past her, barely giving her eye contact.

She was walking the opposite direction but then she stopped, turned around and began to walk next to me. "Where you going?" she asked.

"Girl, I'm about to go visit some relatives," I said, still fumbling with my phone. The Uber app finally downloaded on my phone and I quickly opened it up to check the rates for how much it would cost to get all the way out to the far South Side of the city.

"Oh, okay! I'm headed out as well. Where you headed to?"

"95$^{th}$ street…," I responded. "Why, where you goin'?" I asked.

"Damn, I'm headed out south, too. You wanna catch a ride together and split the cost?"

I thought for a second. I really didn't know Donna like that but I knew this ride was gonna cost me at least $30. Shoot, I probably should split the ride with her. I ain't have nothing to lose. Besides, her and I were the same age and we both knew the ins and outs of the halfway house. She didn't seem like trouble, I presumed. "I guess we can do that," I said shrugging my shoulders a bit.

Donna was a bit on the slender side, kind of reminding me of myself before I got shot and went through all of these rounds of chemo and radiation. She had a head full of hair, unlike myself. Ever since I was loaded up with all of them cancer drugs, I lost all of my hair and had to wear a wig everywhere I went. Dr. Pirtle told me it was gonna be some time before my hair grew back eventually, so in the meantime, I just had to make due with these wigs I was able to buy from the hair store from time to time. Every time I ran into Donna, I caught a glimpse of myself and felt so envious of how good she looked.

"Okay, girl! Well, I'm ready when you are!" she said.

"I am, too," I responded and then the both of us made our way out to the exit of the halfway house. Before we left, we had to check out with the security guard, letting her know where we were going and what time we were gonna be back. If we weren't back in time, we would get in a lot of trouble and could possibly end back up in prison immediately. Although I loved Hope and all the programs they had to offer, they were very strict. In the months I'd been here, I'd seen a few girls get kicked out and sent back to prison for disobeying simple rules. And Pastor Shirley definitely didn't play. Shoot, I wouldn't either...This was a place for redemption, not a playhouse.

Donna and I were now standing outside. "Before I order the ride, I need to get medicated," she said.

"What you mean?!?" I asked, my brow raised out of curiosity.

"I'm about to smoke a joint...," she said as she pulled out a pack of pre-rolled joints from her purse.

My gaze widened with fear. "Donna! No! You can't do that!" I exclaimed, clasping my mouth. "You can go back to jail! Why are you doing this?!?" Now see this girl was straight up crazy! What in the hell did she think she was doing by smoking that stuff?!?!?

"Girl, calm down. I'm a medical marijuana patient. I got approved by the state since I have PTSD."

"Oh...." I fell silent. "You can get medical marijuana although you are on probation?"

"Yeah...You can get an exception from the State of Illinois if you have a doctor's note for a serious, chronic illness..."

"Damn...," I replied.

"I ain't never thought about that...But what about Pastor Shirley? Does she know? I thought Hope had a strict drug policy?" I asked. This girl was truly playing with fire and if she was lying to me, I didn't want any parts of her nonsense. I stepped back from her, almost ready to dip off and get my own ride.

Donna huffed and rolled her eyes, shaking her head as if I had offended her. "Girl, bye. Pastor Shirley smoke all the damn time herself."

"What you mean?!?" Was Donna lying to me?!? This didn't seem right?!? Pastor Shirley?!? She was a sanctified woman! I couldn't see her using no darn weed.

"Girl! Pastor Shirley is the one who told me to get a medical marijuana prescription to help me with my anxiety and my PTSD...Besides, her and I are cool like that."

"Wow...I thought Pastor Shirley was sober." None of this was adding up. NONE OF IT!

"Girl...," Donna chuckled. "I know you saved and whatnot, but I know you not *that* green. Old habits die hard," she said. "Besides, everything that glitters ain't gold."

"What's that supposed to mean?" I asked.

"Girl, Pastor Shirley just puttin' on a front. Child, this nonprofit is a big ass hustle for her. She gettin' all types of grants and whatnot from the State and the Feds to run this place. You never noticed that big ass Benz she drive? Or that Gucci purse she stay rockin'?"

"Wow...I ain't never really paid attention."

"Exactly! Girl...You got your nose up in that Bible too much. You better snap out of the daze. I know you know what's up. I mean, you *just* got saved. Don't be so naïve now..."

"Dang...," I mumbled. I was floored at what I was hearing.

"Well, go on and do your thing," I said. "You just want me to go ahead and order the ride?"

"Nah, I got it. But, let's go over to the alley behind the building. Pastor Shirley don't want me smoking in front of the property," she said.

"Okay...Well, I'll just wait here until you done then," I said.

"You don't want a lil hit?"

"Nah, I'm good, sis. It's all you...Besides, I ain't no medical marijuana patient and I could get in trouble. We get tested every week. That's why I'm surprised you even doing this," I somewhat snapped. I didn't want to come off as judgmental but I had no choice at this point. This girl was on something else. Like I said, I didn't want any part of her foolishness. Hell, I had too much to lose at this point.

Suddenly, Donna busted out laughing. "Riiiiiiight...Girl, you just don't know..."

"Know what?" I responded, raising my brown out of perplexity. Why was this girl trying me right now? I was starting to get a bit irritated. I should've just ordered this dang ole ride by myself. She was doing the most right now.

"How them pain pills treating you?"

"They're doing good...I guess...They make me nauseous from time to time..."

"Girl, you tweakin'. You got cancer and you ain't even considered medical marijuana?!?"

"I'm trying to live life sober. I don't wanna go back to that. Besides, it's bad for my lungs..."

"Okay then...Well, just wait for me here. If you still wanna get a lil taste, just come holla at me," she said with a slight snicker.

"I'm good on that, Donna. Like for real. Anyways, I thought about it...You go on 'head and get yo smoke on. I'm just gonna get my own ride. I'll holla at you later," I said and walked off. Now I saw the devil was REALLY trying me today! I didn't have time for any of this woman's mess, let alone's Satan's mess. Truth be told, I should've walked my behind right back into house and reported her lying behind. But I wasn't no snitch and wasn't going to become one tonight. If she got caught, then oh well. And if Pastor Shirley was doing shady stuff on the low, then that was on her.

"Oh, okay, girl," she replied, rolling her eyes. "Just because you covered in the blood now don't mean you got the right to judge folks."

"I ain't judging you," I replied. "But do you, boo. I'm gonna just go ahead and get my own ride. Have a nice evening," I responded and walked off. I pulled out my phone and order a ride. Within three minutes, a gray Toyota Corolla pulled up to the roundabout of the halfway house and I quickly got in.

"You headed down south?" the handsome Uber driver asked in a thick accent. He was some thick African brother with a head full of waves. His complexion, the color of midnight, radiated with this immense glow despite the fact that it was hazy outside and the sun barely shone.

"Yessir," I smiled.

About a good forty minutes later, thanks to traffic, I was finally out in Roseland. We pulled up to Ms. Williams house.

"Like I said, if you ever want to come to my church, just give me a call," Olufemi, my Uber driver, said as he reached back and handed me a business card. I was glad I took this ride by myself because Olufemi and I had a good conversation about everything. Life. Christ. Love. He was such a charmer. Just too bad I didn't have much longer to live probably. I would've tried to form a friendship with him.

"I will, Olufemi. Thank you so much," I said as I got out of the car. Once I closed the door, he took off. I then nervously made my way up the steps of Ms. Williams house. I guess she knew someone was outside of her door because before I reach the steps, her living room lights came on. Then her front door flung open.

She stood there for a second and didn't say anything. A flat expression was planted on her face. It was almost as if she didn't recognize me. "LaTrisha...?" she asked.

"Hey, Ms. Williams," I nervously smiled as I limped up the steps of the house.

We stood in front of each other for a second until she said, "Well, I ain't mean like I used to be. Come and give me a hug. I ain't gonna hurt you..."

We hugged and then she welcomed me inside...

## CHAPTER SEVENTEEN

Walking up to my Charger, I pulled out my keys. All of a sudden, I heard some footsteps creep up from behind me. "Wassup, nigga!!!" I heard a voice yell. But before I could turn around, I felt something hard come across the back my head and I blacked out, instantly slumping to the ground.

All I now saw were stars cast among darkness. Seconds later, I opened my hazy eyes and could see a group of young niggas, many of them looking no older than fourteen or fifteen, stomping all over me. It was probably these goofy ass Lakeside niggas. They were a small GD set on 79th street. This is exactly why I hated this fucking neighborhood. These niggas weren't on shit anyways.

"FUCK!" I groaned, instantly trying to protect myself from the nonstop blows and kicks.

"GET HIS SHIT! TRY TO GET THIS NIGGA'S KEYS!" one of these wild niggas growled. Oh hell no! They weren't finne get my fucking Charger. These niggas were about to die! I didn't know if any of these niggas was packin' but they were 'bout to find the fuck out that I was. "GET

THE FUCK OFF ME!" I screamed as I reached in my back and pulled out my .45.

"OH SHIT! HE GOT THE HAMMER ON HIM!" another young nigga screamed and suddenly the group took off running like some scary ass hoes. Shit, truth be told, I was thoroughly shocked none of them niggas had a pole on them. In Chicago, everyone lived and died by the motto, "No Lackin'". Goofy ass niggas. "YEAH! GET YO PUNK ASS OUTTA HERE!"

I slowly got up from the concrete and brushed myself off. Then, a huge migraine came out of nowhere, crushing the side of my head. One of those niggas managed to kick me in the side of my head very hard. Shit felt like I had an aneurysm or some shit.

"You alright, young man?" an elderly woman shouted from across the street. Guess she witnessed everything. She was sitting on the porch of her house, rocking away in a chair as if nothing really happened.

"I'm cool...," I mumbled, rubbing the side of my head.

"Be careful around here! These young boys ain't on shit!"

"Thank you, ma'am," I responded as I quickly hopped in my car and jetted down the street to get the fuck out of here. "FUCK, BRO!" I yelled, punching my steering wheel. That shit was probably God paying me back with some instant karma for fucking around with Candreka's sweet pussy havin' ass.

Pissed as fuck, I quickly dialed up Tanisha to let her know what the fuck just happened. Within seconds, she answered the phone. "Sup, nigga! I was just about to hit yo line!" she shouted, sounding happy as fuck.

"BRO! I just got jumped by some young niggas around yo crib! Boy, I almost had to kill them clown ass niggas!"

"What?!?! What niggas?!?"

"Man, I think it was them Lakeside niggas that be hangin' around that convenience store on Essex!"

"Man, fuck them hoe ass niggas! Them niggas no older than fourteen or fifteen! You couldn't handle them lil shorties??!?!"

"Cuz! They just came out of nowhere and knocked me across my head with something! I think one of them niggas had brass knuckles on or somethin' 'cuz none of them had a gun! They took off once I pulled my .45 out!"

"Man, I know them niggas. I'll talk to their stupid asses when I get back."

"Bro, I ain't fuckin' coming around yo crib no more. Shit not safe. We gon' have to link up another way!"

"Dude, you tweakin'. Like I said, I'm cool with them youngins. A few of them work for me."

"Man, whatever. Look, thanks for the weed though. I'm about to go pick up Ariyanna from daycare."

"Before you go....," Tanisha said, her tone instantly changing. "How was it?"

"How was what?!? What the hell you talking about?"

"Nigga, don't act like you don't know what the fuck I'm talking about...Candreka...So, how was it?"

Billions of butterflies began to enter the pits of my stomach. What the hell was cousin talking about?!?! Did Candreka call her and tell her we just fucked or something?!? I was so confused but I wasn't going to sit up here and admit to that shit! But something told me the way Candreka was coming at me was shady as fuck!

"What are you talking about, Tanisha?!?! Yo, I just went over there to cop my weed and to smoke. That's it."

"Man, breh, don't be fuckin' lying to me. I know you fucked my bitch."

"Nah, you got the facts wrong on that one, blood. I wouldn't dare cross my family like that..."

Tanisha suddenly burst into a roaring laugh. Bitch sounded crazy and evil as fuck. My face twisted with confusion. The rage inside of me was ready to explode. I honestly had no idea what type of game Tanisha was playing on me but this shit wasn't funny, especially considering I just got jumped by some dudes that she now was claiming she was cool with. If she was so cool with these niggas, how come any other time I came around they never crossed me or jumped me? Nothing was adding up. Nothing was making any sense at all.

"Yo....Tanisha, stop playing fucking games with me, bruh. What are you talking about?!? Did you have those young niggas to jump me or somethin'??!?!?"

"Hahah! Bro, I knew from the moment I brought Candreka around yo stupid ass, you would eventually fall for her and try to fuck. And you did...But we set you up," she confessed in this diabolical tone I'd never heard pour from her lips. This bitch was sounding more and more maniacal the more she spoke.

"Yo, what the fuck is you talkin' 'bout?!?"

"Dre...I know you fucked. It's cool. Trust me, cousin. It's cool. Listen, it was all a part of my plan."

I still wasn't going to admit to this shit. "What are you talkin' about, Tanisha?"

"Well, cousin, you know I love you a lot like a brother. And I think you got a lot of features and shit I've always wanted in a child."

I didn't say anything in response. I just sat in traffic, listening to this craziness coming from her mouth. I was now on 63rd street, trying to make my way as quick as I could to Ariyanna's daycare. Traffic from rush hour was starting to build up.

"I put Candreka on you so you could get pregnant. I want a baby but I don't trust any other niggas out there...."

"Huh?!?!? What are you talking about?!? Yo, you sound

crazy as fuck right now!"

"Nigga, it's not crazy! I'm pretty much making you be a sperm donor for our kid. Candreka and I plan on getting married pretty soon. We wanted to go ahead and start the baby-making process though 'cuz I know you got a lot going on and whatnot," she said. "But how you like that pussy? Shit fire, huh?"

My eyes widened with fear, my already heightened anxiety began to cripple my muscles, damn near making me want to crash into the car in front of me. "Look, man, I'm so confused right now. You telling me you had Candreka to pretty much seduce me so ya'll could use my sperm and have a baby?!?!?"

"Yup!"

"BITCH! ARE YOU CRAZY?!?!? WHAT THE FUCK?!?!? NIGGA, WE ARE FAMILY! BLOOD! BLOOD COUSINS!?!?!? THAT IS SOME SICK ASS SHIT! SOME SICK ASS MAURY POVICH RATCHET ASS SHIT! WHAT THE FUCK ARE YOU TALKING ABOUT?!?!?"

"Dre! CALM THE FUCK DOWN, DUDE! It ain't that serious. Besides, it'll just be a family secret between all of us. And I don't want your money! Trust me! I got plenty of coins! We plan on leaving Chicago anyways to move to California!"

"TANISHA! WHAT THE FUCK?!?! If you wanted a fucking baby, why the fuck couldn't you just adopt or get another nigga to get that bitch pregnant?!?!? And if you wanted me to get Candreka pregnant, why the fuck you ain't just ask me?!?!?!"

"NIGGA, DON'T CALL MY BITCH A BITCH!"

"MAN! You fuckin' tweakin'! Ya'll tweakin'! That was some foul ass shit! You straight took advantage of me! Ya'll put this fuckin' stress on me over a bag of loud?!?!?"

"Well, that wasn't loud you was just smokin'..."

"Huh?!?!?"

"That was some Percs too...That's why you was fuckin' lit," she laughed. "Anyways, boy, it ain't a big deal. You'll eventually get over it."

"Nah! You on some other shit right now! Bitch, you're fucked up! Get the fuck off my line!"

"Boy! Bye! We'll talk later!"

## CHAPTER EIGHTEEN

"DRE! DEANDRE! DRE! WAKE THE FUCK UP?!?!?"

My hazy eyes exploded open, my gaze instantly attached to Candreka and Tanisha hovering over me. They stood there looking at me as if I was some stranger.

"What the fuck?!?! Ya'll foul as fuck! Why ya'll did that to me!!!" I exclaimed, ready to fight these bitches!

"What are you talking about?!?" Tanisha yelled, her eyebrow lifted and her face scrunched with confusion. Candreka looked thoroughly baffled, too, by my response. "Boy, you tweakin'! You passed the fuck out from the weed!"

"Huh?" I muttered, clasping my chest, frantically looking around like I was some crazy ass paranoid schizophrenic that thought the Feds or Aliens were chasing me.

"Boy! Wake the fuck up and get up! You gotta go pick up Ariyanna," Tanisha exclaimed as she reached down, grabbed me and helped me off the couch.

"Damn, I was passed out the whole time?" I asked as I quickly gathered myself. Damn, that was a fucked up dream I had. What the fuck kind of weed was that? "Man, that fuckin' loud had me on some other shit, G. What the fuck is that shit?!?"

"Boy! I told you that's that fire!" Candreka replied laughing her ass off.

Tanisha didn't find Candreka humorous. "Nevermind all that! Dre, you gotta go before you get charged a late fee! And your phone has been blowing off the hook!"

"Damn, you right! Shit!" I exclaimed as I quickly looked around, making sure I had cell phone, wallet and keys.

"Sorry about that cousin," I said. "I had a fucked up dream or nightmare. I'll holla at you later though."

"Yeah, tell me about it later. In the meantime, go and pick up my cousin before them white folks get on your ass! You so damn irresponsible sometimes," she said.

I lightly chuckled. Man, that was such a crazy ass dream. I couldn't believe I dreamt all of that up. Dicking down Candreka. Getting jumped by some young, wild niggas. And then finding out that cuzzo and her bitch then tried to set me up and get her pregnant. Whatever the fuck was in that loud was gonna for sure have Tanisha's clientele acting like they were in some fucked up alternate universe. I gawked down and saw the loud pack Candreka gave me earlier before I passed out. I handed it back to her and said,

"Ya'll can keep this. I'm good on that."

"Weak ass. Boy, get out of here!" Candreka laughed as she snatched the bag of weed out of my hand and then walked off. I gazed down at her, scanning her up and down, still wanting to possibly tag that muhfucka. But now that I had that dream, that shit was almost like a premonition, warning me not to succumb to that type of temptation.

"Anyways, let me get my ass out of here," I said as I dashed to the front door of the apartment. "Thanks for the smoke session though, 'Dreka," I said and then walked out. Soon as I made it downstairs, I looked around making sure it was no niggas lurking in the cut waiting to jump me. Shit, even though I dreamt that shit, I definitely still had to be on my muthafuckin' P's and Q's around this area. Like I said before, 79th street wasn't no place to fuck around at.

I hopped in the Charger, chucked the engine up and then made my way promptly to Ariyanna's daycare. It was now approaching 4:50 and I had a good ten minutes left before the daycare would start charging me late fees. University of Chicago's daycare didn't play either. They charged $50 for every minute you were late. I remember one time, this Chinese lady told me they charged her $500 for being ten minutes late picking her daughter. I'd be damned if those mothafuckas were gonna try to pillage my pockets for just being a few minutes late.

Luckily, I found a parking spot right in front of the daycare. I hopped out, ran inside the building and went straight to Ariyanna's classroom. From a far, I could see a few other students were still there. Ariyanna was playing with one of her classmates. As I got closer, I guess baby girl sensed that I was there. She turned her head and saw me. "DADDY!" she screamed as she got up and ran into my embrace.

"Wassup, baby girl! You miss me?!?"

"YEAH!"

"Aiight! Well, let's get going!" I said. I looked at her teacher who was still sitting down, carefully watching the other kids. "Sorry I'm late. I had to run some errands," I lied. She looked back at me with a smile. "No worries! See you all later!"

"BYEEE!" Ariyanna said, waving to her classmates. I picked Ariyanna up and then we marched down the hallway and out the door of the building. Once I got to my car, I got her secured in her car seat and then hopped in the front and took off.

"Daddy's gotta surprise for you at Nana's house!" I said, looking back in the rearview mirror. Ariyanna looked at me and said, "TOYS?!?"

"You'll see!" I laughed, shaking my head. I loved my daughter so much. She was such a cutie pie. I'd do any and everything for her.

Some minutes later, we pulled up to the curb in front of my mama's crib. I got out and then made my way to the backseat of the car to get Ariyanna out of her car seat. I quickly turned around and saw my mama flung the curtains back. Some older looking chick who I didn't recognize was standing next to me as mama waved at me and then flung the curtains back.

"Nana's got some good surprises for you inside," I said as I turned my attention back to Ariyanna. Damn...Mama didn't tell me she was gonna have company. That face looked really familiar though but whoever that lady was more than likely one of my mama's church members.

Ariyanna and I walked up to the steps of the house and marched in. Soon as I hit the corner and went into the living room, I froze in place. My eyes amplified in shock.

"Hey, Dre...."

It was mothafuckin' Trish...She and my mother were sitting on the main living room couch. What in the FUCK was she doing here?!?

Why didn't my mama call me and tell me she was going to have this bitch over the house?!? And why the fuck was she over here in the first place?!? I looked over at my mother, a nervous smile came across her face.

"What are you doing here?"

"Dre...Hold on for a minute. Before you get all mad and upset, just listen to her. Don't get all crazy now," Mama begged as she got up to potentially hold me back from going crazy.

Ariyanna was standing next to me, holding my hand. Trish looked away from me and then cast her gaze onto Ariyanna. "Hey, baby girl! You remember me?"

Ariyanna didn't respond. She just snuggled closer to me and shook her head no.

"Answer my mothafuckin' question. What in the FUCK are you doing here?!?! You are supposed to be in jail...," I growled, ready to attack this bitch.

"DEANDRE! NOT IN MY MOTHAFUCKIN' HOUSE, NO YOU WON'T!" Mama roared as she lightly punched me in my chest. "You will not disrespect her, me or your child like that!"

"Mama! Why in the hell didn't you call me and tell me about this?!?! You think this is funny?!?"

"DRE! Stop it! Trish has some things to tell you!"

"Dre! I'm dying...I have cancer."

My face twisted with bewilderment. "What are you talking about?!?!"

"Dre...I don't have much longer to live," Trish confessed as she wiped tears away from her face. "I got out of prison not too long ago and I've been living in a halfway house. I've been praying and hoping to reconnect with you and eventually get a chance to see Ariyanna before it was too late."

I stood there frozen and silent. I didn't know what to say exactly. Shaking my head, I didn't want to hear any of this bullshit right now. I took a quick scan of her and saw just how different she looked. She was no longer the slim, sexy woman I used to know. She had this horrible wig sitting on top of her head. Her entire outfit wreaked of Salvation Army. I started to feel partly bad for her because, damn, she had to be telling the truth. No one would just make some shit up like this. But I was just still so floored that I was blindsided by all of this.

"No, no, no. You not gon' do this to me right now. Not in front of my daughter. This is messed up."

"Dre...Please listen to me. I'm not lying about any of this," she begged. "I've been begging you for the last year or so to let me see Ariyanna."

"I don't care about none of that. You should've thought about your relationship with your daughter when you were making all of them piss poor decisions. Now you need to leave or I'm calling the police," I shouted. Ariyanna clutched my leg harder. The anger in my voice probably was scaring her. "Daddy, who is this?" she asked.

"Nobody, baby girl," I replied.

"I'm ya mama," Trisha said smiling, looking straight at baby girl.

"Ariyanna, go to Nana's room and wait for me. I need to talk to Nana and this lady for a minute."

"Can I watch TV?" baby girl asked.

"Yeah," I said and she quickly made her way into the back to my mama's room.

"You need to really leave before I do something I'm gonna regret!"

"Dre! Please, stop all of this right now! You need to calm down and ya'll need to talk!" Mama begged.

"Mama, I don't wanna hear all that. And truth be told, you had no right to invite her over here and let her infringe on me and Ariyanna like this."

"I tried to call you, Dre!" Mama said. "But you weren't picking up your phone!"

Suddenly, Trish shot up from the couch.

"DRE! YOU AIN'T ARIYANNA'S FATHER!" she screamed.

My head shot back for a second, my eyebrow raised. Silent, not a single muscle in my body twitched. "What did you just say?"

She quickly covered her face and shook her head. "I said, you not Ariyanna's father…"

"What the fuck are you talking about?!?" I roared, clenching my fists.

"You may need to take a DNA test…I was sleeping with other guys when was together. I'm sorry."

Mama looked at me and then back at Trish. "Wait! Wait a minute! Why you didn't tell me that when you got here?!?!" mama screamed at the top of her lungs.

I snapped. "BITCH! I'MMA KILL YOU!"

I suddenly let loose and lunged at Trish, quickly throwing my hands around her throat. I swear to GOD I was going to murder this bitch!

## CHAPTER NINETEEN

"BITCH, I'MMA KILL YOU!" Dre screamed, lunging at me. Without hesitation, he threw his hands around my throat.

"No! No! Please, stop Dre!" Dre's mother screamed and cried, trying her best to pull him off of me. Still sitting on the living room couch, I was now pinned down with all of Dre's weight. Choking me as best he could, I attempted to punch his grip off my neck but he didn't relent. I kept yelling and crying, I was seconds away from passing out. I kicked and punched him, but my blows were like throwing grapes at a giant. Dre was hellbent on killing me. I virtually had no energy to muster up a fight. If his mama didn't succeed in pulling him off of me I knew I was going to for sure die tonight.

"DRE! GET OFF HER! PLEASE STOP!" his mother continued as she tried to yank him off me.

"I'M GONNA KILL THIS BITCH!" Dre continued, tightening his grip around my slender throat.

Suddenly, he let me go and exploded into rage. "AHHH-HHH! I SWEAR TO GOD YOU BETTER NOT BE

FUCKING WITH ME, BITCH!" he screamed as he paced in the living room floor, his fists clenched. He then dashed to an adjacent wall and started punching it, damn near putting a hole in it.

"DRE! CALM DOWN!" his mama cried and begged once again, running over to him to attempt to stop him from hurting himself.

"GET OFF ME, MA!" he yelled into her face. He then threw his attention immediately at me. "GET THE FUCK OUT NOW, TRISH! LIKE FOR REAL! YOU GOT FIVE SECONDS TO GET YO STUPID ASS OUT OF HERE OR I WILL FOR REAL KILL YOU!"

Crying uncontrollably, I got up from the couch and limped over to him. "Dre! Please, just listen to me! I don't know for sure if you are or not the father! Please just calm down!" I tried to plea with him.

"Just leave, Trish. Just get the fuck out of my house. I told you not to come over here with no mess and this is what you do. Get the hell out now before I call the mothafuckin' cops, you nasty ass bitch!" his mama growled as she ran up on me, ready to beat my ass well.

I buried my face into my hands. "Ca-ca-can I just se-see Ariyanna one more time?" I inquired stuttering, tears streaming down my face and into my palms. I pulled my palms away and stared at Dre's mama who was now standing inches away from me. She, too, looked like she was no ready to fuck me up.

"GET YO MOTHAFUCKIN' ASS OUT OF MY HOUSE, BITCH! Hell to the fuck no you can't see her!" his mama roared, pointing to her front door.

"Okay," I said as I grabbed my belongings off the couch and then grabbed my cane. Still crying and sniffling, I limped toward the front door and opened it. Before I headed out, I turned around, looked at Dre and said, "Dre, if you wanna make sure about everything, we should do a DNA test ASAP."

"GET THE FUCK OUT, BITCH!" his mama yelled again. Dre didn't even give me eye contact. He just stood there, frozen, tears running down his cheeks, his facial expression was flat.

"Sorry," I mumbled as I made my way outside and down her front steps. I quickly pulled out my phone, ordered an Uber and within minutes, someone came and got me.

🐚

Sitting in the backseat of the Uber, I contemplated everything that had just transpired. I know, I know, I know. This was truly all of my fault. I was responsible for this entire situation. I should've been more upfront with Dre from the very beginning and we could've avoided this entire fiasco.

Don't judge me (which I already know you were probably doing) but like you already knew, I had a past. A bad past.

When Dre and I were together, yes, there were plenty of times where I had cheated on him. I had only done so out of retribution.

Well, let me stop. That was a lie.

Yes, I was a hoe. A big one at that. And back then I had such a huge thirst for nonstop sex. Even when Dre sexually satisfied me, I still had this knack to go out and mess around with other guys. It is what it is though.

Listen, I made my fair share of mistakes. Everyone has. But now that I was on the verge of dying, I wanted to make sure that I made amends with Dre and his family. Now that the cat was out of the bag, Dre had to know this secret before I went on to be with the Lord.

You might be wondering who the real father was. Shoulder shrug. Well, truth be told, I honestly didn't know who could've been Ariyanna's real daddy. Shoot, maybe there was a slight possibility it could be Dre. However, around the time I got pregnant, I had slept with about ten or eleven men in total.

"How are you doing tonight?" my Uber driver asked, looking back at me in the rearview mirror.

"I'm fine," I said as I threw him a quick, fake smile. I wiped my face and then stared back out of the window, taking in the Downtown scenery from the expressway.

"Is everything alright?" he asked. "You seem kind of sad," the older Arab-looking man said in his thick accent.

"I'm fine...Thank you. I prefer not to talk on my rides," I said.

"Sorry," he replied and then threw his gaze back onto the semi-busy expressway.

Going back into my thoughts, I had to think about who could've possibly been Ariyanna's father.

Let's see...First, there was Dre. Then there was Mike. He and I went to high school together. There was Terry. Paul. Lil G. Lamont. Oh, and then Frank. I used to love me some Frank. He was this fine light-skinned dude who I knew since middle school. Then there were some other men I had messed around with who I met at the club or on Tinder but I didn't know their names...Truthfully, it could've been more than ten men. During that time in my relationship with Dre, I was also having sex with a few guys for money here and there. Like I said, please don't judge me. We all have a past. I know you do, too...

But listen, I didn't want to ponder over my mistakes and all the relationships I had in the past. That was water under the bridge. I had to shake these thoughts away because that was exactly how Satan moved. Infiltrate your spirit and then have you almost wanting to renege on your faith. Now, I was covered in the red blood of Jesus. And I even made that known to Dre's mama when I first got to her house. I told her how I found redemption and salvation sitting in that jail cell, almost rotting to death. And I wanted the opportunity to tell Dre about my change, too. Not that I was trying to get back with him or anything like that. But I was beyond my past now, ready to make things right with everyone. My sole mission right now was revealing the truth about the possibility of Dre not being Ariyanna's father.

Anyways, I was now headed back to Hope, still crying, quietly sobbing. Luckily, I wasn't making a scene. I didn't want this Uber driver to notice how messed up I was. I needed someone to talk to ASAP. Someone to give me consolation. And the only person who I knew who could help me get through all of this was once again Monique. Hell, she was the one who even encouraged me to call Dre's mama.

I quickly pulled up her contact info in my phone and dialed her. Within seconds she picked up and answered with, "Hey, girl! How you feelin'?"

"I ain't doin' too well...," I said.

"What happened? You called Dre's mama?"

"I did...In fact, we talked and I went over to her house. I just came back."

"Oh, no! What happened?"

"Dre came over with Ariyanna..."

She gasped.

A minute later, my Uber driver pulled up the roundabout of Hope. By now the sun was setting, and darkness began to cover the skies. "Hold on for a second, girl, I'm about to get out of my Uber ride...," I told Monique. I looked at the driver and said, "Thank you, sir." I got out and then walked over to an empty bench near the building entrance's awning. "Okay, I'm back," I said to Monique.

"Girl, what happened?"

"Well, I went over there to see Ariyanna. Dre's mama and

I talked for about a good hour before he came home. Soon as he saw me, he started to flip out."

"Why?!?"

I closed my eyes and exhaled. Truth was, Monique didn't know the secret I was keeping either. "Girl, please don't judge me when I tell you this but I don't think Dre is Ariyanna's father...," I confessed.

"WHAT?!?!? Girl, what in the hell are you talking about??!?"

"Sis, I don't know if Dre is actually Ariyanna's father. I hadn't told anyone about this 'cuz at the time I was just a mess. When I got pregnant, I just wanted the baby to be Dre's 'cuz out of all the dudes I was messin' with at the time, Dre was the one who had his stuff together."

"Oh, no, bitch! You have to go to be mothafuckin' kidding me right now! What the fuck is wrong with you?!? And you even lied to me!"

Quickly going back into a frenzy of tears, I clamped my mouth and shook my head. "I'm so sorry, Monique. I was too embarrassed to tell anyone about this. Please don't judge me!"

"Bitch, get the fuck off my line. You're a lying ass bitch! Chadwick was right! Said all of this newfound Christianity of yours is some fake ass shit! Bitch, you ain't a real ass woman! How could you tell a lie like this? You're fucked up! I don't even know why I continued to be friends with you all this time. That is some low-life ass loser shit for real, girl. Ughhh! So Dre was just taking care of another nigga's kid all these years?!?! What the fuck is wrong with you?!?!? Why wouldn't you tell him that!"

"DON'T CURSE AT ME!" I screamed, still crying frantically.

"Bitch! FUCK YOU! GOODBYE! Don't call me no more! Fucking liar!" Suddenly Monique hung up.

"AHHHHH!" I suddenly burst into tears, drooling and

slobbering as intense pain overcame me. I just lost a friend. WOW! This was way too much!

Sitting on the bench, I rocked back and forth wondering what I was going to do next. Numbness overcame me and I briefly contemplated running back to my room and downing the pills once again.

"Girl, what's the matter? You alright?" I heard a female voice say. I looked over my shoulder and lo and behold it was Donna.

Not saying anything, I kept crying and shaking my head no.

"What's wrong, sis?" she said as she sat next to me and held me.

"I...I...I won't be able to see my baby no more..."

"Shhh, shhhh. Come on now, let's get it together. Don't make a scene," she said.

"I'm dying and I won't be able to see my baby no more," I moaned.

"Come on, sweetie. Let's go somewhere else and talk about this. Your nerves are all bad," Donna said.

She grabbed me and we both stood up from the bench and took a walk away from the house and to a back alley behind the building. "Come on now, tell me what happened...," she said, wiping my face free of tears.

"My cancer is back big time and all I wanna do is just see my baby. I'm hurting right now. I don't know what to think," I said.

Donna raised her brow and then reached in her back pocket. She pulled out a pack of her pre-rolls, pulled out a joint and said, "You need this right now. You are too messed up. Just relax and forget about everything we talked about earlier."

Still crying, I shook my head no, but the truth was I

needed something right now just to distract myself. "I can't," I cried. "I can't do that."

"Girl, you're gonna drive yourself crazy if you don't just relax. Stop playing now," she said as she took the joint, slapped it in her mouth and then pulled out a lighter from her pocket. She sparked up the joint, took a huge pull and then exhaled away from me. She then took the joint of her mouth and handed it to me. "Just take a few pulls and calm down. You're a wreck right now, LaTrisha. A lil weed ain't gon hurt you," she said.

I glanced down at the joint. Lord knew I was trying my hardest to resist. If I took that joint and smoked on it, I knew I was gonna get in trouble. But this pain was so intense, I felt like I was going to die from a broken heart right here and now.

*Fuck it*. A voice said in the back of my head. I took the joint out of Donna's hand and threw it in my mouth. I missed the smell of weed. Damn, and this joint was pulling so smoothly too.

# CHAPTER TWENTY

I really couldn't believe this shit. Like, I really couldn't. I was floored at the fact that first, Trish had the mothafuckin' audacity to bring her raggedy ass over to my mama's house and try to see Ariyanna. She knew good and goddamn well that she wasn't legally allowed to do that. Second of all, even if she wanted to see Ariyanna, she should've taken her ass down to the family judged and filed a motion to see her. Let the fucking courts intervene and force me to let you see Ariyanna, bitch.

Sitting on my mama's couch in her living room, my head was buried in my sweaty palms. I had been crying my heart out now for over an hour.

"It's gonna be okay, Dre...Come on now, stop all of this crying," mama consoled as she rubbed my back trying to get me to calm down.

"Mama, I can't! I can't calm down. Didn't you just hear what she said?!?! My baby may not be mine!?!? What the fuck is she even talking about??!?"

"I know, sweetie. I know...I'm so sorry I even let her come over here. I don't know what in the hell I was thinking. I mean, she called me up with that sob story. At first I didn't wanna hear shit from her. I was so mean to her when she first called me. But my conscience began to eat me alive and I had to quickly call her back. I didn't want that type of guilt on my heart and soul if she were to pass away suddenly," mama explained.

Not saying anything, I just stared off into space, still in disbelief. I wasn't going to believe. No. NO! Hell no! "Man, I swear, mama. Ariyanna has got to be my kid. She looks and acts just like me!" I exclaimed. Some minutes later, Ariyanna came creeping around the corner and then ran into my lap.

"Why you cryin', daddy?!?" she asked. I guess she didn't hear that crazy ass fight Trish and I just had. She must've been deep up in mama's room watching the hell out of cartoons or something. Thank God.

"I'm just upset…That's all, sweetheart," I said as I cracked a smile, taking an intense stare at my baby girl. Ain't no way in the hell she wasn't mine. She had mostly all of my features. Her smile. Her eyes. Her hair. All of it belonged to me.

"Don't be sad, daddy! I love you!" she said, cracking open a big smile. Just seeing her flash that wide grin, exposing her tiny teeth, just made my heart crack wide open even more. I had such deep love for this girl that I was willing to kill and die for her. I mean, wouldn't any noble man do the same for their seed?

"I know, baby girl! I know!" I said grinning back, wiping my face free of tears.

She leaned in and gave me a tight hug. "Don't cry! Let's play with my toys!" she screamed, beaming angelic innocence.

Mama looked at me and said, "We just gotta do the right thing, Dre. I know this is all hard to take in. It really is… Especially considering the other stuff you got going on with that other woman. But the right thing you need to do right now is calm down, get some rest and then eventually take a test just to make sure," mama said.

"Yeah, you right...," I replied standing up. I picked up baby girl and planted a kiss on the side of her face.

Mama stood up and then said, "I mean, I am so confused myself. When Trish first got pregnant, why in the hell didn't you take a DNA test? You just assumed the baby was yours??!?!"

Damn..She was right. I didn't take a DNA test. Shit, truth be told, it never crossed my mind. "I don't know...I just assumed she was mine. I mean, I just assumed Trish wasn't out there like that. And the timing and everything made sense," I said. "I mean, mama, I trusted her. I never even cheated on her."

Mama lowered and shook her head. "I told you that girl was no good. I really told you all of this. But oh well. Look, I hope once all of this mess is settled and done, you truly stop messing around and find someone with a solid head on their shoulders. Now is not the time to even think about getting into no new relationship with nobody. You just need to focus on raising your children, your job, and finishing school. You got too much good stuff going on. You got your own place now. You got a car. Good credit. Dre, your only downfall, son, is your weakness for women. And no good women at that. Let this be a life lesson. Keep ya dingaling in your pants," Mama said as she walked deep into the kitchen and cracked her fridge open. "I need me a damn drink after this damn day dealing with you young kids. I swear ya'll gonna give me a stroke."

"I'm sorry for all of this, mama," I said as I made my way past the kitchen. "I'm gonna figure everything out. I promise."

Some days had passed.

It seemed like every day that went by, I became more and more shallow and cold. Between finding out that I now had a son with Shelly and then consequently finding out that Ariyanna may not even be my kid, I just had to get away from all of the madness. I had to take some more time off from my job just to go through a reset. Besides, school was starting to become increasingly difficult and I had this major exam coming up for this crazy ass international economics class that I was taking.

It was Friday evening. I asked mama if she could watch Ariyanna for the weekend while I studied for this exam. Currently, I had a B- in this class. I kind of slipped up a bit over the last few weeks and ended up getting a D- on this last quiz I took a week ago. Professor Horowitz told me that I needed to pull off at least a 90 or higher in order to get at least a B+ in the class, so I was on top of it now.

For the past hour or so, I had my head buried in this thick ass textbook reading about international trade policy with China. I had been sitting in the living room, my books and shit splattered all over the place. Since I wasn't the type of nigga who needed music to study, not a single sound could be heard in my place. But boy, lemme tell you, I was seconds away from passing the fuck out! Not only was I distracted from my own incessant thoughts thinking about all of this baby mama drama, but this material was boring as fuck! But I knew I had to absorb all of this material if I was going to pull of 90 on that exam.

"In 1984, The Chinese Government then expanded its relations with the United King—"

*Ding Dong! Ding-Dong! Ding-Dong!*

All of a sudden, I paused reading aloud the text and my eyes shot toward my front door. My doorbell was ringing off the hook. "The fuck?!?" I groaned as I threw my book to the side and got up from the couch, quickly sauntering over to the front door. The doorbell kept going off, almost as if whoever it was on the other side was in some sort of emergency or playing with my fucking doorbell.

"Yo! I'm coming!" I screamed. Truth be told, I should've had my blickie on me in case these were some fool ass niggas trying to rob me. Lately, my neighborhood had been victim to a string of robberies and home invasions. So, I'd be damned if I was gonna let some niggas try to stick me up. But I didn't know where my gun was at and besides it was a bit late.

Once I got to the door, I looked out the peephole and saw Candreka standing in front of the door, still frantically ringing the doorbell. Like from side to side as if she was running from someone, she began ferociously banging on my door as she kept ringing the doorbell.

"Candreka?!? What the hell!" I growled and immediately opened my front door.

"DRE! Please! You gotta help me! Tanisha is gonna kill me! PLEASE HELP ME! PLEASE!" she screamed as she pushed past me and hid in a corner near my kitchen.

Confused yet slightly nervous, I looked out the hallway and saw that Tanisha was no where to be seen. What the fuck was Candreka on?!? Quickly closing the door, I dashed through my living room toward the corner where she was hiding. "What the fuck is wrong?!?" I asked as I scanned her up down. And. Oh. My. Mothafuckin'. Goodness'. Candreka's ass was tore the fuck up. Bitch looked like she got stomped on by some niggas. I leaned down and grabbed her swollen, bloodied face. I didn't notice her face at first when she stormed into my townhouse. "Yo! What the fuck?!?!? Tanisha did this to you?!?" I asked.

"Yes! She's crazy! She's gonna kill me!"

## CHAPTER TWENTY-ONE

*amn, damn, damn.* Donna was right.

Lord knew I needed that hit of weed.

As the THC entered my bloodstream, I could immediately feel relief and relaxation come over me. This feeling was like none other. Baby! I felt like I had felt like I had already died and walked straight through the gates of heaven. Although my tender lungs had gone some time without smoking weed, they were still used to the thick smoke.

For the past hour or so, as Donna and I puffed on that joint, we chatted about all the craziness I just endured while we were still in the back alley. I had damn near forgot about all the drama I just went through earlier in the day.

"You want another hit?" Donna asked as she took the joint of her mouth and handed it to me. We were now on our second joint and the munchies were starting to kick in.

"Sure," I replied. "I'm kind of hungry though."

"Let's finish this and then go back inside. Maybe we could order a pizza since the kitchen is probably closed already for the night," Donna said.

"Okay, cool," I said, grabbing the joint from her fingers. Before I slapped the joint between my lips, I paused for a moment and wondered if I was doing the right thing. My guilty conscience began to kick into high gear. "Damn, I can't believe I'm doing this."

"Doing what?" she asked.

"Smoking this joint," I said nervously. "But I feel...I feel so good right now," I confessed. My gaze was heavy. I just knew my eyes were visibly red. Although Donna told me we were smoking on something called an Indica, which gives more of a body high, I felt so light on my feet.

"Well, if you feel so good, then why are you nervous? Girl, just stop being so paranoid," she said.

Suddenly my guilt fled away. Donna was completely right. And she was right earlier when she mentioned the cocktail of drugs the doctors had put me on. All of the pain medicine my doctors had been loading me up on was nothing compared to weed. Those Vicodins gave me bad headaches when I came off of them. Sometimes I'd get the chills or a bad fever if I skipped a few days of not taking them.

I told myself time and time again that I would never ever put another blunt or bottle of alcohol up to my mouth, but now I was questioning that stance. *Nonsense*. Hell, if I was dying, I at least deserved to have something to give me peace of mind and body relaxation. This weed was definitely doing the job and I knew weed wouldn't make me feel like I was coming off a hard drug once I stopped.

"This is so different from what I'm used to smoking," I said after I got done taking a toke and passed the joint back to Donna.

"Hell yeah! This is straight from a medical dispensary. You ain't gonna get this on the streets," she said.

"Damn, for real? So, it's very different from what I used to smoke on the streets?"

"Hell yeah! Girl, this is lab-created by some white folks. That stuff you used to smoke got all types of pesticides and shit on it," she laughed as she finished the joint. "Anyways, you really need to go talk to Pastor Shirley and tell her what's going on and go see if you could get you a medical marijuana card."

"Damn, I might just have to do that," I said. I couldn't believe this. These past two years I swore I was going to change everything around and here I was, feeling like I was back to square one. But then again, not really. Guilty conscience was poking and prodding me to just stop and walk my behind back into the House and shake this devilish nonsense off. But, the more the weed set in, the calmer I became, the better I felt. Truthfully, I ain't felt this way in quite some time. The pulsating migraine I had earlier seemed to wither away. And the pain that would come from time to time in my hip from my surgery melted away like butter in the microwave.

"Anyways, girl, I am sure eventually everything will work in your favor. And also, girl, you really need to talk to another doctor. Have you thought about getting a second opinion? I mean, I know you probably like your doctor and all, but sometimes doctors don't know everything. You should see what other types of alternative treatments you could get," Donna said as she blew the last remaining smoke out of her mouth into the cold wind blowing outside.

Damn, I actually hadn't thought about going to a different doctor. I didn't even know if I could even do that. I was technically on Medicaid and I didn't even know if the State would allow me to go and get a different doctor.

"That sounds good and all but I don't know...If I ain't got that much left to live, I don't wanna risk and go to a different doctor. I mean, I don't even know if I'd be able to pay for it," I said.

"Girl, don't worry about all that. Shoot, I can help you! There are plenty of resources you could probably look into! Girl, we live in Chicago, not Tupelo, Mississippi! I am sure it's some people out here in the city who could give you some alternative treatments!" Donna exclaimed as we began exiting the alleyway, making our way back to the front entrance of the building.

"Well, we'll see...I mean, for right now I just wanna focus on seeing my daughter. At this point, I don't even know if I care anymore about living," I confessed.

Suddenly, Donna who had been walking by my side, stopped dead in her tracks and then tugged me into her embrace. She looked me dead in my eyes, her gaze intense like a heart attack. "GIRL! DO NOT SAY THAT! You know you do not mean that!" she explained. "You gotta remain positive! The doctor didn't say you were gonna die tomorrow!"

All of a sudden, tears escaped from the corners of my eyes and I lowered my head out of fear. "I don't know, Donna. This is just a lot. I mean. This is such a crazy life. I've been praying forever for a change and it seems like nothing is working. Like damn, is God even real?"

"Oh, girl Please stop it! Yes God is real! But at the same time, you can't just be nilly willy about all of this. Stop being some pessimistic. Look, I'm gonna help you. Your doctor is gonna help you. Once we sit down and talk to Pastor Shirley, the *real* Pastor Shirley, she's gonna help you, too!"

"Girl, how are you so sure about all of this?"

"Just trust me! Now come on! Let's go inside and start doing some research on how we can find some other treatments and stuff. I'm not gonna let my sister just succumb like this. We're gonna fight to the very end!" she said, a big smile stretched across her face.

"Okay," I replied nonchalantly. Damn, it was so crazy how I had a sudden, unexpected change in friendship. I lost one friend and gained another in a matter of an hour. Truth be told, with the interaction Donna and I had earlier, I didn't even think a friendship with her was possible. But for the last hour or so, she proved to be more informative and hopeful about my situation than Monique and even Neicy. Granted, deep down, I still felt so bad about lying to Monique about everything. And although Neicy and I were now cool, I still to this day blame her to a degree for even getting up in my business with Dre. Then again, maybe all of this had to happen for a reason. If Neicy didn't butt her way into my business, I probably would've still been out there on the streets.

After we walked inside, we checked back in with the security guard. Funny thing was, although we reeked of straight weed, the security guard didn't even care.

"Let's go see if Pastor Shirley is in her office so we can talk to her ASAP about everything," Donna said. "I think I saw her Benz out front."

"Okay...But damn, don't you think we should put on some spray or something or change out of these clothes?"

Donna looked at me and rolled her eyes. "Girl, please. Stop tweakin'. I'm telling you. Pastor Shirley is *cool*."

"Girl, I don't know...This just seems so...I don't know. I don't know about all of this," I said as I began to become very suspicious and doubtful all over again. It was like on one hand I truly wanted to trust everything Donna was telling me. I mean, she really had no real reason to lie to me. I barely knew her. She barely knew me. A part of me was telling me to go ahead and have faith and trust in the Lord. *This woman was obviously put into your life for a reason*, I thought to myself. But another part of me, the inner street *nigga,* in me was very much doubtful. My intuition kept telling me something wasn't right. But then again, my intuition had been off so many times, I truly didn't know what to think anymore.

"Look, do you want my help or not? I'm kind of going out of the way to help you. I ain't got no real reason to lie to you," Donna said.

I froze and then stared at her, not able to say anything back.

She raised a brow. "Well? So what you gon' do?"

"I'm sorry. Let's go. I'm tripping," I replied, a nervous smile stretched across my face.

By now it was nearly nine pm and most of the house activities were over. Everyone had to be in the rooms by ten pm for bedtime. Pastor Shirley's office was on the far end of the building on the first floor. I'd been in there a few times.

Some seconds later, Donna and I arrived at Pastor's office. Donna then knocked twice.

"Come in," Pastor Shirley said inside of her office.

Donna then looked at me and scanned me up and down with this slightly devilish grin. She opened the door and walked in. Following behind her, at first I didn't see Pastor Shirley since I was standing directly in front of Donna. But soon as Donna moved out of the way, Pastor Shirley was sitting at her desk with a big black bonnet sitting on top of her head as she filed her nails. Some young, skinny dark-skinned guy with dreads, looking no older than thirty, was sitting in front of her desk, looking like he was rolling up weed. What in the hell was going on?!?

"Just the chick I wanted to see," Pastor Shirley said, not giving me any eye contact.

"Huh?" My face twisted into confusion. Donna spun around and looked at me shaking her head. That same devilish grin returned to her face. "You's a dumb ass bitch," she laughed.

"Wait! No! No! I didn't do nothin'," I yelled to Pastor Shirley.

"Hoe, it's too late!"

## CHAPTER TWENTY-TWO

"Yes! She's crazy! She's gonna kill me!" Candreka cried, clasping her battered face.

"Oh my God! Where is she?!?! Do you know where she went?" I asked, my heart thumping out of my chest.

"I don't know where she's at!" Candreka cried.

"Why the fuck you came over here?!?" I angrily asked.

"I don't know! You were the first person I could think of who was closest to where we stay!"

With no idea what was going on, I damn near feared for my life as well! This shit was crazy as hell! What in the fuck did these two really have going to make my cousin beat her girl's ass this way! And I didn't even realize cuzzo even had it in her to do this type of damage. All the years I'd known my family, never once did I ever see her get into a fight, let along damn near kill someone. Granted, Tanisha had some tom boyish ways, but she wasn't the type to fight broads nor niggas. If anything, she acted like a straight up female. She could run her mouth and be passive aggressive but she wasn't the type of chick who would put hands on another person.

"I don't know where she's at!" Candreka cried.

All of this shit was totally unbelievable. A part of me for a split second thought perhaps Candreka was lying. Shit just seemed too shady.

"Why would she do this to you!?!?" I asked as I leaned down and helped her off the ground. *Call Tanisha, Dre. Somethin' ain't right. This bitch is lying. Something suspect as fuck!* I thought to myself

Shivering like was one some dope, she stared at me with her eyes bugged out as if she'd seen a ghost. "I...I, ummm...I..."

"You what?!?"

"I got pregnant..."

Suddenly my face twisted with surprise. "You got pregnant?!?!? Huh?" It took me a moment to process what the fuck she just said. "I thought yo ass was a lesbian!?!?"

"I am! But I fucked dudes from time to time!"

"Shit! What the fuck?!?!? How did she even find out?!?! Why didn't you just abort the damn baby?!?!"

"I was going to but she went through my phone and saw the text messages I was getting from the dude."

"What dude?!?! What the fuck, bruh!?!?! What is REALLY going?!?" I stood back, shaking my head. None of this shit was adding up. "I think I need to call Tanisha to see what the fucking real story is. None of this is making sense!" I quickly pulled out my phone, ready to dial up Tanisha, but before I could do so, Candreka shot up from the corner and tried to grab the phone out of my hand. "DRE! PLEASE, NO! PLEASE DON'T CALL HER!"

***Knock! KNOCK! KNOCK!***

"WHERE SHE AT?!?!? I KNOW THAT BITCH IN THERE! Open up this goddamn door!"

"Shit! She knew you came here?!?! What the fuck?!?!?" I yelled, looking at Candreka with shock. But she was just as shocked. "OH MY GOD! FUCK! She knew I came here 'cuz I forgot we both got GPS trackers on our iPhones!"

"Damn!"

Tanisha kept pounding at my front door, damn near ready to bust that shit down. "Open up this mothafuckin' door, Dre! I know she in there! You got my bitch pregnant! I KNOW YOU DID! I know it was yo fuckin' ass!"

Suddenly I stood in my place not able to move. "Fuck she talkin' 'bout?!? I got *you* pregnant?!?" Hell nah! Shit, even though I would've loved to fuck the shit out of shorty, I definitely didn't get this broad pregnant. No sir! Not even in my wildest dreams, especially considering that crazy ass dream I had earlier when I passed out at their crib some days ago. But damn, maybe that dream turned out to be some weird premonition.

I didn't know honestly what to do next. "I gotta see what she want, Candreka! I can't just let her stand there! She gon grab the attention of my neighbors! Shit, the police probably already on their way!"

"No! NOO, Dre! Please, no!"

"Man, look! This my cousin! I know I can talk to her. This just all one big ass mistake. And besides, whatever the fuck you two got going on, I don't want no parts! And I definitely gonna clear my name in this shit!"

"Dre! Please, no! She's dangerous!"

Smacking my teeth and looking shorty up and down, I said, "Nah, this family. She ain't gonna do shit to me."

Candreka suddenly shoved past me and dipped down the hallway.

"Where you going?!?" I asked but then I ran to my door and looked out the peephole. My eyes widened with fear though when I saw Tanisha standing there with a big ass glock in her right hand. "DRE! OPEN UP THE DOOR! I SWEAR I'MMA KILL THAT BITCH!"

"YO! What the fuck is you doin', Tanisha?!?! Nigga, what is you smoking?!?"

"DRE! OPEN UP THE GODDAMN DOOR! SO YOU THE NIGGA WHO WAS FUCKING HER, HUH?!?! THAT'S WHY SHE RAN HER ASS OVER HERE!?!?"

"NAH! Hell nah, cuz! I don't know why the fuck shorty came over here! But you need to put that gun away before the cops come and see you! Girl, you know you in fucking Hyde Park. These white folks gonna call twelve with the swiftness!"

"DRE! That no good bitch fucking broke my heart! That bitch is no good! And I thought we was family! You fucked my wife, Dre! You out of all people!?!?? Really?!? You?!?!?"

"Bruh! You tweakin' the fuck out right now! I ain't did shit with shorty!"

Tanisha and I kept going back and forth, right at my damn door! Cuz was definitely bugging but I knew one thing for sure, I definitely wasn't going to open that goddamn door!

"Yo! Bruh, you need to calm the fuck down and go home! You with the shits and you 'bout to go to jail!"

"DRE! PLEASE! JUST OPEN THE DOOR! I WANNA TALK TO HER!" Tanisha screamed and cried, waving the gun all over the place.

"Nah! I ain't gonna do that, Tanisha!"

Out the corner of my eye, I could see Candreka come down the hallway and hide behind a corner. I glanced her way and told her silently, "Go back to the room. She got a gun!"

Then, blue lights began to pierce inside of the living room through the windows. Twelve was now on the scene. One of my neighbor's probably just called the cops, just like I expected.

I looked back into the peephole and said, "See, cuz! The fucking police are here now!

"Fine! FINE!" Tanisha screamed, still waving the gun.

"Ya'll gonna regret this shit! All the shit I did for you mothafuckas! And this is how you repay me?!?!"

Tanisha then stormed off and then went out into the middle of the street, approaching the police officers. I flew into my living room and then pulled my blinds up to see what the fuck was about to happen next. Once again, from the corner of my eye, I could see Candreka catiously make her way back into the living room and then she stood next to me. "What is she doing?!?" she cried.

"I don't know! Damn!" I replied angrily.

Two squad cars were right in the middle of the street, their lights filling the darkness outside. Suddenly, one of the officers hopped out the car, a gun hoisted in his hand was aimed straight at cousin. "Ma'am! Put the gun down and put your hands up in the air!" the middle-aged looking white cop screamed.

Tanisha was completely silent, but she kept walking toward the two cars, the gun still in her hand. It was as if she didn't hear a damn thing the officer said. Then she spun on her heels and looked straight into my townhouse's living room window. The blinds were fully open now and she could see Candreka and I standing next to each other.

"Man, bruh! WHAT THE FUCK ARE YOU DOING?!?" I screamed, throwing my hands up. I was now getting so nervous cousin was about to do something so stupid and unthinkable.

"Please, baby! Just put the gun down!" Candreka begged, crying and shivering next to me.

"I LOVED YOU! YOU BETRAYED ME!" Tanisha screamed, looking dead at the both of us as we stood there silent and unmoving. This was like some scene out of a movie. Like straight from Set It Off. Within seconds, three more CPD squad cars arrived on the scene and without hesitation, two more officers jumped out of their vehicles and had their pistols aimed straight at Tanisha.

"Ma'am! I'm not gonna say it again! Put the fucking gun down NOW!" the same officer screamed.

Tanisha then spun on her heels.

"I can't sit here and watch this! She's about to do something stupid! I just know it!" I exclaimed. I had to go out there and dissuade her from trying to do some stupid shit. Fighting the urge, something told me not to go, but I had to. This was my cousin! My favorite cousin at that. We were so close, we were almost like brother and sister, so I couldn't stand to see her put herself in this crazy ass situation. Not even a second passed and I suddenly dashed to my front door, hoping I had enough time to get out onto the street and talk some sense into cousin's head.

***POW!***
***POW! POW! POW!***

"NOOOOOO! AHHHHHHHH!" I heard Candreka scream.

Guess I was a second too late. By the time I opened the door, I saw Tanisha laid out in the street.

"NOO! What the fuck did ya'll do?!?!" I suddenly exploded into rage.

"GET BACK, SIR! STAND THE FUCK BACK!" one of the officers yelled at me, aiming his gun straight at my chest.

"That's my cousin! Ya'll killed my cousin!" I screamed, now uncontrollably crying. Candreka ran outside, and she too was crying and screaming.

"She raised her gun at me!" one of the officers said.

A crowd began to form outside on the sidewalk. One of the officers sauntered over to Tanisha's lifeless body and then kneeled down and picked up the gun she was carrying. Carefully examining it, he shook his head and then muttered, "This is a fucking BB gun!"

## CHAPTER TWENTY-THREE

"Ma'am!"
"Ma'am!!!!"
"Hellooooo!!! Ma'am!"
"Please wake up! I'm at your destination!"

Suddenly, my eyes shot open at the sound of my Uber driver's voice. Staring back at him, I didn't know how long he had been trying to get my attention.

"Are you okay?" he asked me, looking very concerned.

I didn't know what time it was or how long the man had been trying to get my attention. After I left Dre's house, I got into my ride, popped my medicine and dozed off.

"Yeah, ye-yeah, I'm fine. I just took my medicine a little bit too early and I passed out. I'm sorry about that," I apologized. "I'mma leave you a tip on the app."

"Thank you very much. Enjoy the rest of your night, ma'am," the driver said. I quickly gathered my belongings and then made my way out of the car. By now it was definitely dark outside and I had a good hour to get inside to check in.

I couldn't believe I passed out in the back of that man's car and had such a vivid dream, really nightmare, about smoking weed with Donna and then getting into some mess with Pastor Shirley. That was probably God speaking to me, telling me that Donna was definitely no good and that I needed to stay away from her as much as possible.

Although I knew I dreamt that craziness while I was in the backseat of the Uber, I still on the edge. That dream felt so real. So, making my way up into the front of the building, I quickly looked around to see if Donna was lurking around the corner. And she wasn't. Thank the Lord.

After I walked inside the building, I checked in with the security guard and then made my way back to my room. Although I was a tad hungry, the kitchen was already closed. I could've ordered some take out, but I wanted to make sure I was on my Ps and Qs when it came to my diet. Dr. Pirtle wanted me to make sure I still ate my fruits and veggies and stay away from fried foods. That takeout was nothing but the devil, so I'd just fast for the rest of the night and make sure I got a nice lil breakfast in the morning after prayer.

Nonetheless, I was still so devastated about everything. Yeah, truth be told, I should've been more upfront with Dre and his mama about the reality of Ariyanna's paternity. But hey, that was water under the bridge. I said what I had to say and I was truly determined to make the situation right. Oh, and as far as Monique, my bestie, not knowing about who Ariyanna's father was. Well, honestly, she was the only person who knew the truth. And that was also I was something I was grateful for. She never judged me about the mix-up. Although from time to time she told me I should've pressed for a paternity test just to verify everything, the reality was I didn't want to go there. That would've been a bad thing to do.

Why?

Well, there was another secret that I was keeping from everyone.

There was also a possibility that Chadwick, Monique's now fiancée, could've been the father.

PLEASE DO NOT JUDGE ME!

It was just a mistake. I swear to God it was.

Although now I considered myself a saved and sanctified woman of God, there was one thing that I was going to for sure take with me to my grave. And that was that truth. Now I understood fully why God gave me that dream in the back of that Uber. Hell, if I would've called up Monique and really confessed to her the possibility that Chadwick was one of many suspects, she would end our friendship. Hell, she might try to kill me.

Once I got back into my room, I changed out of my clothes and put my pajamas on. This entire situation with Dre was bothering me so much, especially considering that at the end of the day that probably wasn't even his child. If I was going to die, I deserved the right to see my child and if Dre wanted to take it there, now I was gonna be forced to do something I knew would get under his skin. I was gonna fight to see my baby, meaning, I was now gonna get the courts involved. If Dre wants to play that game with me and deny my right to be around my baby, well, I can play that game.

Now in my pajamas, I got down on my knees and said a prayer. I asked the Lord to continue to give me guidance and assurance that everything was going to be okay. That everything was gonna work out in his holy favor.

# CHAPTER TWENTY-FOUR

**TWO WEEKS LATER...**

"Amazing Grace, how sweet the sound. That saved a wretch like me!" An older black lady poured her heart out, singing that familiar gospel tune at the side of Tanisha's golden brown casket at the cemetery.

Sitting directly in front of my cousin's casket, I was a total wreck. So many tears flooded my face. Mama was sitting to my side holding Ariyanna.

Some moments later after the singer got done singing, some workers from the cemetery came over and began to lower Tanisha's casket into the ground. Holding a single rose in my hand, I stood up and threw the rose on top of her casket. Man, I still couldn't wrap my head around any of this mess. I couldn't believe my cousin, my sister really, would go out like this. All over Candreka's shady ass. Thank God I never acted on my impulses and tried to make a move on her nasty ass. Something always told me this bitch was shady as fuck.

Speaking of the mothafuckin' devil...

As I looked over my shoulder, I saw her standing several feet away. She was by herself, dressed in some tight-fitting black dress. Some shades adorned her face. Holding her arms by her elbows, she just stood there and watched the casket make its final journey into the muddy pit.

I glanced over at her, wiping my face free of tears and sweat. On this Saturday in Chicago, it was exceptionally hot and sunny outside, which kind of sucked because the weather was so nice. In fact, it brought me back to memories with Tanisha. Usually this time of the year, she'd be hosting all types of kickbacks and barbeques at her crib.

Still staring at Candreka, I almost had it in me to run up over there and choke the shit out of her. This was all her fucking fault. She fucked around on my cousin, got pregnant by some nigga and then cousin decided to take her own life. Well, she technically didn't take her own life. She let the muhfuckin' jakes do it. Apparently, she had raised her gun up and almost aimed it at the officer who shot her. Crazy thing was I believe she knew what she was doing. She knew had a BB gun on her and she knew the cops would mistakenly think it was a real gun. Truth be told, I think the one thing that really blew my mind was to also find out that cousin was high as fuck that night. When the county morgue did an autopsy and some toxicology tests on her, they discovered she had lethal amounts of cocaine and meth in her system. *Like damn, Tanisha, what the in hell did Candreka do to you to make you go this crazy?!?* I wondered to myself, still debating whether or not I should go over there and cuss that bitch the fuck out.

After Tanisha got killed that night, Candreka hadn't been seen or heard from in quite some time...until today. I thought she wouldn't come to the funeral but it looked like she felt like she had to pay her last respects. Bitch.

*Calm down, Dre. Don't do it. It ain't worth it. Don't do cousin like this*, my mind ruminated, trying so hard to dissuade me from making a big ass scene at the cemetery.

Quickly looking away to distract myself, I then turned my attention back to my mama and Ariyanna. "You ready?" I asked her.

"Yeah...I'm ready," she replied in a nonchalant tone. She, too, wasn't dealing all too well with this fucked up situation. Tanisha was almost like a daughter to her, so from the moment she found out what happened, she was completely devastated. I reached down and grabbed Ariyanna from out of mama's lap and then the two of us followed the rest of our family members back to the road where limos, the hearse and other cars were parked.

"Dre...," I heard a familiar female voice say from behind me. I turned around, holding Ariyanna.

It was Trish.

I froze for a second and tightened my lips. I had to look up to the blinding sun in order to make sure I wasn't hallucinating. What in the FUCK was she doing here?!?

I looked back down and she was now a few feet away from me. Damn! How long had she been here?!? I wondered. I didn't see her at the church nor did I see her in the crowd moments earlier.

"What are you doing here?" I asked and then looked at my mama. She looked ready to pop off, like she was ready to explode like a volcano in Hawaii. "I know you ain't coming here to my niece's funeral to start no mess!"

"No, Ms. Williams. I'm not. I'm just here to pay my respects. Tanisha and I were cool, too. I just thought I'd come by and say how sorry I am for everything. That's all," she said, then she smiled and waved at Ariyanna. "Hey, baby girl." Trish then limped off, using her cane for assistance.

Mama and I looked at each other. For a split second, once again, my anger almost came out, but then I realized that was a bit honorable for Trish to come out and show her support. And she wasn't lying. She and Tanisha were cool at one point in time.

A part of me felt somewhat bad seeing Trish in that condition. Although I was still mad as hell that she would come to my mama's house on that bullshit.

"You okay, broski?" I heard Myron, my best friend, say as he came from behind me. I looked at him and said, "Yeah, I'm cool. Just didn't expect Trish to bring her ass here."

"Yeah, that was kind of foul...She on some other stuff, bruh," he replied shaking his dread-filled head.

"Yeah, whatever...," I responded, staring at her as she walked toward a car. Looked like she took an Uber to get here.

After we all headed back to our cars, we then made our way back to the church for Tanisha's repast. It was like any ole typical black funeral repast. Old ladies served fried chicken, yellow rice with gizzards, collard greens and buttery pound cake to funeral goers.

Mama, Ariyanna, me and some other family members were sitting at a main table inside of the church hall munching away. I was feeding Ariyanna when suddenly I saw once again Trish enter the dining hall of the church. This time, her best friend, Monique was to her side. "I'll be damned," I mumbled under my breath, my eyes widened with slight anger. Monique was all drama, too. She was the type of bitch who put all types of crazy thoughts up into Trish's head. Where in the hell did she come from? Man, see now something kept telling me these broads were up to no good.

"Mama, she came back here," I said as I leaned into her side.

"Who did?" she asked. She wasn't paying attention since she was chatting it up with one of my uncles.

"Trish...now she with Monique," I replied.

"Hrrrm...Let them be," she said.

With my eyes still glued to these broads, I just had a feeling that they were on some shady shit. Although, of course, I wasn't talking to Trish, but damn, why didn't she at least call me and tell me that she was going to becoming to my cousin's funeral?!? If she knew her and I were already on thin ice as it was, she could've at least given me the heads up. Granted, she *didn't* have to really tell me shit since she did know Tanisha and they were cool. But this was my family and she knew this. For a second, I even wondered how in the hell she found out Tanisha died. Then again, maybe word got around. Regardless, I had the urge to get up and confront her. And if anything, with paternity of Ariyanna being out there, I wanted to go ahead and nip that shit in the butt.

"Where are you going?" Mama asked as I began to get out of my seat.

"I'mma go talk to Trish. I just don't like the vibes she's giving me. She just gonna show up to the funeral and act like it's all cool and whatnot. Something ain't right," I said.

"Dre, just sit down and leave them alone. I don't want no mess today. Handle that craziness another time. Now is not the right time," mama said.

"Mama, please. I know Trish. She might think she a changed woman now but I can sense her shadiness from a mile away. She's up to something," I explained.

"Whatever," mama replied. "Give me my grandbaby and any mess you start, take it outside," she said.

"I will," I replied as I handed mama Ariyanna. I leaned down and pecked a kiss on the side of baby girl's face. "Daddy will be right back," I said and then strolled over to Trish and Monique. They were now standing in line, waiting to get served some food.

"What ya'll doing here? Like for real?" I asked.

"What are you talkin' about, Dre?" Trish asked, looking a tad perplexed at my question.

"Please, don't' play dumb with me. If you knew you were coming, why wouldn't you call me?"

"She don't owe you an explanation! Besides, you ain't nothin' but a bully!" Monique interjected. "You see the condition she's in. You know what she got going on and this is how you decide to treat her?"

I smacked my teeth and looked Monique up and down, "Bitch, mind your own damn business!"

Suddenly Trish clasped her face. A few of the older women who were serving food heard me and looked at me as if I was smoking crack in front of their faces.

"Uh-uh! Not in here. Ya'll need to take that outside!" one of the older ladies said. "This is a house of God!"

"Dre...You wrong for that," Trish replied shaking her head. Damn, this bitch was really on some other shit now. I couldn't believe she was gonna stand there and act like some holy roller. Bitch, I know all about your mothafuckin' ass. You weren't gonna be able to floss that shit on me now that you out of jail. Lying ass hoe. This Jesus shit was probably all a front anyways.

I couldn't take it anymore. "We need to talk," I said. "Let's go outside," I commanded as I grabbed her arm and try to pull her out of line.

"Get your hands off me," she growled, pulling her arm back.

"Monique, come with me in case he gets flip," Trish said.

"Oh, you already know I will!" Monique responded.

"Fine..." I walked off and the two bitches followed me outside into the parking lot of the church.

Once the coast was clear and no one was around, I looked at Trish and said, "So, what the fuck is really going on, breh? Like, you first gonna come to my mama's crib unexpectedly and try to see Ariyanna knowing you weren't supposed to do that. Then, you gon' sit up there and try to run me some story about you dying and that I may not be the father to my child? You fuckin' playing games with me. You already know how angry I get!"

"Nigga, you ain't gon do shit!" Monique spat as she shoved Trish out the way and scanned me up and down. "You need to calm the fuck down before shit get really serious, bro. You not gon sit up here and talk to my best friend this way!"

"Man! I don't even know why the fuck you here! You need to mind your own business! Like I was doing, TAKING CARE OF MY DAMN DAUGHTER!"

"That's if she's even yours!" Monique spat back.

"Ya'll please stop it! This is not how I wanted to talk to you, Dre! Monique, I told you this was a bad idea!" Trish suddenly burst into tears.

"Man, whatever," I said smacking my teeth. "You used my cousin's funeral as an opportunity to come talk to me. You should've been woman enough to call me," I said.

"Dre! The last time I tried to talk to you, you damn near tried to kill me!" Trish screamed, tears still flying out of her widened eyes. "Remember?"

"Yeah, yeah, yeah! So what you want?"

"Dre! I am not playing. I am very sick and I think it's only right that you let me see Ariyanna and you need to take a test just to make sure she's yours! Please, we gotta do this before it's too late!" she begged.

"Nah! I ain't doing that. I got fully custody over *my* child. She's mine. I know it. Everyone knows Ariyanna looks just like me. So stop playing games, man. She has my personality and everything. And like I said, you technically not her mother no more. The courts took that right away from you. So, I suggest you two broads get on your merry way and leave me and my family alone to grieve," I roared.

"Dre...Please...This ain't right. But if that's the path you wanna go down, this is for you," Trish said as she reached into her purse and handed me an envelope.

"What's this?" I said as I snatched the envelope out of her hand.

"Let's go, Monique. I'm done with him," Trish said and then the two of them walked off.

"What in the hell is this?" I mumbled to myself as I quickly opened the envelope. I pulled out a piece of paper and then began to read over it. "Dear Mr. Williams..You are here by notified by Cook County Family Court, Division #23, to appear before Judge Lynn Tolliver in regards to a motion filed by LaTrisha Johnson to establish joint custody..."

"WHAT THE FUCK?!?!?" This bitch just served me papers!

# CHAPTER TWENTY-FIVE

"WHAT THE FUCK?!?!?"

I heard Dre scream from afar as Monique and I took off as fast as we could, despite the fact that I was limping. But it seemed like with the adrenaline running in my system, my limp wasn't as debilitating as usual. With me just serving Dre those court papers, I just knew he'd use all of his speed and might catch up to us and try to inflict as much harm as he could. I just knew he would finally let loose and kill me. And probably even try to kill Monique.

"Come on, girl! Hurry up before he tries to run up on us," Monique commanded as got close to our Uber ride and then hopped in. "Take off, sir! Please! Someone's chasing us!" Monique told the driver. The older Mexican-looking driver quickly followed.

With my heart damn near ready to explode out of my chest, I couldn't believe Monique had persuaded me into confronting Dre in this manner. I was a bit apprehensive about doing things this way, but she told me it was the only best course of action to take to get Dre's attention.

The Uber driver sped off down the street and then we got

onto Stony Island Avenue, the main thoroughfare not too far away from the church we were just at.

"I told you it would work!" Monique laughingly screamed, sticking her tongue out. "Mission mothafuckin' accomplished!"

*Accomplished...*

"Ughh,!" I groaned, rubbing the side of my head as a pulsating migraine began to pound my right temple. While Monique felt we accomplished something, I, on the other hand, felt a bit shady doing this to Dre. But truth be told, this was his fault. He was unreasonable and I felt like I had no other choice to take it there. I had to force my hand to at least get to see my baby.

"Girl, aren't you excited!" Monique roared.

"Yeah, I guess," I replied nonchalantly, staring out through the passenger window, still somewhat scared about that interaction. "But sis, I just know Dre is gonna go crazy now. Him and his no-good mama," I complained.

Monique smacked her teeth. "Girl, don't worry about none of that. He ain't gonna do shit," she laughed. Glancing over at me, I guess she noticed that I wasn't all too pleased how everything just suddenly went down. "I'm sorry I cursed," she said. "I'mma do better."

"I'm not mad about that actually. I'm just mad that I feel like I cornered Dre. Especially at Tanisha's funeral. And especially considering how she died. Now my guilt is eating me alive. I don't know if that was the right thing to do," I said.

"Girl, you really overthinking all of this. Just relax. Besides, with no time left to lose, we don't have time to get caught up thinking about Dre's feelings. Was he thinking about yours when he put you through all of this drama?"

"No," I replied.

"Was he thinking about you and your health when he tried to kill you a few weeks ago?"

"No."

"Well, okay then. Don't worry about it. So long as I'm around, trust me, he ain't gonna do shit to you or me. I guarantee that, baby! And Chadwick ain't gonna let a nigga try to put their hands on me. I know that for sure," Monique explained, fumbling through her purse and then pulled out her cell phone. "Speaking of which, I need to see if bae want something to eat. I guess since you're gonna be spending the weekend with us, what you want to eat?"

"Just a salad," I said, still thinking about everything.

Damn...Monique was kind of right. To hell with Dre. I had to do what I had to do.

That night after I got back from Dre's place and tried to explain to him the precarious situation we were all in, I realized that I had to take things a step further. I called Monique and told her exactly what went down and she formulated today's game plan.

She told me she had a friend who worked as a paralegal for a nonprofit in Downtown that dealt with family issues. At first, I was doubtful a court would hear my petition to grant me visitation rights given my now ex-felon status and that I was currently staying in a halfway house. However, Gary, her paralegal friend, talked to his boss and then they got into contact with me and told me that a judge might show me some leniency given my grave health situation. The nonprofit said they would work pro bono on my behalf, so they immediately went down to a Cook County judge and filed a motion asking a judge to grant a hearing in regard to restoring my visitation rights and possibly establishing joint custody. I also told Gary about the possibility that Dre may have not been the father after all, so they said once we got to our hearing, they would ask the judge to mandate a paternity test to see if Dre indeed was Ariyanna's father. And if he wasn't, well, there was a good possibility that if I had gotten completely back on my feet by that point, I could gain full custody over baby girl.

Our initial plan was to try to corner Dre and serve him papers at his job or at school. But I didn't want to take things that far because I didn't want to make a scene for him at his job. Although I was bitter at him for putting me through all of this hell, it would've not been Christian-like for me to return that bitterness to him. Although expensive, we then decided to possibly hire a private process server to serve Dre those papers but then we found out Tanisha had died. That totally threw Monique and I off guard. I was going to back down from everything but then bestie said that we could probably go to the funeral, pay our respects and then serve him papers there. He wouldn't dare make a scene, she suggested. And I guess to an extent she was right even though it did seem like he was about to chase us down in that parking lot and murder us right then and there.

We were now on Lake Shore Drive, headed north back to Monique and Chadwick's place. I got permission from my probation officer and Pastor Shirley to spend the weekend with them. Truth be told, I felt kind of bad because deep down, there was still this huge possibility of Chadwick being Ariyanna's father. Lord knew I didn't have it in me to tell Monique that secret, so I tried my best to suppress that thought, hoping the Lord will forgive me and understand this predicament.

Thirty minutes later, we got to Monique and Chadwick's place and made our way upstairs to their apartment. We walked inside and Chadwick was sitting quietly on the living room couch watching television while he sipped on a beer.

"Hey, babe!" Monique announced as she trekked into the living room carrying my suitcase.

"Sup," he replied, not giving any of us eye contact.

"Hey, Chadwick," I said nervously then tightened my lips.

He looked over at us and then nodded his head and said, "Hey."

"You okay?" Monique asked. "Everything alright?"

"Yeah, I'm fine..." He took a sip of his beer. "How was the funeral?"

"It was sad. But it was a nice service. Tanisha looked so pretty in her casket," Monique said as she made her way into the kitchen. Honestly, I couldn't move. I just stood there in between the foyer and the living room, not knowing if I even had permission to sit down. Besides, I didn't even know if I felt comfortable sitting in the same space as Chadwick.

"Go ahead and sit down, Trish! Why you just standing there?" Monique said laughing as she ran some sink water and began washing dishes.

"Sorry, I just was thinking for a second. Actually...I need to use the bathroom," I muttered. "I'll be right back." I then limped down the apartment hallway, needing to quickly calm myself down.

You know, years ago, I would've been able to ignore the obvious tension in the room and pretend like Chadwick and I didn't have anything going on. But now I was more conscious about my past decisions. I recently spent so much time thinking about all the madness I'd been through. Hell, I even contemplate the madness I put others through. So, none of this just sat right with my spirit.

Once I made my way into the bathroom, I pulled my dress and panties down and began to pee. While on the toilet, I closed my eyes and said a prayer, asking the Lord to show me through all of this.

"In Jesus name, I pray...Amen," I mumbled and then stood up.

Once I flushed the toilet and washed my hands, I made my way back out into the living room. Monique was now snuggled up next to Chadwick on the couch. "Have a seat, girl! Make yourself comfortable!" she said.

I nervously moved deeper into the living room and then sat down on the love seat.

"So, Chadwick wants some wings and pizza. The place we order from doesn't deliver, so I was thinking about running down the block to go get it."

"I'll go and pick it up," Chadwick said. "I need to get out of the house anyways."

"Nah, baby. You stay. I gotta go run some other errands," Monique interjected.

"Nah, it's cool. You've been out all day. Don't you wanna rest?" he asked.

"Yeah, I hear you, but I also need to stop by Jewel and Walgreen's to get some feminine products. I know you don't wanna have to pick those things up, do you?"

He thought for a moment. "Yeah, I guess you're right," he said nonchalantly.

"I'll go, too!" I beamed and was already ready to get up but Monique threw a look of concern. "Girl, no! You need to rest, too!"

"I'm fine, girl."

"No! You've been on your feet all day. You need to let your hip rest," she said as she kissed Chadwick on the cheek and then got up. "I'll be back in an hour or so. In the meantime, make yourself at home, Trish. Don't act like no stranger. Chad ain't gonna bite," she laughed as she made her way near the foyer. "Just give me a ring if ya'll need me to pick up anything else," she said.

"Okay," Chadwick replied.

"Okay," I replied as well.

Soon as Monique headed out of the door, I just sat back and kept my gaze locked onto the television. Awkward silence entered the room and all you could hear now was ESPN blaring from the hi-def television in the living room.

Not into sports, I pulled out my phone and then pulled up my Bible app. Lord knew I needed to read some of his holy word to keep my mind distracted from the tension.

"So you just gonna sit over there and not say anything?" Chadwick suddenly asked.

I glanced up and saw him looking dead at me, his eyes turned into penetrating slits.

"Hey," I responded nervously. "How you doin'?"

"Bitch, I told you the last time I didn't want your ass in my house or near my presence. And now you gon' snake your way back here?"

"Chadwick, it wasn't my idea to come over here. Monique begged me to stay the weekend. I had no other choice. I'm sorry," I fretfully said, my body beginning to quake with fear at the sound of the tension concealed in Chadwick's tone.

"Yeah. What the fuck ever," he replied shaking his head, his eyes still attached to the television. "You a lil lying ass, shady ass bitch. And fuck all of that holier than thou bullshit you on now. Fake ass hoe. Gon come up in my mothafuckin' crib and spend the night here. Raggedy ass hoe. I don't give a fuck if you dying or not," Chadwick growled. "Yo ass need to be rotting away in a jail cell."

"Chadwick, how could you say this? I ain't never did nothing so mean to you. What you and I had was the past. Just occasional flings. And remember, you came onto me. I ain't never pushed myself onto you."

"Bitch, fuck you," he spat.

All of a sudden, I grew angry. "I'll be damned if I'm gonna be disrespected. And for your information, you just as guilty as I am. Especially since you know there's a possibility Ariyanna might be your daughter," I spat back to him.

"What did you say?" his face twisted with confusion.

"Yeah, I said Ariyanna might be your kid."

"Oh, bitch, here you go again with your lies. Man, I was wearing a condom that night. And besides, even if the girl was mine, you weren't even woman enough to confront me. You raggedy ass, loser ass mother."

Suddenly Chadwick rose from his seat. I quickly grew nervous as to what he was going to do next. "I know you not finne put your hands on me!" I growled.

"Hell no. Bitch, you aren't even worth the kill. Look at you. Your hair is falling out of your head. Your body is all shriveled up and frail. That chemo got you looking forty years older. Bitch, your skin is drier than a California raisin. Bitch, you're about to die, ain't no point in trying to kill you. If you do end up dead, which I hope you do, thank God Ariyanna is being taken care of by a nigga who got his shit together and not by some deadbeat nigga. And now that I think about it, I want you gone tomorrow. You can spend the night tonight but I want you out of my place tomorrow. If you don't, then I'mma tell Monique the truth about everything. And yeah, she'll be upset. But I'm a real nigga. I don't give a fuck if Monique breaks up with me. I can always find me a new bitch. But you on the other hand. What you got? A sister who barely likes you? Monique is the last person in your life who truly cares about you. Once that's gone you might as well be dead."

Sitting there in shock, I couldn't believe Chadwick would stand there and say those hateful, hurtful things to me. What in the hell did I ever do to deserve that type of verbal lashing?!? But to an extent, I realized he was right. I put myself in this situation and couldn't even be upfront with my own friend. And I knew if I told her the truth, she would disown me.

"Fine, you know what. You're right. In fact, I can just

leave now. I don't think I feel comfortable being over here," I said.

"Yeah. You should've never felt comfortable in the first place, you raggedy ass bitch. See your way out my mothafuckin' door."

Swallowing my pride and fighting back tears, I mustered up my strength to get up from the couch.

"Before you leave, call Monique and tell her why you leaving, too. I wanna hear this lie you gon tell her since you not woman enough to tell her the truth about anything at this point, you loser," he said.

Shivering, a few tears trickled out of my eyes. I couldn't believe I was letting Chadwick have this much power over me but he was right. There was just no way in hell I could tell Monique the truth about what Chadwick and I had going on some years ago. And Chadwick obviously had nothing to lose at this point. I did. Monique was all I had left. Ariyanna was all I had left, too, but there was still a possibility a judge may not even take me seriously.

I pulled out my phone and dialed Monique. Within seconds, she picked up.

Chadwick looked at me and lowly mumbled, "Put her on speakerphone." I followed suit.

"Hey, girl! What's up! What you need?"

"Hey, girl, I hate to break it to you but I actually gotta head back to Hope. I got a call from my probation officer telling me that I gotta report back for a mandatory drug test. Also, Pastor Shirley wanted to see if I could work some overtime this weekend since she was loaded up with revivals all weekend," I lied. "I really need the money, too, especially if I gotta get this apartment soon."

"What?!?!? What the hell are you talking about, Trish?"

"I know...I'm sorry. I'mma see if I can make my way back over here," I said wiping my face.

"Ughh! Trish! No! Come on, girl! Call them folks back and tell them this ain't right! You already made plans. Plus, we still got so much to talk about for the court hearing!" she exclaimed.

"I know, I know, I know. But listen, sweetheart, these aren't my rules. And I gotta follow them to the tee if I don't wanna get in trouble," I lied once more.

Chadwick, still looking at me, produced this devilish grin and shook his head. "Pathetic," he muttered.

"Ok, well, it's cool I guess. Glad we had a chance to get Dre those papers though," she said.

"Yeah. True. But anyways, I'll holla at you later when I get back. I'll probably take the train back since it's right there. Save some money, I guess."

"You don't want me to order you an Uber?"

I looked at Chadwick and he gawked back at me. This look of disgust came across his face. "Hell no," he whispered in a dark tone.

"I got it, girl. Don't worry about it," I said. "You paid for enough stuff already."

"Alright, girl. Well, give me a call later," she said.

"Aiight, girl. Love you."

"Love you, too, girl. Stay safe," she said and then hung up.

I threw my phone back into my purse.

"Now see your way out my mothafuckin' house, bitch," Chadwick growled, pointing toward the front door.

"I wish you the best, Chadwick. May God open up your heart," I replied, wiping my face free of heavy tears.

"Yeah, whatever, hoe. Save that shit for those stupid ass jail bird hoes you live with. Now get the fuck out my shit," he said and then threw his gaze back onto the television.

I limped over to my suitcase, which was still standing next to the door near the coat rack. I grabbed it and headed out the front door and made my way down to the Redline train station. I was so ready to die right now. Like for real. I felt so horrible knowing Chadwick used our secret to manipulate me into leaving. And he was successful. I knew what he was trying to do. Create a wedge between Monique and me so that way I wouldn't eventually tell her the truth about our relationship. Guess he knew deep down inside I still wasn't able to come to grips with revealing I betrayed the trust of my own best friend.

Limping down the semi-busy sidewalk, everything I learned about faith and God over the past two years seemed to slip down the drain. The more steps I took, the more I realized none of this mess was real. Honestly, there were times where I struggled with all of this newfound religiosity.

"Fuck it," I grumbled as I came to a pause in my walk. I leaned down and opened up the top part of my suitcase, pulled out my bible and then threw it in a trash can sitting in front of a café. "I'm done with this shit," I said. "I ain't no real Christian. Fuck this shit."

## CHAPTER TWENTY-SIX

**TWO WEEKS LATER...**

"Man, I can't believe this bitch gon' serve me papers! I swear ta God if I get my hands on her, I'mma kill her! Like, I just might go to jail over the bitch," I angrily spat, sitting at the bar.

My homeboy, Myron, and I were at Rayco's, this upscale bar and lounge in the South Loop, throwing back these endless shots of Henny.

We had been meaning to check out this place for a while, but since I had a busy ass schedule, we hadn't had a chance to check it out. Between school, work, raising Ariyanna and then dealing with all of the drama with Shelly, Tanisha, and Trish, the last thing I had on my mind was going out and hanging with the guys. But now, as this life shit became more and more intense, I just needed to get out of the fucking house and get pissy drunk. I could've just stayed back at the crib, ordered me some pizza and blew a bag of weed but weed wasn't doing it for me anymore. Besides, now that my cousin was gone, I didn't even know if I had in me to put a blunt to my face. Every time I tried to take a hit of some Kush, I just kept thinking about her. Damn, I was missing her so much.

It was a chilly Thursday night. I asked my mama to watch Ariyanna for the night so I could just chill and relax. Get my mind off Tanisha's unexpected death.

This lounge though…It was aiight…Barely filled, only a few other patrons were inside the joint. Shit, there were more workers here than actual customers.

"Man, that shit is crazy, broski. I mean, so what you gon' do next? I mean, at the end of the day, I don't even see how a judge could even grant her visitation rights, let alone split custody if the bitch just got out of jail," he said.

I shook my head. "Tell me about it. Tell me fucking about it. The shit ain't even adding up. I mean, where the fuck did she even get the bread to even get an attorney? I'm just so confused about all of this. But I know that fat ass bitch, Monique, put her ass up to this shit," I complained, damn near ready to fall out my seat.

"Bruh, I feel you. I always knew Trish was a lil sneaky ass hoe," Myron grumbled, throwing a shot back. "So what you gonna do next?" he asked.

"Man, I'm finne get an attorney. In fact, I need to hit up that same nigga I had the last time. And then we gonna march right into that courthouse and put an end to this shit. Once and for all."

"But what about the DNA test. You gon take it?"

I scrunched my face. "Hell nah! The fuck?!? Why? I know Ariyanna is my daughter. Truth be told, I just think Trish dropped that shit on me to fuck with my head. Everybody can see Ariyanna looks just like me," I said.

"Man, bruh. I think you should take a test though, real talk. I mean, everyone knew Trish used to get around," Myron said shaking his head, somewhat laughing. "And do you really wanna be taking care of another nigga's kid?"

Huh? His comment kind of threw me off for a second. I was confused by what he meant by that. "What the fuck you mean she used to *get around?* When we were together, I didn't know that shit. I thought the bitch was loyal as fuck."

Myron raised a brow. "You *really* thought that? Like for *real?*"

"Hell yeah! The fuck is you talm'bout?"

Myron lowered and shook his head. He reached in and grabbed his other shot. We had them lined up, back to back. "Bruh, I know you fucking lying right now. You gon sit up here and tell me you didn't think Trish was a lil hoe?"

"No...Not really. I mean, she was a freak. But I didn't think she was out there like that. She was kind of fucked up in the head, but I didn't think she was messing around with niggas like that."

Myron started to laugh again but this time I was getting fucking agitated. What the fuck was he really trying to imply?

"Yo, bruh, what the fuck is so funny? Ain't nothin' funny about this, bro."

"Man, calm down. Lighten the fuck up. But damn, bro, I didn't think you were that green. I mean, everyone on the block knew that Trish was a lil nasty thot. No one thought you two would actually get serious," he said.

"Man, fuck you. You foul as fuck and out of pocket right now, bro," I replied shaking my head. This nigga's commentary was beginning to sober me the fuck up. If I had it in me, I'd quickly reach down and grab this empty barstool next to me and bludgeon this nigga to death.

"Anyways, fool, you need to lay off the drinks. And I need to head back to the crib. My BM been blowing my shit up. Just relax, man. I'm sure ain't no judge in their right mind gonna let Trish get visitation rights, let alone get custody. The bitch ain't even stable. She JUST got out of jail," he said as he leaned in and tried to give me dap. I wasn't feeling him at the moment, so I just waved him off. "I'll holla at you later, nigga," I said.

"Damn, it's like that?" he said, his twisted with a bit surprise.

"Man, whatever. Go on and check on ya BM. Make sure she faithful," I replied, somewhat irritated.

Myron scanned me up and down then shook his head. "Yeah, aiight. Peace," he said, sauntering off and out of the bar.

"Fuck nigga," I groaned under my breath.

With one more shot sitting in front of me, I contemplated for a moment whether or not I needed that shit. Then again, I didn't drive here. I took a Lyft to get here. "Fuck it," I groaned as I grabbed it and tossed that muhfucka back.

"You want some more rounds?" this lil thick ass white bartender hoe asked me as she began wiping down the counter in front of me.

"Nah, I'm good," I said. "I'm about to head out. Thanks for the drinks," I said as I pulled out some cash and slapped some twenties on the counter.

"Thanks," she the bartender replied as she picked up the cash. Although I wasn't into white bitches like that, shorty was kind of cute. She had long, silky black hair that ran down her back. Not too tall or too short, she had the build of a cheerleader. She had to be no older than twenty-five, maybe twenty-six.

Curiosity seeped in. "What's your name?" I had to ask.

"Melissa. You?" she asked, throwing this sexy ass smile back at me.

"Dre...Nice to meet you," I said, slightly throwing her a flirtatious grin.

"I like your hair," she commented. "Really goes well with your face."

"Really? What makes you say that?"

"I'm a stylist...I love hi-top fades. Anyways...Have a nice night," she said and spun on her heels.

"Wait, you just gon' walk away like that?" I asked.

"Well, I have other customers waiting for me."

"Oh, okay. Well, let me get your number."

She smiled. "Sure..."

---

"FUCK THIS PUSSY! FUCK THIS WHITE PUSSY!" Melissa screamed as I kept drilling that lil white pink pussy with all eight inches. I had this Becky cumming on my shit so much, I thought I was about to drown in her juices.

"You like that shit, huh?!? You like that black dick, huh?" I growled, pulling her hair back as I continued to shove this dick all deep up in her lil tight ass white pussy.

Man, I was in heaven dicking down this white broad. This was the first time EVER in my twenty-seven years of existence that I had a taste of some white pussy and I was so disappointed in myself that I never tried this shit earlier on.

It's funny 'cuz a bunch of my guys always used to try to encourage me to get me a white bitch but I absolutely refused. Had no real reason why. But then I always thought white bitches were gonna smell like spinach and tuna. But Melissa, goddamn, her lil pretty white pussy tasted like a marshmallow pie.

"Hell yeah! GIVE ME THAT BLACK DICK!" she screamed as she threw her lil booty back on.

Man, her guts were so juicy and tight, I knew I was gonna bust seconds from now.

"AHHHH! I'm cumming! FUCK!"

"PULL OUT!" she yelled

"Fuck!" I tried to quickly pull out but before I could I could feel some of my seed slip through the tip of my dick.

When I managed to get my dick out, I bust the remaining nut on her back.

"Goddamn!" I yelled, taking in deep breaths. A nigga was sweating profusely like I was in a dry sauna at the muhfuckin' gym and shit.

I left the bar after I got Melissa's number, and shorty hit me up an hour after I got back home. She didn't even hesitate in letting me know she wanted to fuck, so I invited her over with the swiftness just to see if this white pussy was hittin'. And it sure was. That shit was fucking fire. I ain't never had some pussy like this before in my life.

"I need to run to the bathroom," she said as she quickly shot up from my bed and made her way into the bathroom.

"Aiight," I replied, rolling my sweaty, naked body over into the bed and then pulled the sheets over me. Some minutes later, Melissa emerged from the bathroom and danced her slender naked white ass back into the bed. "Damn, that was some good sex. I haven't been fucked like that in a while," she said.

"Yeah…Shit, I haven't had sex like that either," I commented. Honestly, this was the first time in a long time I had been with a chick. Maybe I was being a bit delirious about just how good her pussy was now that I think about it. Hrrrm.

"So, are you in a relationship? You seeing anybody?" she asked.

"Nah. You?"

"Nope. I'm single…," she replied. "Well, anyway, let me get going. Thanks for the fuck," she said.

"Damn, you gonna dip out just that quick?" I asked.

Melissa raised a brow. "Umm, yeah…"

"Oh okay," I replied. "Well, maybe we can go out sometimes. I know ple—"

"Look, DeAndre…Thanks but no thanks. I don't really date black guys," she interrupted me, throwing her hands up.

"What? Are you serious?"

"Yeah. Serious as a heart attack. But thanks for the screw though," she said as she quickly threw her outfit back on.

I was stunned she'd even say some slick shit like that but I didn't care. "Wow. Okay. Man, get the fuck out of my house, white bitch. Get your shit and get ta steppin'. Pussy was trash anyways," I said.

"Oh, whatever!" she said and quickly dashed out of my bedroom. "Fucking asshole," I heard her shout before I heard her open my front door and slam it.

"Man, what the fuck ever," I groaned as I got up and made my way into the shower. Welp. At least I got to bust a big ass nut.

After I took a shower, I took my ass straight to bed. I had some important shit to take care of in the AM. I had already put in some PTO tomorrow so I could go straight to this lawyer's office and get working on this damn hearing I had coming up with Trish. Bitch thought she was gonna succeed, well, I was about to put a stop to that.

## CHAPTER TWENTY-SEVEN

"Cum for me! baybee! CUM! SQUIRT DE PUZZY JOOS! SQUIRT!" Olufemi screamed as I watched him jack his big, black Nigerian dick from my iPhone.

Although I should've had my ass up on this early Friday morning, I was laying back in my bed, salivating at the sight of Olu's big, pretty dick. I had my phone angled up, pointing directly down at my naked body. He and I were video-fucking each other through Facebook messenger.

My legs were spread wide open so Olu (as he wanted me to call him) could see this pretty pussy of mine. I was a bit embarrassed that my lil pussy was covered in a mound of hair, but Olu said he loved a hairy twat. And indeed I did have an afro growing on my shit.

Truth be told, I didn't' know what the fuck was going through my head these last two years. Yeah, I tried to become a Christian and turn my life around but I realized that shit just wasn't in me. I prayed. I fasted. I meditated. I did everything I was supposed to do yet my life was a fucking wreck. So to hell with all that bullshit. If a bitch only had a few more months left to live, I might as well go out with a bang. Besides, Chadwick was right. I was a liar. I couldn't even come to grips with my truth. I was a nasty hoe. And if I was a nasty hoe, I might as well live up to it. So here I was in, in my bedroom, finger-fucking myself as Olufemi watched.

If you don't remember, Olufemi was the Uber driver who picked me up a few weeks ago. Although he claimed he was a bonafide Christian, I knew deep down his ass just wanted to link up with me to get some pussy. At first, I resisted his invitations to come out to his church or to hang out with him. He seemed a bit odd to me, but then again, I guess it was because he was from a different culture and shit. But now, after talking to him for a few days, I was ready to give in. It just sucked because I wished he was back in the states. Otherwise, fuck the virtual fucking shit. I would've been at his crib right now, jumping up and down on that dick. Olu told me he was in the US on a student visa and he had to go back to Nigeria, otherwise, he would've gotten into trouble.

Yeah, I ain't gonna lie. Playing with my pussy was feeling so good. Although I was still dealing with my cancer, and I could feel myself getting weaker and weaker as days progressed, getting as many orgasms as I could was my main mission right now.

"I'm finne cum again, Olu! Fuck, my pussy is so wet! Do you see that?" I moaned as I stuck my fingers in and out of my wet ass coochie. Then I pulled them out and stuck them in my mouth to lick up all the pussy juice dripping from my fingertips. Damn, I ain't came like this in a minute!

"CUM! I'm CUMMING!" he screamed and next thing you know he blasted his thick white nut all over the place. GODDAMN! I ain't never seen a nigga bust so much nut out of his dick! Damn, I wish I could be there to suck up every single damn drop, too! Truth be told, when I was a lil nasty bitch back in the day, I used to love the taste of cum. Ughhh! Olu was just so damn sexy!

"FUCK!" he panted as he wiped his hands off with a towel and then blew me a kiss. "That was good. Very very *gud*," he said in his thick accent.

"I know right. Ughh! I just wish you were here, Olu," I replied back, producing a big sad puppy face.

"I'll be back, baybee...I'm gonna take care of you. You no die. Cancer will be gone a few more months. I promise. And then I will take care of you for the rest of my life. I promise, baybee," he said.

"I love the sound of that, Olu. Anyways, it's starting to get late and I gotta get going to my doctor's appointment. Thank you for a great time."

"I love you, Treesha! I love you, baby," he said, once again blowing me a kiss and then winked at me.

"I love you, too, baby," I replied and then hung up the phone.

***Knock! Knock!***

"What's going on in there?"

Suddenly, my eyes shot open with fear and I quickly turned my attention to my door. "Oh my God," I whispered to myself. That sounded like Pastor Shirley.

"Coming! Hold on for a minute," I said as I quickly got up and cleaned up my bedroom. Completely naked, I didn't have time to try to put on an outfit. "Hold on, Pastor Shirley. Let me put my robe on," I said as I limped over to my dresser where I sat my nightrobe. Once I put it on and tightened it, I sprayed some air freshener in the room to get rid of the smell of pussy. I walked over to the door, took a deep breath and then opened the door.

A nervous grin came across my face. "Hey, Pastor Shirley! It's early in the morning! What's going on?"

"Everything alright in here? Karen, the girl next door,

called down to the security guard's desk and said she heard a bunch of noise up in here. Like some screaming and whatnot. Said it sounded like a bunch of people were fighting in your room," she said, throwing me this curious gaze.

I exploded into fake laughter. "Oh, no, Pastor Shirley. That was probably just my cell phone. I had been watching these crazy Facebook videos after I got done with bible study," I lied.

"Speaking of which, how come you haven't been coming to any of my meetings or to services? I feel like these last two weeks you've been in MIA. Everything alright?"

"Yeah, I'm fine...," I lied once more.

She didn't say anything back. Her eyes just turned into curious slits. "Let's talk for a minute. Can I come inside?"

I really wanted to say no so I quickly thought of an excuse. Honestly, I did have to get ready soon for my doctor's appointment. Today, Dr. Pirtle was supposed to be running another battery of tests to see how far along the cancer was truly spreading and what next treatment options I could go through in order to slow the disease. She told me at my last doctor's appointment that if the disease reached a certain threshold, I needed to consider going into hospice.

"I would, Pastor Shirley, but I gotta get ready for my doctor's appointment."

"Oh, I know. I won't be long," she said.

"Okay then," I said and then welcomed her into the room.

With deep curiosity etched into her chubby face, she scanned my room, her hands attached to her waist. "What's that smell?" she asked.

"Probably just my laundry," I lied.

"Okay," she replied as she made her way over to my computer desk, pulled out a chair and sat down. "Sit down," she said. I sat on the edge of the bed and gawked at her with anxiety. "What's wrong, Pastor Shirley?"

"I'm concerned about you…I've been noticing some quick, sudden changes in your personality."

"What do you mean?" I asked. "I'm fine, Pastor Shirley. I truly am. I've just been so busy lately."

"Girl, you ain't fooling me. I'm old enough to damn near be your grandmother. I heard about the situation you got going on with your child's father and I had been meaning to speak with you about that," she said. "How's that going?"

Damn. I wondered how she heard about my personal business. Then again, I forgot. I did run my mouth to a few of these girls here and, as usual, a catty ass bitch probably went and ran her mouth. I should've seen that coming. Honestly, I should've told Pastor Shirley what I had going on but I didn't want her that deep up in my business.

"Well, I got my hearing coming up pretty soon. I just wanna be able to get visitation rights before my health further deteriorates," I said. "I just don't know how long I have left to live," I said. "Honestly, Pastor Shirley, I'm losing faith. I think I lost faith," I said.

"Oh, child, you can't lose faith. Not now! Look at how you far you've gotten in your life! You're gonna walk back on God when he's been walking with you this entire time?" she asked.

I couldn't say anything in response. Although I knew Pastor Shirley was partly right, now wasn't the time for her to try to intervene and stop me from second-guessing everything. I'd pretty much made up my mind that this Christian shit was just a little bit too much for me. Truth be told, I was somewhat faking it, deluding myself into being this person that I knew deep down I truly wasn't. But I just thought perhaps the more I faked it, the more I'd make it. But I realized I didn't even have it in me to lie to my own mothafuckin' self.

I lowered my head and began to cry. Hopefully, these fake ass tears would usher her ass out of my room ASAP. Besides, I only had a few more weeks to deal with her and then I'd be off on my own.

"I know, Pastor Shirley. I know. I'm trying."

"Well, you just gotta keep praying, honey. Life ain't easy. It will never be. God didn't say any of this will be easy. This is all a part of the test to see how much faith you have to keep pushing on."

"I know,"

"But do you?"

Awkard silence came into the room. To a degree, I felt like, damn, maybe she could sense I was somewhat being fake about my faith.

"I *think* I do," I replied.

Not saying anything back, she rose from the seat and strolled over to me as I still sat on the bed. She looked down at me and then said, "Stand up. Give me a hug."

As we embraced, she leaned into my ear and whispered, "I've been there, done that. Just promise me that if you only have so much time left, that you make the best of it. Don't leave here and end up making the same mistakes. At the end of the day, I don't care whether or not you really believe in God. I just want you to be better. To be whole as a woman. As a *black* woman. Don't mess up this second chance at life. Don't lose your redemption being impulsive. That's the fastest way that will land you back in jail. And possibly for good."

My core was shaken as I didn't expect to hear those words fly out of her mouth. She released me, smiled and then turned around, making her way to the door. "Good luck at your doctor's appointment," she said and then exited my room.

*Knock! Knock!*

Two knocks at the exam room's door instantly shot me out of a daze I was in. For the past twenty minutes or so, I had been sitting inside Dr. Pirtle's office inside the exam room, hoping that maybe today I'd get some better news. The door opened and Dr. Pirtle waltzed in. It was now Friday afternoon.

"Hey, LaTrisha! How's it going?"

"I'm fine, Dr. Pirtle. How are you today?"

"I'm good! Very good!" She fumbled through a manila folder and then pulled out a single sheet of paper, which probably were some test results I presumed. As she carefully scanned the paper, she bobbed her head up and down. "Wow…"

"Wow what?" I quickly asked. Nausea filled my stomach.

"Well, it seems like the immunotherapy we gave you is working," she said. "This is promising. If we can slow down the cancer and put it into regression, I think we should also try something else I've been researching lately for my other patients."

"Oh my God! What's that?"

"Intravenous Vitamin C therapy…"

"Huh? Vitamin C? Like oranges?"

Dr. Pirtle began chuckling. "No, dear…Well, yeah, Vitamin C is found abundantly in citrus. But actually, with intravenous Vitamin C therapy, we give you heavy rounds of liquid Vitamin C or sodium ascorbate. There are some clinical studies out there that show that when Vitamin C is introduced in the bloodstream, it quickly converts to hydrogen peroxide then kills cancer cells. Kills bacteria and viruses, too."

"Wow. I'm kind of confused but I guess it sounds good, right?"

"Yeah. In fact, one of the good things is treatment is

somewhat inexpensive. Then again, we'd have to see if Medicaid would cover it. We wouldn't be the ones to administer it though. I found an IV therapy center out in Skokie that does these Vitamin C megadose treatments," she said.

"So, wait, I'm still confused, Doctor. Are you saying I ain't really dying?"

She smiled. "I guess you can say that. If we continue with the immunotherapy and then add in some additional alternative treatments like the Vitamin C megadose treatment, I think we'd be able to kill off all of the cancer inside of your body."

"Oh my God! Thank you, Dr. Pirtle. Oh My God! I've been so scared about today! I didn't know what the hell I was gonna do!" I screamed, tears beginning to rush down my cheeks.

I shot up from the exam bed and gave Dr. Pirtle a tight hug. Although she wasn't exactly giving me one-hundred percent good news, any sign of good news at this point was one-hundred percent to me. The feeling of knowing that my chances of living were now higher sent me into a frenzy and I couldn't hold back any more tears. I cried like a baby and she consoled me, telling me everything was gonna be alright. "I told you, sis! Just gotta be patient sometimes," she said.

"Thank you so much, Doctor. I don't know what I would've done without you," I replied, sniffling like a nine-year-old badass kid that just got a whooping.

"Well, let's go ahead and do some more routine tests and then I'm gonna have you talk to Harriette out front about whether or not Medicaid will approve the Vitamin C therapy, okay?"

"Okay," I replied, wiping my face free of tears.

## CHAPTER TWENTY-EIGHT

One thing a mothafucka was gonna learn about DeAndre Williams was not to fuck with three things most valuable to me – my money, my mama and my kid. So, you already know from the moment Trish hit me with them court papers, I was about to go full offense on her and shut her shit down ASAP.

Doing as promised, I ran my ass right down to the same attorney I used the last time I had to deal with Trish's ass. Mr. Harrington's office told me I could come in first thing in the morning so we could get this situation squared away, once and for all.

Flying down Lake Park Avenue in the Charger, I quickly made my way to 53rd street and found a parking spot in front of Mr. Harrington's building. Once I got out, I flew inside the building and made my way up to his floor. I was immediately stunned when I saw that his office looked remarkably different from the last time. Looked like this nigga went through some serious upgrades. Damn, he must've won a big ass lawsuit or something. Now walking with cautiousness, I proceeded inside the doors and sauntered up to the receptionist's desk. This time, some sexy ass petite Asian bitch with some plump ass lips was working the front desk. Shit, a nigga should try to get her number. Then again, I got this vibe that she was probably into white boys. I cleared my throat and said, "Hey there. Good mornin', beautiful. I'm here to see Mr. Harrington."

"Are you DeAndre?" she asked, throwing me a somewhat unimpressed look.

"Yeah, I am..."

"Have a seat. He'll be with you shortly," she said. Damn, lil bitch had an attitude I see.

About ten minutes later, some light-skinned, mulatto-lookin' ass nigga bumbled around the corner and then proceeded into the waiting area. Dressed like he was straight off a GQ magazine, this fake ass Omari Hardwick-lookin' ass nigga reached out to shake my hand. "DeAndre?" he asked with this shady ass smile on his face. "Yeah," I said, not smiling back. "Who are you?"

"Oh...Sorry...Ditya probably didn't tell you but I'm Mr. Harrington as well. Well, Sherman Harrington, Jr. My father retired last year. I took over the firm. Sorry for the miscommunication," he explained.

"Oh. Damn. Yeah, I didn't know," I replied as I stood up and cautiously shook his hand. "Follow me," he grinned and then led me all the way to the back to his office. The last time I was here, there weren't any other lawyers working here but seemed like things had changed quite a bit. The rest of the offices were filled with other lawyers and as we passed each individual office in the hallway, I could hear the murmuring of people chatting. Presumably, attorneys talking to their clients. Or maybe some clients explaining their fucked up legal situation.

"Damn, seems like business is booming," I said as Harrington, Jr., led me to his office door and then opened in.

"Hell yeah!" he replied as he invited me inside the totally renovated office. This shit was decked the fuck out. The last time I was here, the office was barely filled with some basic ass Office Depot furniture. But now, this young nigga had what seemed like some expensive ass Italian shit all up in this mothafucka. A big red oak desk was centered in the middle of the office. A hi-def 5k television blasting CNN was glued to a wall adjacent to a massive bookshelf that was filled with at least a thousand books.

"Have a seat," he said as he pulled out a seat in front of his desk and then made his way around and sat down himself.

I sat down, and I was already starting to get bad vibes from this nigga. "So what brings you here?" he asked.

"Well, the last time I came here, your dad helped me out with a custody situation with my daughter. He got business squared away ASAP. I can go ahead and pay the retainer right now to go ahead and handle this mess," I said.

"Okay. Well, what's the situation now? Don't you have fully custody?"

"Yes. I do. But my child's mother, she's out of jail now and she hit me up with papers."

"You have those?"

"Yeah, I do," I replied as I quickly pulled out the court summons from my jacket and slid them across buddy's desk. He grabbed them and carefully scanned them. "Hrrrm. So she filed an emergency motion with the court to look into re-establishing her visitation rights and then she's also challenging for split custody."

"Exactly. How in the hell can she even do that? She was just in jail for selling dope."

"But she's the mother, right?"

"Yeah."

"Is she rehabilitated? Working?"

"Hell if I know. She just showed up to my mama's crib.

She talkin' about she became a born-again Christian and she works part-time for the same halfway house where she lives. She ain't even—"

"Let me stop you right there," he interrupted. "First, get rid of the anger and the attitude problem. If you're serious about winning this case and showing a judge that this lady is unfit to be your child's mother, then you need to not act like you have a chip on your shoulders. Ninety-percent of the family court judges in Cook County are women and sixty-percent of them are Black women, brotha. Last thing you wanna do is walk inside any of these judges' courtrooms parading your bitter masculinity," he said.

My face twisted with confusion, I had the sudden urge to deck this asshole in his face. But I was so vulnerable right now. I had no other choice but to listen to what this pretentious asshole had to say. "Okay," I replied.

Attorney Harrington then continued to scan the summons and then he tossed it to the side. "So here's the thing. Your daughter's mother is going to gain the sympathy of a judge. Your child's mother went two years without being able to see her child. A judge is going to give in and try to establish some sort of visitation protocol. Supervised or unsupervised, it's gonna happen, unfortunately. Now as far as split-custody, well, I doubt a judge will give in to that. The hearing is still some weeks away. If your child's mother can prove she is stable, has her own place, a good job and has good references, there *is* a slim chance her petition could get approved."

Shaking my head, I lowered it into my palms. I found myself in sudden disbelief. This nigga was telling me everything I didn't want to hear. But then, I also had to drop this other dime on him. "She's also claiming the child may not mine, too," I confessed.

"Nigga, *WHAT*?!?" he roared.

I gawked at up this fool.

He gasped and a look of embarrassment came across his face. "My bad, brotha. I...I just didn't expect to hear that...," he apologized.

"It's cool."

"Brotha...You mean to tell me you *never* took a paternity test when she first got pregnant? Were you all married or engaged or something?"

"No."

"So what in the hell made you think the child was yours? Did you have any suspicions she was sleeping around?"

All of a sudden, I grew annoyed as fuck with this dude's line of questioning. "Man, look, dude. I know I fucked up. I was immature as hell back then when I got her pregnant. There's a lot I am learning now. But I don't need the judgment, bro. Especially if I am gonna be paying you mad cash to get me out this jam," I angrily spat.

"Hey, man. I'm not judging you. I'm just letting you know the smart thing to do in all these situations is to always get a paternity test. Even *if* you think the kid looks like you, you never know. Anyways, we can start working on this case ASAP. You have your deposit already?"

"Yeah," I replied and pulled out some stacks of twenties that equaled out to a thousand dollars. That was what it cost me the last time and I assumed this time handling this case would cost the same.

"Here you go," I said as I slide the crispy bills onto his desk.

"What's that?"

"$1,000. That was what I got charged the last time," I said.

Next thing you know this nigga exploded into a huge chuckle. "$1,000?!? That was what my father charged you?"

"Yeah..."

"DeAndre. Brotha...I went to Harvard. Not Howard. My

rate is $1,000...per hour. That includes paralegal fees, case research, court filings, and other expenses. A case like this will take at least twenty billable hours. You're gonna have to come up with at least a $20,000 retainer if you want me to continue..."

"$20,000?!?!? Nigga, is you crazy? Man, you got me fucked up! $20,000 the fuck for what?!?"

Attorney Harrington's smile became flat and unmotivated. He simply slid the crispy bills back into my direction. "Sorry, but that's my rate. Honestly, dad was probably just doing you a favor since he was already semi-retired when you worked with him. You can always try Legal Aid. DePaul has a good—"

"Man, fuck you," I said as I grabbed my cash off his table, stood up and walked out of that mothafucker's office.

Nigga had me all the way fucked up if he thought I was gonna drop twenty stacks to get me out this bind. Storming out the office, I didn't even wanna give the lil Asian bitch a glance (although I should've tried my hardest to get them digits). Soon as I got back to my Charger, I hopped in and angrily sped off down the street. "Fucking asshole," I grumbled shaking my head as I turned up the in my car. Truth be told, a nigga needed a fucking drink now. A stiff one at that. I should've stopped by Kimbark Liquors and picked up a bottle of some Henny but it was still too early in the day to get drunk. But then the thought hit me.

Shelly.

I forgot all about her. She did tell me she was a family attorney. And we were supposed to link up some weeks ago to start making some parental arrangements, but with all the drama that happened, our plans fell through. I guess now was an opportune time in order to arrange that playdate with Junior and Ariyanna. And then I could pick her brains about this situation.

Once I came to a red light, I quickly found her contact in

my phone and dialed her. Some rings later, she answered, "So, you are finally calling me back, I see..."

"Hey, sorry about everything," I apologized. "I've just had a lot going on. Are you busy? Can we talk?"

"Dre...I'm in the middle of work but I'm glad you called. Give me a few minutes and I'll hit you back, okay?"

"Okay. Sorry for calling you during work."

"It's cool," she said and then hung up.

As annoyance continued to bubble within me, I finally got back home and parked. I had been meaning to hit up Myron and apologize for our conversation last night. He, too, was probably in the middle of working now but I went ahead and gave him a ring. Seconds later, he answered, "Wassup, bro? You still on bullshit?" he asked.

"Nah, nigga, look, my bad for acting that way. This shit is just too much for me man."

"Yeah, I feel you, broski, but let me hit you back later. I'm trying to de-escalate this call with one of my reps," he said.

"Aiight, man. Hit my line later."

## CHAPTER TWENTY-NINE

"I never understood what you even saw in that hoe ass nigga, to be honest with you," Myron laughingly said to me as he hung up his cell phone and shook his head.

"That was him who just called?" I curiously asked. I felt so bad being in the car with Dre's best friend, Myron, knowing that this nigga was playing both sides.

"Yeah...That was that bitch ass nigga," Myron giggled. "Anyways, so you finally hit his ass with them papers. I know that nigga didn't see that shit coming. Wack ass fuck nigga."

"Yeah, I did. And thank you for calling me up and telling me what happened to Tanisha. She and I were cool but since Dre and I were getting into it, we kind of lost contact. It was so fucked up what happened," I said.

"Yeah, yeah, yeah. Well, she was on some other shit. Her ass was kind of crazy. It was just a matter of time before some crazy shit happened to her anyways. I didn't expect her to go out like that," Myron said shaking his head. He then stuffed a mild-sauce covered fried drumette into his mouth and chewed away.

He and I were sitting in his car in a parking lot of an Uncle Remus' Fried Chicken shack in Broadview, a suburb west of the city. The crazy thing was ever since I had got locked up, Myron was the only person who had steadily been in contact with me. From the moment I landed in jail, this nigga was sending me all types of letters, cards and even putting money on my books. I was thankful that he was looking out for me but I tried to minimize my contact with him because I didn't want to give him any impressions that I wanted something out of him.

Now, there you go again. I know you judging me, but before you jump to conclusions, I'll just go ahead and tell you...Yes, Myron and I was fucking around when I was with Dre. And truth be told, I kind of don't regret it because Myron was the one who told me that Dre was messing with all types of bitches when we were together. Although I never caught Dre in the act, the way he moved just always made me feel like the nigga was constantly running in the streets, messing with other females.

Anyways...

Myron was kind of like my first payback dick. He was the first dude I had fucked when I began to get suspicions that Dre was fucking around on me. But that was the past, now I was simply trying to maintain some cordial friendship with Myron. He was truly a good guy and he meant well, although he cheated on his baby mama with me. I never liked that bitch anyways and she was so disrespectful to Myron. To this day, I never understood why he was still with her. He worked two jobs, paid all the bills and took care of his twin boys while her fat ass stayed at home and ate chips and watched Judge Judy. Fat ass hoe. I couldn't stand a bitch like that. Ughh! Let me stop. I did tell myself after I got back my results that I was going to try my hardest to rekindle my faith in Christ and not revert back to my old ways. Pastor Shirley was right. I needed to hold out hope and stop just easily giving in into temptation.

"It's just so unfortunate I had to go down this route with him but it is what it is. I deserve to see my baby girl," I said.

"Yeah, well, let me ask you a question. The nigga is claiming that you told him that Ariyanna may not be his. That's true?" Myron asked, smacking his teeth.

I froze for a moment and didn't know if Myron was asking me some sort of bait question. But then again, this dude was in love with me. I was pretty sure he was looking out for my own good. "Yeah...I just never told him. He used to do me so wrong back then," I said. "But I figured he was the only guy who had his shit together, so I said fuck it. I'll let Ariyanna be his. I guess he's a good father tough," I confessed.

"Damn, that's kind of fucked, don't you think? I mean, Dre is an asshole and he got anger issues, but you don't think it's wrong to let the nigga continue to think the baby might be his?"

"I mean, yeah, I see what you saying and all, but that's water under the bridge, Myron. I already told him I wanna do a paternity test when we go to court so that way he can move on. I can get my baby back and then he can focus on another child. Besides, I'm pretty sure he messing with a new woman anyways," I said.

"Yeah..." He took another bite out of his chicken then wiped his sexy tan face with a napkin. Myron kind of reminded me of a lighter version of 50 Cent, except with dreads. "But still. But it is what it is though. Fuck him," he mumbled then took another bite out of his chicken wing.

"Well, I got some other good news though!" I excitedly said, wanting to kind of change the subject.

"What's that?"

"Well, you know, I thought I was dying. My doctor told

me today that my cancer is starting to retreat. We're gonna be starting a new treatment plan on Monday!"

"Yayyy!" Myron said as he reached over and wanted to give me hi-five. "I'm so glad to hear that, Trish. You deserve good news. I know all of this mess has been a lot for you," he said.

"Thank you," I replied as I picked through my fried catfish. I sure did miss eating Harold's. Now that I was going on a different treatment plan, I figured I could cheat a little and eat something different for a change.

"Anyways, I appreciate everything you did for me when I was locked up, Myron. You are a good man. Why are you still with Quisha?"

Myron suddenly lowered and shook his head. "Shit, I ask myself that every damn day, truth be told. Only reason why I keep her raggedy ass around is because she's a good mother to my kids."

"Is she really though? I mean, she don't work. She doesn't keep herself up. I mean, I'm not one to judge given my situation, but damn, you got a lot going for yourself. You're back in school. You about to move into a new house. Don't you wanna do better? It ain't like ya'll married or anything."

"I know...But it's whatever," he said, stuffing another wing in his face. Then he took a swig from his Pepsi.

Myron and I continued to talk and eat. A part of me wished he wasn't with that fat ass hoe, otherwise, I would've tried to make my move on him. He was such an endearing sweetheart and I knew he'd make a great husband one day. Not just with that Quisha bitch. After we got done eating, Myron drove me back to Hope.

"Aiight, Trish. Well, holla at me anytime. You know we family and all," Myron said as I got out of his Pontiac and headed back inside Hope.

I checked in with the security guard and then made my way to the mailbox to check to see if I got any mail.

"Hey, girl..."

I looked up. It was Donna.

"Wassup?" I said, quickly throwing my attention back to my mailbox.

"How's everything? You still mad at me?"

"No, not really. Anyways, I gotta get going. I'll holla at you later," I said once I grabbed my mail and then shoved past her. I ain't have time for any of her foolishness. Soon as I got back up into my room, the first thing I was gonna do was get straight on my knees and thank God for bringing me out of this mess. Although I found myself slipping back into my old ways, I had promised God in Dr. Pirtle's office that I was going to try to get back on track and stay committed to his word.

꽃

"And in Jesus' name, I pray...Amen," I mumbled once I finished praying. I opened my eyes and grabbed my phone sitting off to my side on my bed. I had been on my knees for the last hour or so, praying my heart out, thank God for those miraculous test results he gave me. Pastor Shirley was right and now the first thing I was gonna do was go down and attend one of her bible study meetings tonight. Fridays were usually movie night for Hope, but Pastor Shirley often held a bible study in case people didn't want to watch movies.

Now that the Holy Ghost was moving through me and healing my body, I could feel my sense of energy return. My hip wasn't bothering me as much. Hopefully, within weeks I wouldn't need to walk with the assistance of a cane anymore. I got up off my knees and stretched. "Whoo! Chile! I feel good!" I laughed. "God is great!"

It was now nearly seven PM and Pastor Shirley's Bible study was going to start in about ten minutes. I quickly searched my room to see if I had an additional bible to bring with me. I threw my other one away that day Chadwick kicked me out. Then suddenly I started to hear my phone vibrate on my bed.

"Who is that?" I mumbled to myself as I dashed over to my bed and grabbed the phone. I looked and down and didn't recognize the phone number. It was a 773 area code though, so that had to be someone in the city. "Hello?" I answered.

"Hey, LaTrisha Johnson?" the female voice said on the other end.

"Umm, yes, this is she," I replied.

"Hey! This is Rebecca from Property Solutions International! We were calling to let you know that we approved your application for an apartment and we could get you moved in as soon as possible!"

"Really!?!? Oh my God!" I shouted, clasping my mouth. I didn't see any of this coming but one of the caseworkers for Hope had told me since I was weeks away from leaving the halfway house, she was gonna work to help me find an apartment.

"Yes! Are you still interested?"

"Of course!"

"Okay, well that is good to hear! In order to secure the apartment, we are going to need you to put down a $1,000 deposit. We can go ahead and take the deposit right now through debit card, credit card or check over the phone. How would you like to pay?"

"Wait! What do you mean I have to pay a $1,000 deposit now? The leasing agent told me they would waive the deposit if I filled out an application and got approved immediately."

"Ohhhhhh…Yeah, well, that promotion actually expired last week. You would've needed to be approved on that same day. Your background check took a while to complete," the lady said.

"Damn! That ain't right. I don't even think I have $1,000 just to chuck up. Besides, I am just getting back onto my feet. I clearly explained that to the leasing manager! Ya'll lied to me!"

"I'm sorry, ma'am, but in order for us to go ahead and secure the unit for you, you're gonna have to put down at least $1,000. That's our rental policy," the lady said.

"Ughh! Okay. Well, when is the latest I could pay the $1,000?"

"Well, technically we would need it now but we can make an extension until tomorrow evening. After that, the unit that you wanted will go back up on the market. Your application will still be good for at least thirty days but we can't put a lock on the unit. And that was the last one in our building," the lady said.

"Damn, okay. Well, let me see what I can come up with. I'll have to give you all a call tomorrow," I explained.

"Okay, well, give us a call back promptly," Rebecca said.

"Thank you. Have a nice night."

"You do the same." I then hung up.

"FUCK!" I yelled, stomping my foot. But then I quickly clasped my mouth. "Sorry, Lord," I apologized. I need to get my mouth in order. But I couldn't believe that damn leasing agent would be kind of deceptive and bait me into getting approved for an apartment knowing I didn't have the money right now for that much of a deposit.

Given my background, this place was one of a few property management companies in the city that were willing to work with people with criminal backgrounds. Luckily, since my credit wasn't all too messed up and I had a job guarantee from Hope (Pastor Shirley was moving me to full-time as an office assistant in a few weeks), I was able to get approved for a two-bedroom apartment down in Woodlawn for $700 a month. I had been desperately searching for a place to stay now for some weeks and Monique's paralegal friend told me the quicker I could get a place, the better it would look in front of a judge. With my hearing now just two weeks away, I needed this place ASAP.

Pastor Shirley's class was starting in a few but now I didn't have time for none of that. I had to get to work. With only about $600 in my name right now, I needed to see if anyone I knew could help me get my hands on $1,000. Without hesitation, I pulled out my phone and dialed Neicy to see if she could help. Once I pulled up her contact, I quickly dialed her and she answered within a few seconds. "Hey, little sis! I was just meaning to call you! How'd your doctor's appointment go?"

"Hey, sis! It was good actually! I got some good news. I found out the cancer might be going into remission with this new therapy Dr. Pirtle got me on!"

"Oh my God! Why didn't you call me and tell me earlier?!?!" she asked.

"Yeah, I know! I've just been so overly excited. I'm sorry I forgot to call you. And I've been running a million errands just trying to get things straight before I head out of here," I said.

"Yeah, I hear you on that! Oh my God! I'm gonna cry right now though! I've been so worried," she said.

"Yeah, I know. Me, too."

I paused for a moment. I didn't want to waste any time and I needed to let her know what was up. "Hey, big sis. Look, I'm calling because I need a big favor…"

"What's that?" she asked.

"Well, I just got a call from this property management company. I got approved for the two-bedroom apartment I was telling you about but they want me to come up with $1,000 if I want to move in ASAP. And I ain't just got it. You think you could lend me $1,000?"

"I thought they said they weren't going to charge you a deposit?"

"That's what I thought, too!" I said.

"Damn…Well, LaTrisha, I wish I could but I ain't got it. I just got my hours reduced because of this damn city furlough and I'm holding onto every coin I can," she explained. "Damn. Damn! DAMN! Shit! This just ain't right!"

"I know right. I just don't know what I'm going to do at this point."

"Well, let me see if I can pull money from my 401k. I mean, you say you can pay me back, right?"

"Yeah, I can…Well, if I do pull money out of my 401k, I won't be able to get to it until Monday. When do you need the money?"

"Damn…Like tomorrow. She said she could only hold the unit until tomorrow."

"Fuck…Shit…I'm sorry, I didn't mean the cuss," Neicy apologized. "Well, let me call around and see what I could do. But quick question, I mean, why do you need to get the apartment now? Why not just stay with me?"

"Neicy, I need the apartment to show the judge that I'm stable and back on my feet. And besides, I love you, but it's probably just best I get my own place…"

"Yeah, you're right," she said. "Well, let me see what I can do. What about Monique? Did you call her?"

"I should call her right now probably."

"Okay, well you do that and then I'll see what I can do. Maybe I can talk to some of our kinfolk and see if they could help out," she said.

"Okay, sis. I'll hit you up a bit later. We got some other things to talk about," I said, damn near wanting to cry as panic began to set in.

Once I hung up with Neicy, I quickly called Monique but her phone went straight to voicemail. That was odd. I called her again. I didn't get an answer. "Damn it," I said to myself, fidgeting with my fingers.

Some fifteen minutes had passed and now I was pacing up and down in my room, wondering what I could do next. Then there was Myron...But, ughh! I didn't want to call him up and ask for money knowing that I was taking money out of his pockets that would go to his kids. I would feel so wrong doing that. Quickly running out of options, I didn't know what else to do at this point.

Then the lights went off in my head. Olu. Maybe he could help me out. I quickly pulled up my Facebook messenger app and searched to see if I could find him online. However, when I went to his profile, I saw that he couldn't receive messages anymore. What the hell?!? Then I went to my main Facebook app and saw that he and I weren't friends anymore. Either he deleted and blocked me or his profile got deactivated. That probably explained why we hadn't talked for a few days. "Damn it!" I groaned aloud but this time I didn't care if I cursed.

I sat down on my bed and rocked back and forth, quickly trying to come up with a solution to get this stack. I looked around my room to see if I had anything to sell.

Nothing.

But then there was my laptop. Nah. I would only get maybe like $100 for it. And I knew that for sure because I sold an old laptop before at a pawn shop in Wicker Park and got less.

Tears began to slide down my face and then I saw Neicy calling me back on my phone. I didn't want to answer because I just knew she probably didn't have a solution either but then I went ahead and answered anyway.

"Wassup? Any good news?" I asked.

"Well, I reached out to Antonio and he said he got like

$200 on him. But that's it. Everyone who I could think of who would have it said they didn't have it..."

"Damn! Man, just when I was trying to do the right thing..."

"Uh-ugh! No! Don't think that way, Trish. Be positive. Besides, we still got time before your hearing anyway."

"I know, girl, but nothing's guaranteed."

"Yeah. Well, let me see who else I could call. Just keep praying, okay?"

"Okay," I replied and then she hung up.

## CHAPTER THIRTY

This Friday was already turning out to be one big headache for me. After I talked to Shelly earlier, she called me back some hours later and invited me to come over tonight. She told me that she had her aunty watching Junior over the weekend, which actually kind of sucked because I did want him and Ariyanna to meet each other for the first time. I also did want to start to spend more time with him.

As the sun began to fade and chilly gusts swam through the city, eight-thirty pm struck the clock inside of my Charger as I made my way up to West Loop to meet up with Shelly. I was a bit apprehensive about going over to her place. Why? Well, I had a feeling she was going to try to be on some slick hoe shit and try to get the dick. Truth be told, a nigga would hit the pussy if she was giving it out but that would be all the fuck I wanted out of her. Nothing more, nothing less. We could co-parent and fuck once in a while, but I didn't want any type of real relationship with her.

I hopped off the expressway and got onto Halsted. Shorty lived off Green Street in this luxury condo building. For a split second, I kind of wondered the possibility of us being together. Shit, from the looks of it, Shelly had to be making some mad bread as an attorney. With my ambitions of getting into law school in the near future, I should try to pick her brain so she could give me some career advice. The more I thought about it, hell, if we did become a couple in the near future (shit, you never know what the future holds), we could some on power couple type shit.

I pulled up to her building and following her instructions, I dialed to get into her garage. Once I got in and parked, I quickly hopped out of my ride and made my way to her floor. I got to her door and I rang her doorbell.

"Coming," I heard her say and then some seconds later her door opened.

Instantly my eyes fell onto her petite and well-proportion body. Shorty was definitely giving me Nia Long vibes. Man, she was sexy as fuck and if I wasn't such an impulsive asshole, I could've really made something work with her from the very beginning. Anyways, I smiled and said, "Sorry I'm running behind. I had to stop by mother's place to check up on Ariyanna," I said.

"Oh, okay! No worries. Come right on in," she said, inviting me into her posh condo.

Walking in, my eyes curiously scanned her vast living room, taking in the expensive ass leather couch set she had. A big ass hi-def television was plastered to the wall. A rerun of the Cosby Show was blaring in the background. I cut my eyes over to the big ass, open kitchen. Damn, Shelly must've hired an interior designer to come in and deck this shit out because the motif and layout looked like some fancy shit straight off HGTV. She definitely wasn't a white fridge-type of bitch. Shorty had nothing but stainless steel appliances all up in this mothafucka.

"Damn, so tell me the secret," I commented with a big ass grin slapped on my still curious face.

"Secret to what?" she asked as we both stood still between the foyer and the living room.

"Like, your secret to getting all of this...Like, you never struck me as the lawyer type."

"Why you say that?"

"I don't know...'Cuz when we linked up that time, you were kind of..." I didn't want to say it.

"Kind of what?" she looked perplexed. Last thing I wanted to was to piss her off, so I quickly tried to formulate the right words.

"Well, you know, ratchet..."

"Hah! Well, Dre, I was drunk and high as hell that night. Every woman who has had a lot to drink and smoke would have their inner hoe come out. Plus, sometimes you just gotta live," she said. Her face then twisted with judgment as she looked me up and down and said, "And you're one to talk. You're the walking definition of a man hoe. Anyways, sit down and make yourself comfortable."

My head flew back and my brow raised. "What? Man hoe?" I replied as I made my way into the living room and sat down while she trekked into her kitchen.

"Yeah...Man hoe. Do you want something to drink? I have lemonade, cider, water, Gatorade and milk."

"You got any henny? I need a stiff drink," I said.

"Hrrrm...Well, I'm not really much of a drinker anymore but you're more than welcome to go run to the liquor store. There's one a block up."

"I'm fine," I replied. "I guess I'll have some lemonade."

"Cool. With ice?"

"Sure..."

Some moments later, Shelly emerged into the living room with two tall glasses of ice-chilled pink lemonade in her hand.

She handed me one. "Please use the coaster on the table. Don't mess up my nice ass shit," she laughingly said.

"Bet." I took a quick sip and then sat the glass on the coaster. She sat next to me and then said, "So, let's talk about co-parenting I guess…"

"Shelly, before we get into all of that, I actually need your advice."

Her head flew back with a raised brow. "What? You want legal advice?"

"Yeah," I replied.

"How much you paying? I don't work for free…"

"Ah, come on," I replied smacking my teeth. "One lawyer is already trying to charge me twenty-stacks. You on that shit, too?"

"Umm….Dre…Welcome to the legal industry, partner. You said you wanted to be an attorney, right? You know how many people are gonna try to pull what you are doing right now? Trying to get free legal advice on the low? I studied and worked too hard to give my advice out for free. So my rate is gonna be a play date with me, Ariyanna and Junior every Sunday for the next ten weeks."

I lowered and shook my head. "Fine," I replied.

She stuck her hand out and said, "Shake on it."

Cautiously extending my hand out, I shook hers and then said, "Please let this advice be worth it."

"So what's your question?"

"Well, I got this crazy situation going on with Ariyanna's mother. She just got out of jail and she wants to try to re-establish her visitation rights. She also wants split custody now. She's also claiming that Ariyanna may possibly be another dude's child. I don't believe her though."

"What?!?! Dre! You mean to tell me that you and this woman have a child together and you never did a DNA test? Are you crazy?"

"Please...Just spare me the judgment for a moment. I know I sound stupid as fuck not doing a paternity test but at the time I was just way too much into my emotions," I said.

"Anyways...So, she just got out of jail? How long ago?"

"I think like six or seven months ago. I'm not too sure. I hadn't been keeping tabs on her."

"Where does she live now? What does she do? Does she have a job?"

"I think she stays at a halfway house. Her and her sister kind of don't get along. But she's claiming she also has cancer and she's dying. She's a born-again Christian and now and all of this extra shit. Bitch just sounds—"

"Excuse me?" Shelly interrupted, looking instantly annoyed.

"What?"

"I'm not gonna let you sit up here and call another woman, especially another black woman a bitch. I don't care what situation you have going on with your child's mother but if you and I are gonna have some sort of working co-parenting relationship, I'm not going to allow you to berate another black woman."

"Sorry," I mumbled.

"Well, continue," Shelly said, taking a sip of her lemonade.

"Well, anyways, she's talking crazy."

"First, before you do anything, you shouldn't even waste your time with the courts if you don't know whether or not you're Ariyanna's father. I mean, even if you are technically not her father, you should still know. Second of all, it's also good to know in case someone tries to file a paternity suit against you. You never know who's lurking in the shadows," Shelly explained and then took another sip of her drink. "Now that I think about it, this story sounds crazier by the minute. I think I need some Hennessey, shit...Let's go to the liquor store," she said.

"Okay," I replied.

Some moments later we both left her condo and headed down to the liquor store a block away.

---

"So, like I said, what I can do is talk to my girl, Dominique, to see if she could help you out. I am sure she's within your budget for an attorney. I can't handle your case because it would be a conflict of interest," Shelly explained.

We had got back an hour ago and while we took shots of Hennessey, Shelly gave me nonstop advice about how to handle the situation with LaTrisha. Although I was a bit irritated that she used a playdate arrangement as a fee in exchange for advice, I was glad we got that out of the way.

"I appreciate everything, Shelly. I really do. I just feel so bad that we never really got to know each other. You seem like a down-to-earth chick. Like, I really feel kind of bad now," I said.

" Bad about what?"

"That we didn't take things further."

"Yeah, well, that was the past. We just need to focus on co-parenting our child together. I just want our son to have an active father in his life."

"Yeah," I replied and then paused for a moment. I gave her a seductive stare and then said, "Well, maybe we could possibly rekindle some things. No rush but I'd like to get to know you. Seems like we have a lot in common, ya know?"

Not saying anything back to me, Shelly just stared at me with this weird smile fixed on her face. "Ummm...No...I think the fuck not," she said. "You're cool and all, Dre. And I guess during that time we hooked up, the sex was...great. But I don't think you're really my type?"

"Why not?" I had to ask. Damn, shorty was rejecting me

and I didn't even know if I was hearing her right. I had never been rejected by a female before when I gave an initial advance.

"Well, for starters, you're a bit too hood. I mean, don't get me wrong. I've fucked with hood guys before. But you all are dangerous and reckless," Shelly said. "I prefer someone who's already established. I mean, I know you're getting your shit together but I'm not the type of woman who's gonna sit back and wait for a guy to grow up. And you're a bit immature. And you also are a bit misogynistic," she said.

"Damn, really? I'm all that?"

"Yeah. You are...I mean, yeah, I'm not gonna lie. I thought about us having a future when it seemed like we were getting our situation with Junior squared away but that thought quickly fled my mind. If there was a slim chance in hell I'd want to be in a relationship with you, let alone go out on a date with you, there are a lot of things you'd need to change about your personality."

"Such as?"

"Well, for starters, your language. I mean, yeah, I curse a lot, too. But the way you reference women. Females. Bitches. Hoes. You have scorn for women. What does your mother think about your relationship with women? I'm quite sure deep down she hasn't been too thrilled with the way you treat women," she said.

Right then and there, once she mentioned my mother, I grew very fucking pissed. Granted, I could take some light criticism, but the way Shelly was unloading onto me had me very fucking irritated.

I shook and lowered my head and then began to chuckle.

"What's funny?" she asked.

"You. You're funny." I continued, "It's almost as if this shit is a joke. Like, on one hand, you wanna sit up here and offer me all types of advice to get me out of my situation but then you wanna sit up here and belittle me as if I'm some child. You know you got some fucking nerve. Immature? Man, you're the one who's immature. You waited a whole ass two years to drop this kid on me. If you really about your business, you would've confronted me right then and there when you found out you were pregnant. Anyways, Shelly, it was cool you invited me over and everything but I'mma head out now. You enjoy the rest of your night, sweetheart."

Soon as I said what the fuck I had to say, I stood up and began trekking through the living room.

"Don't forget about Sunday, Dre," Shelly said.

"Oh, I won't. I'm still responsible...baby mama," I said back, my tone filled with annoyance.

"I bet you won't...baby daddy," she replied. "Loser..."

"Yeah, yeah, yeah. Whatever," I said, making my way to the door and then walked the fuck out. Bitch.

❦

A good thirty minutes later, I hopped off Lake Shore Drive and made my way back to my townhouse. Shelly had me pissed as fuck and I could already see her and I weren't going to be getting along. Fuck her advice and her friend. I didn't need that bitch's help any damn way. Truth be told, I should've never told her shit and should've just done my research and found a different lawyer.

Anyways...

After I got on the block, my gaze widened and attached to two Chicago police cruisers parked in front of my shit. Slowing down, I wondered why the hell they were. Once I pulled into my driveway, I got out and glanced their way. One of the cops proceeded to get out of his cruiser. He was some older fat nigga, looking just like Carl Winslow.

"DeAndre Williams?" he asked.

I froze. "Yeah…That's me. What's up?"

The other cop hopped out his shit. He, too, was some fat nigga but he kind of reminded me of Judge Joe Brown. Man, these niggas were looking like some straight characters. But as the two of them strolled closer to me, my heart began to thump.

"We need to take you down to the precinct for some questioning," the Carl Winslow-lookin' muhfucka said.

"For what?" I replied, my face twisted with surprise.

"In connection with a rape."

"Rape?!? What the hell are you talking about?"

"Look, brotha. You ain't under arrest yet but someone is claiming you sexually assaulted them. We need to take you down for questioning. You either comply or we're gonna slap some handcuffs on you," Judge Joe Brown grumbled.

"Fuck! Man, I swear me and that white girl had consensual sex. I didn't rape her."

"Okay, well, tell that to the detectives. If your story checks out, then you don't have nothing worry about, guy. Just take it easy. Now, do you want us to take you to the station or do you wanna follow us?"

"Man, ya'll can take me and then bring me back 'cuz in five minutes I'm finne clear my fucking name," I said shivering. That goddamn white bitch! I swear! And something told me not to mess with that white bitch!

"Ok, well, get in the back of his car," Judge Joe Brown said to me, pointing to Carl Winslow.

"Fine," I replied and trailed the fat muhfucka to his cruiser. He opened the backdoor and I hopped in. Within five minutes, we made it to Chicago Police headquarters on 35th street.

# CHAPTER THIRTY-ONE

Still pacing the floor in my room, I didn't know what else I could do. No solution to the out-of-nowhere rent situation was coming to my head.

A part of me wanted to run down to Pastor Shirley's office and ask her for help, but given that bible study was going on, I obviously couldn't do that at the moment. And then one bible study got done, there was no telling if she would say yes or no to my pressing financial need. Some days ago, when I started to make preparations to leave the halfway house program, Juanita, one of the workers here told me a lot of women end up right back in jail or in worse situations because they didn't do a diligent job of trying to securing housing. I was determined not to end up being a part of that number, so I needed to think of something quick.

Still pacing around, I almost wanted to breakdown and cry but now wasn't the time for me to get weak like this. "Please, God, please, give me a sign. A solution. Something. I need it right now, Lord. Please come through for me, I promise I will totally turn my life around if you come through for me. You've already brought me this far, please don't turn around on me now," I begged the Lord, hoping he'd hear my cry.

Not thinking of what else I could do, I realized there was no other thing I could think of but indeed ask Pastor Shirley for help. Hell. We had already had a talk earlier and her talk was very encouraging. Maybe I should go to bible study, I thought to myself. And that indeed I decided to do. My leg was starting to hurt me again, so I grabbed my cane, phone, and a bible and then quickly made my way out of my room.

Glancing down at my phone, it was now approaching nine PM. Pastor Shirley's bible study class usually went on to around ten pm. Once I got down to the conference where bible study was going on, I slowly creaked the door open, peeked my head in and saw the group of women along with Pastor Shirley sitting down in a circle.

Pastor didn't notice me walking in, so as she continued lecturing, I slowly walked up to the circle and then found an empty seat and sat down. She paused for a moment, looked at me and said, "Hey! So glad you could join us, Sister Johnson. We're reading from the second chapter of Galatians," she said.

"Thank you, Pastor Shirley," I smiled and then cracked open my bible.

🐚

It was nearly ten-thirty pm when we got done with bible study. We prayed and then we all gave each other a hug. As a few of my housemates began to exit the conference room, now was the time for me to go ahead and ask Pastor Shirley for some emergency help. I said a quiet prayer in the back of my mind and then approached her as she gathered her belongings.

"Pastor Shirley, can I speak with you for a moment?"

She paused and glanced up at me then turned her attention the other way. "What seems to be the issue? How did your doctor's appointment go?"

I exhaled. I had to get my thoughts together. Every word I said now mattered. Although Pastor Shirley was a very nice and understanding woman, I still couldn't help but think about what Donna said about Pastor Shirley that afternoon when she tried to get me to smoke with her. *Was this all one big front?*

"Great actually! My doctor said that the cancer actually is slowing down in growth and might be reversing. We're gonna be trying some new therapies."

"That's so good to hear! I'm glad that things seemed to have turned around," she said.

"Yeah...Well, I'd like to say thank you for those encouraging words you gave me earlier. I've just been battling with some depression and anxiety lately."

"Understandable. I'm glad our talk this morning gave you a little boost."

"Yeah..." I paused. "Pastor Shirley, the other reason why I wanted to speak with you is that just some hours ago I got a call from this apartment complex. I got approved for a unit that I could move into ASAP," I said, my hands shivering with anxiety.

"Oh, that is great to hear! See, I told you faith works! You just gotta keep believing and be encouraged no matter what's going on!" she exclaimed.

Biting my lip, I had to get out what I really needed from her. "Yeah, well, there's just one dilemma though. I need a thousand-dollar down payment by tomorrow."

"Don't you have money saved up from working?" she asked with an eyebrow raised. "You virtually have no expenses living here."

"Yeah, kind of, sorta," I confessed. "But not enough.

Besides, I've been still having to buy medicine and other things I need for myself. I'm not making that much working here..."

"Well, have you talked to your family? Any relatives can come to your help?"

"I did but my sister doesn't have the money and nor do some other folks."

"Well, I'm so sorry to hear that, LaTrisha—"

"Pastor Shirley, do you think you could advance me the money on my next paycheck?" I quickly interrupted.

"Excuse me?" Her tone suggested I seemed to kind of catch her off guard.

"I know, Pastor Shirley. I'm sorry and I know this is probably the wrong place and time to ask but I'm in a serious bind now. I would've just waited until Monday and spoke to Juanita or one of the other case managers here but I figured since you were here, I could go ahead and ask. I mean, you're the boss and all."

Pastor Shirley rolled her eyes and said, "LaTrisha, I wish I really could help but I can't just take money out from the organization's budget and just give it to individuals. And the rules are pretty clear. We offer housing assistance through CHA. Juanita should've told you that. So, if you seek housing on your own, you would have to come up with your own deposit. Why didn't you just get a CHA-approved apartment if you knew you wouldn't have the money to get your own place?"

I hesitated for a moment but kind of grew irritated wondering why this woman wouldn't even consider my plea. And it wasn't like I was asking her steal? Hell, if anything she could've dug in her own pockets and helped me. "I know, I'm sorry, Pastor Shirley. But those CHA-approved apartments just didn't look safe. Some of them were too far south, too. I'm trying to get cust—"

"See, that's where I'm gonna stop you right there," she said, suddenly interrupting me. "In life, sometimes you don't have a choice about things. You gotta take what you're able to get. We can't have everything we want out of life, missy. Hope is already on a limited budget. Although I'm the executive director, I still have to get every single dollar we spend approved by our board of directors. On top of that, we get federal grants in which every single dollar has to be accounted for. And all of it goes to our programming..."

"But Pastor Shirley, I understand—"

"I'm not done yet, LaTrisha. See, you know what the problem is with people like you. You all want your cake and you want to eat it, too. Honestly, I saw this coming from a mile away. And you had no intentions really on coming to bible study. You came down here to get money. Plain and simple. Well, that's not gonna happen."

My mouth flung wide open. I was in disbelief that she was standing here chastising me for no apparent reason. Like, I didn't see ANY of this coming. But she continued verbally lashing me and said, "When I got out of prison, whatever resources I could get my hands on, I took it. You had the opportunity to work with one of our caseworkers and get into a CHA-approved apartment ASAP. You chose to go another route and we are supportive of that...just not financially. That's up to you and you knew that. So now you need to deal with the consequences of your poor decision making. You wouldn't be in this predicament if you would just be patient. But nope, now that you want this particular apartment, you think it's my responsibility to help you pay for something you really didn't need?"

Still not able to muster up the words to defend myself, I just stood there frozen and shocked. I didn't expect Pastor Shirley to be this cold and brutal with me.

She rolled her eyes and shook her head saying, "Anywho, I

gotta get going. I've been trying my best to give you all the resources you need. I can only do so much." Once she had all of her stuff in her hand, she walked past me and made her way to the conference room door.

And that was when it hit me. Donna was probably right. Maybe not one-hundred percent right, but obviously Pastor Shirley had two, possibly three sides to her. Pastor Shirley was now showing another side of herself to me that I didn't even think she had in her possession. Just wow. WOW! Like I said, I didn't see any of her response coming at all. Before she left out of the room, I quickly had to say something though. See, I wasn't going to let this woman who I thought was my spiritual guide and mentor just run all over me in this way. I simply asked for some short-term help and suddenly this fat bitch made it seem like I was asking for a million dollars, a brand new house and a Mercedes...which was ironic, because that was how this big bitch was flaunting herself to us women. Sorry, I know I said I wasn't gonna be cursing but fuck all that. I was thirty-eight hot now. This shady hoe had us all geeked believing once we made the right life changes, we could accomplish what she had. Well, it seemed like maybe I had been fooling myself all along. Perhaps Donna was letting me know that Pastor Shirley truly was in this prisoner rehabilitation business simply for the money and not to help people.

"Before you go, Pastor Shirley, I just wanna say that you just pulled a fast one over me..."

Suddenly, Pastor Shirley scrunched her face, scanning me up and down with her judging eyes. "Excuse me, LaTrisha?"

"Yeah...Here I was, putting so much faith and stock in your word, thinking that if I truly needed help, you'd be there to help me. Honestly, I didn't want to come down here and ask because I wanted to get things resolved on my own. And I was somewhat bracing for rejection or some excuse. But the way you just talked down to me. That shit was totally uncalled for. You're a fake ass bitch. And not even a good fake either because half the shit you wear looks like something you got out of a flea market. And now I feel like everything you told me earlier seemed like a lie. Yeah, maybe you do care to an extent. But it seems as though your care only goes so far. So long as it doesn't interfere with your paycheck. But it's cool though. I'll find a way to get that apartment. Have a good night," I said.

Pastor Shirley let out a slight chuckle shaking her head. I could tell I got under her skin. She stood there for a few more seconds until she finally said, "Like I said, I wish you the best of luck. We can only do so much."

"Yeah, whatever, bitch," I replied rolling my eyes. I knew I was totally out of character and out of line but the old Trish was back. I was tired of oscillating with this new found holy persona. Fuck this shit. Fuck this place. Fuck it all.

Pastor Shirley lowered and shook her head. I guess she couldn't formulate the right response. She just stared at me and then finally walked out of the conference room. Some seconds later she came back and then said, "Lights will be out in thirty minutes, so I suggest you make it back to your room in time. Besides, since you'll be leaving on Sunday, I guess you'll need to start packing soon."

"Sunday?" My eyebrow suddenly raised. Was this fat bitch now really going to fuck with me?

"Yeah...Sunday. You were scheduled to leave in a few weeks. Let's go ahead and make that this Sunday since you think I'm full of shit," she said and then walked back off. "Let's see how much help you'll get now that you won't get it from Hope anymore..."

## CHAPTER THIRTY-TWO

This was the first time ever I had stepped foot inside of the police headquarters on 35th street, let alone a police station. This shit was like a massive armed fortress right on Chicago's South Side.

Following the two fat ass police officers into the headquarters, they quickly brought me to the detective's unit and I was told to sit in this small, chilly waiting lobby for a few minutes until a detective from the sex crimes unit would come and speak with me.

It was nearly ten PM and it felt like I had been waiting for hours for someone to come interview me about this bullshit ass allegation. I couldn't believe that white bitch would lie. See, this was exactly the reason why I didn't mess with those Becky bitches. Now my ass was caught up. Shit was un-fucking-believable. I mean, goddamn, you hear about this shit on the news, but you don't ever expect that some shit like this would happen to you. You know what I mean? Most of the time, you think the niggas that get caught the fuck up with these white hoes were probably some sheisty ass niggas any damn way. But now I see this shit could happen to anyone, including a dude like me who always treated women with the utmost respect. I'd never fucking rape a woman.

But I guess now in this moment, my convictions didn't matter at all. A woman accused me of raping her and now I gotta defend myself. This was some crazy fuck shit, I swear ta God! Truth be told, you already know a nigga was scared as fuck. Somehow though, I just knew if I told my story from A through Z, the white bitch's lies wouldn't stand.

Some minutes later, some tall, light-skinned nigga looking around fiftyish sauntered into the lobby. With this cheap black JC Penny's suit on, I knew this nigga was a straight-up square. At the moment, I had been going through my phone, going over the brief exchange of text messages between me and Melissa. While I waited, three other dudes, all white, were in the waiting area as well.

Crazy thing was the light-skinned nigga didn't hesitate in walking straight toward me. Guess he knew I was the suspect since Melissa probably told these muhfuckas "a black guy did it…" I could already hear that white bitch's voice crying in the back of my head, sobbing like a toddler as she recounted her lies. I still couldn't believe that white bitch would set me up like this, I thought to myself as I kept my eyes latched onto this pig.

"DeAndre Williams?" buddy asked.

"Yes. That's me."

"Good Evening, sir. I'm Detective Wright. Please follow me. I just have some questions in regards to a report that was filed this morning."

"Sure thing. I can clear my name," I responded.

Pursing his lips, he didn't say anything back. He just scanned me up and down, his eyes turned into judgmental slits. I stood up, adjusted my shirt and wiped lint off my pants. I then followed this Detective Wright back to a room past a few cubicles and other offices. Once inside this medium-sized dimly-lit room, which I presumed was an interrogation room, he pulled out a chair at a table and said, "Have a seat. Make yourself comfortable. I promise this won't take long."

"Okay," I replied and cautiously sat down. Anxiety was burning in my spirit. I should've been praying my ass off…

Detective Wright pulled out a chair adjacent to me and then sat down. A manila folder was already sitting on top of the table. He grabbed it and then opened it, quickly scanning a piece of paper.

"So, the reason why you're down here is because we had a young woman come down here and file a report stating that she had been sexually assaulted by you in your residence last night or rather this morning."

"Lies. I didn't do shit to that woman. She and I had consensual sex," I immediately stated. I wasn't going to let this nigga get me caught the fuck up.

"Okay, I'm not accusing you of anything. I'm just letting you know why we have you down here."

"Yeah, but still. I'm telling you that's a lie, Detective," I confidently stated. "As I said, the woman, Melissa, and I had consensual sex. I wouldn't dare do such a thing." "It's funny, too, 'cuz this all probably stems from the fact that she and I got into an argument before I kicked her out. I asked her if she wanted to kick it later on the week. I thought she was cool. But then she told me, 'I don't date black guys.' That obviously made me mad, so I kicked her out of my house. I told her that her sex was trash and so that probably explains why she's trying to get revenge…Something told me not to mess with that white girl."

"Hrrrm…Ok. Well, she's already been administered a rape kit. Before we dig any deeper into questions, are you willing to submit to a DNA test?"

My head shot back in surprise. This bitch was really going there. Wow! "A rape kit? What exactly does that entail?"

"Well, it depends. But we collect a wide variety of samples from the victim. Vaginal fluids, sperm, hair, clothing fibers, etc. We also take pictures of any bruising or marks that might indicate physical trauma," Detective Wright said.

"Right! Exactly! There you go. I didn't dare put my hands on her. I didn't even punch or try to fight her. If anything, she was ultra-aggressive when we had sex," I said. I already knew I was exonerated.

"Hrrrm...Well, she has plenty of bruising on her back and thighs. When she came in this morning, her lip was also busted, sir."

I clasped my hands over my face and shook my head not believing what I was hearing. "Sir, I swear I didn't do this. It sounds like she may have had another run-in with someone or she's clearly trying to frame me," I responded.

"Look, I'm not here accusing you of anything. All I am doing so far is getting your story and then we will further investigate."

"Man, this is crazy as hell! I wouldn't dare have to rape a woman to get any! That's just not my style."

"Well, how am I supposed to know that, Mr. Williams? How do I know you're just not making this up? You know how many times I hear guys using your explanation? Of course you are obviously going to defend yourself," the detective shot back.

Fuck!

I couldn't say anything back. I felt like this nigga was somewhat trying to catch me in a tongue twister. I could see the want all in his eyes to trap me.

"But, brotha—"

"I'm not your, brother. And answer my question...Do you

or do you not want to take a DNA test now? We can really do this the easy way or the hard way."

"Man, this is so messed up! I feel like I walked into a trap. I need to speak to my attorney!" I demanded.

"You're not under arrest yet, Mr. Williams. I'm just asking preliminary questions and gathering evidence. The case may or may not proceed into prosecution. Typically in cases like this, there is already a fifty-fifty chance they will proceed, but with DNA tests and administration of rape kits, we can generally determine what looks like a valid case. So again, do you or do you not want to take a DNA test?"

"Man, fuck it. I'll go ahead and do it, but I wanna speak to my attorney after this."

"You'll be more than welcome to do so," Detective Wright replied. "And as I said, you aren't under arrest. We are just asking questions…"

"Yeah, aiiiight!" I replied, doubt rolling off my tongue. I knew where all of this was headed. There were the questions at first. Next thing you know, my ass was gonna be thrown in a fucking Cook County jail cell, awaiting trial for some shit I knew for sure I didn't fucking do.

"Follow me. We'll have someone from the lab to come and draw blood and saliva. Then you'll be free to go back home. But once we get results, we'll bring you back in for further questions," Detective Wright said.

"Okay."

Moments later, Detective Wright took me down to the lab where a tech drew some blood from me and took a saliva sample. After I got done, Detective Wright told me that I should expect a follow-up call from him in the next twenty-four to forty-eight hours and that I'd better lawyer up.

Soon as I walked outside of the police headquarters, I called for a Lyft and made my way back home, floored that now I was days away from losing my mothafuckin' freedom over some bullshit rape allegations.

It was now nearly midnight and I was in my dark living room, sitting on my couch, wired to the tee. The television was blaring a rerun of Good Times. I couldn't sleep. Shit, how could I? Fear was running through my blood at a million miles per hour.

I was beating myself up mentally, telling myself I should've never fucked with that white bitch. Every life lesson I learned from my mama and others went down the drain. Shit, I could even hear Shelly's ass in the back of my head chastising me for my treatment of women.

This shit was just so unimaginable, and for a brief moment, I thought I was a dream. Hopefully, this entire rape investigation would end once the detectives pieced together enough clues to know Melissa's ass was definitely lying her ass off.

This was the first time ever in my life I'd ever been accused of raping a woman. Like, for real. Granted, I knew I wasn't the perfect guy and I made my fair share of mistakes when it came to my relations with women, but I wasn't no mothafuckin' rapist.

I was so mentally fucked up, I didn't even have the capacity to call anyone else and let them know what the fuck was going on. Shit, I was still trying to process all of this my damn self.

My chest began to tighten and I swore to God it felt like I was about to have a heart attack. "Calm down, Dre. Calm down. You tweakin'. You're gonna be fine. You're not gonna get in trouble," I kept telling myself, stupidly assuring myself that nothing would come of all of this shit.

Bro, it would be a white girl who would do this to me. I felt so violated. Felt so vulnerable. I could literally see my life flashing before my eyes. I could see myself in prison, locked up for a decade, not able to see my own daughter and shit. Nah, this wasn't going to be me. I had to get myself out of this jam. I had to do something immediately.

"Oh fuck no!" I suddenly screamed when the reality of everything hit me. "This bitch ain't finne set me up. White bitch wanna lie on me, I'm gonna lie on her ass, too," I thought to myself, trying to figure out a way how to snake my way out this jam. I shot up from my living room couch and paced the floor, trying to think of a solution.

Tapping my chin, I mumbled aloud to myself possible solutions to this dilemma. But there really wasn't. It was just my word versus Melissa's. And in this day and age, rape allegations by any woman, especially a white woman, would land any dude in jail. I just knew I was guilty before proven innocent.

A situation like this made me regret not taking school seriously. By now I could've been a lawyer and figured out how to get out of not only this fucked-up situation but even that bullshit I had going on with Trish. Although Detective Wright said that so far he was just gathering evidence and that there was a chance the case wouldn't go anywhere if the evidence didn't line up, I didn't want to believe that. That was just police talk. Reckless police talk at that. Hell, if I was a cop, I wouldn't even tell a suspect none of that shit. But none of this tangential-ass thinking mattered at the moment. I had to think of something NOW!

Then it hit me...

The only way to disprove I didn't do shit to this white bitch was that I needed a witness. Someone who could vouch I didn't do shit to this bitch.

But how would I get a witness? There was no one else in

my bedroom. It was just me and Melissa. I mean, Myron and I kicked it at the bar that night. But he and I weren't even paying attention to the bitch. She didn't even cross my mothafuckin' radar until I had about a good ten shots up in me.

Think, Dre. Think. Think. Think. You're smart, nigga. Figure this shit out. You need a witness.

My thoughts kept rolling as I continuously paced the floor. Nothing came to me. Absolutely nothing.

But then it hit me...I needed someone who wouldn't mind covering for me. Someone who could understand the situation I had going on. My mind kept going to Myron. But I didn't know if I could trust that nigga anymore. That shit he said last night at the bar had me still second-guessing that nigga...

For some odd reason, my mind kept floating Trish. I didn't know why. She would be the last person I'd call, even if I was dying from cancer and she had the mothafuckin' cure.

But then a sudden light bulb went off in my head.

She needed me right now more than anything. And truth be told, there was a slight possibility she could help me out. Maybe...Just maybe I could work out a deal with her and she could help me get out of this situation. But how would that work, idiot? I thought to myself. Yeah, how would that work? What the fuck would Trish lie about??!? And that bitch was all the way in a halfway house. I don't even know if I still had her cell phone number. I don't even know if she would even wanna deal with me in this manner.

"Fuck it," I said. I was going to call her and see if we could squash our beef in exchange for helping me. I didn't know how yet but I hope she'd at least give it a consideration. I knew I was being a tad irrational and stupid as fuck thinking she could help me...But I guess it was worth a try, right?

I lunged back over to my coffee table and grabbed my cell phone. I went through my contacts and luckily I never deleted Trish's phone number. I just had her number blocked. After I unblocked it, I quickly dialed her and held the phone up to my ear.

The phone kept ringing and ringing. And after about six rings I was ready to hang up. Then the phone went to voicemail.

"Fuck!" I growled. "Goddamnit!"

But literally, a second later, she called me back.

"Hello? Dre?"

My eyes widened with anxiety. "Hey, Trish..."

## CHAPTER THIRTY-THREE

Fuck Pastor Shirley. Fuck this church. Fuck God. Fuck everything. Well, I don't know about the *Fuck God* part but yeah, like I said, fuck everything. I was over this shit. Pastor Shirley was nothing but a fake ass holy hoe.

That bitch thought she had one up over me. Gon kick me out her raggedy ass halfway house program early. Bitch, fuck you. I got her ass alright. I hoped karma would come back ten-fold on her ugly, fat ass.

Anyways, soon as my anxious ass left the conference room, I made my way back to my room and began to come up with an alternative plan. Truth be told, I wanted to breakdown, scream and even possibly fight a bitch, but I knew I had to keep my composure.

Pacing back forth in my room, the walls felt like they were closing in. I closed my eyes, said a prayer and then got a hold of myself.

"Fuck all of this shit," I mumbled to myself.

I needed to go back to do what I knew I did best. Sell this sweet pussy of mine. Granted, I may not look the best at the current moment, but for the right price, any man could get his hands on this lil fire ass twat of mine. That seemed like that was going to be the only way I would get my hands on this $1,000 I needed to secure that apartment ASAP. I definitely wasn't going to let this dilemma boggle me the fuck down. No, ma'am!

Still frantically pacing my room back and forth, I needed to figure out what websites I could hop on and find me a client. Shit, I needed to find me some lonely ass cracka. From my previous experience, I knew it didn't take much to make a cracka cum and those were the types that paid top dollar. Hopefully, I could find me a white man with a nice, ole big dick, too, 'cuz these last two years of trying to be all saved and sanctified was drying my pussy up. I needed to fuck. Fuck all that shit. Yeah, I knew I sounded hella reckless right now, but like I said, I didn't give a fuck. Fuck all of this shit. All I had to worry about right now was not violating my probation requirements. And all that meant was I couldn't smoke no weed or do no drugs. I could drink though. Shit, I'd find me a nice white man, get pissy drunk and pop this pussy all over him for a stack.

Right now I didn't need to pack. I needed to hop on my laptop and get on Craig's List or Backpages to see who wanted to get down with this sweet brown. But before I could make it over to my desk, my phone started buzzing in my pants pocket. Maybe that was Neicy calling me back letting me know she found someone who could lend me the $1,000. But it wasn't. It was actually Monique...Damn! Right on time 'cuz truthfully I was just talking shit about selling pussy. I didn't even know if I even had it in me to succumb that low and do some nasty, foul shit like that. I knew bestie could come through and lend me the $1,000 with no questions asked.

I answered the phone and quickly said, "Oh My God! Girl, please! I need your help!"

"Bitch, fuck you!" she angrily replied.

I instantly froze in place and then I already knew what the fuck was about to happen. *Fuck! Fucking Chadwick told her ass about us*, I thought to myself. "Excuse me?" I replied, faking as if I didn't know what convo was going to be about.

"Bitch, don't act like you don't know why the fuck I'm calling you. How could you do this to me? You fucked my man and had a kid by him? Bitch, you are as low as they come. You are pathetic. All that I did for you and you weren't even woman enough to come to me and tell me all of this? Bitch, I hope you die," Monique cried through the phone. She sounded so upset, that I damn near could hear the painful tears falling from her eyes.

"Monique! I wanted to tell you but I didn't know what to say! And Chadwick threatened me!"

"Yeah, yeah, yeah, bitch…You know, I really can't be mad at you. I feel like this is karma for me anyways."

"Huh? Monique, look, I can't explain! I really can," I responded, wiping tears from my face. Now I felt so low that I betrayed my best friend. I should've just been more upfront and honest with her. But this was all my fault. And I deserved all of this. But what the fuck did she mean by this was her karma?

"Nah! You don't have to explain shit. But I'mma just drop this dime on you and then you can be on your merry fucking way. Yeah, you may have fucked Chadwick and got pregnant by him. But guess what, bitch. I fucked Dre. Yup! Fucked him so many times, I lost count."

My mouth dropped and my eyes widened with surprise. "Huh? Nah! You did what?"

"Yeah! I fucked your baby daddy. And the dick was so good. And you remember that time you got that bad case of gonorrhea and you just knew Dre gave it to you? Well, guess who gave it to him, bitch? It was me."

"Monique! You know what, hoe! Fuck you! Fuck you and fuck Dre! Bitch, no wonder you were so hellbent on trying to get back at Dre! Bitch, you were chasing some personal vendetta! Something told me you were on some other shit, too! And I can't believe I trusted yo ass after all these years! Bitch, if I catch you in the streets, I'm gonna whoop yo ass!"

"Yeah, whatever, hoe. How you gon do that with that bad ass hip of yours. Big Mama diabetic foot ass bitch! You big and bad, pull the fuck up hoe! But you can't 'cuz you ain't got shit and you will never have shit, broke ass, illiterate ass hoe!"

"FUCK YOU! Get off my line!" I screamed, suddenly hanging up the phone.

Enraged, I almost wanted to stop what the fuck I was doing, hop in an Uber and go all the way to the North Side to put my foot up that nasty bitch's ass. I couldn't even believe she would have the mothafuckin' gall to call me and confront me about Chadwick but then gon turn around and confess that she was fucking Dre and she was the reason why I came down with gonorrhea them years ago! That bitch was foul as fuck and now all of this made sense of why she harbored resentment for Dre.

"I'mma kill that bitch!" I growled, now back to pacing my floor. But I had no time to lose over this shit. Now that Monique was unexpectedly out the picture to provide me help, I was back to square fuckin' one. "Fuck it!" I said and dashed to my desk to hop on the net and find this white man. I needed that cash like yesterday! I needed it now. Fuck morals. I had to do what I gotta do. But I swore after I got done doing what I was about to hopefully do, I was gonna get my act right. I was over everything and everyone. Once I got my baby back from Dre's evil ass and got me a good ass job with benefits, a bitch was finne be straight.

My phone started buzzing again. Bet you it was Monique's ass calling me back to try to curse me the fuck out. Yeah, I didn't give a fuck about cursing anymore by the way. Like I said, I was too stressed the fuck out to be worried about trying to control my language. Fuck all of this shit. I grabbed my phone off the bed but then I was surprised to see the number flashing across my phone. It was mothafuckin' Dre calling me. What a fucking coincidence! But why in the fuck was this clown calling me this late at night? Did Monique call him and tell him she told me about them? Shit, truth be told, I was surprised he was calling me in the first place. I hesitated at first, debating whether or not I wanted to answer the phone. Rapidly tapping my right foot against the floor, I wondered what I should do next. Hrrrrm...Fuck him. He was probably on some late-night bullshit and probably wanted to explain his situation with Monique. But I didn't have time for any of his shenanigans or his bullshit explanations. "I'll see yo ass in court, lying ass, fuck nigga," I mumbled to myself and threw my phone back onto my bed. I always knew he was cheating on me with another bitch. I just never thought it would be my own best friend. But you know what, you should never put anything past anyone these days. It be ya best friends, too, that'll do you in the most. Fucking bitch.

But then I paused for a moment and thought to myself.

"Hrrrrrm," I mumbled, tapping my chin, still thinking why in the fuck was Dre calling me.

As the phone get buzzing, a weird idea floated into my head. Maybe...Just maybe...And I knew this was going to sound like a crazy ass idea. But maybe I could work out some deal with him if he lent me the money I needed to get the apartment.

By the time I decided to answer the phone, I saw the call disappear. But then I quickly called him back. "Hello? Dre?" I immediately answered once the call connected.

"Hey, Trish...," he replied, his tone sounding off and dark.

"Umm, why you calling me? We really shouldn't be talking to each other until we go to court," I said.

"I know, I know. But look, I had been doing a lot of thinking over the past few days."

"About what?"

Thinking? What was he thinking? I found it very odd he was calling now that Monique dropped that secret on me. Nigga was probably feeling hella guilty now. Granted, I made my fair share of mistakes and I cheated on him, too, but that was only out of long-held suspicion that he was doing me dirty with other bitches. And lo and behold, my intuition was right all along. And now I didn't regret a damn thing. Fuck him and fuck Monique.

"Well, listen, I'm not calling on some bullshit. You are right. You deserve to be in Ariyanna's life. It's wrong for me to deny you that right, especially if you trying to get your shit together," he explained. "I think we can work something out for the best of everyone. You know, at the end of the day, you already know how I feel about my daughter. I never wanted to put any harm on you. I just felt a certain type of way about the reckless ass decisions you were making," he said.

"Yeah, I hear you, Dre....I know I fucked up and made some mistakes, too, but the thing is, you don't do a good job of fessing up to the shit you put me through, too. Yeah, I cheated on you. Cheated on you several times, but you always made it seem like you never did any bullshit either. So, tell me, before we get any further into this conversation. Tell me, did you ever cheat on me while we were together?"

Dre became silent. Yup, this nigga already knew he was guilty. Caught red-handed.

"Yeah...Yeah, I cheated..."

"Okay, and who you fucked while we were together? Do I know the bitch?"

I was just waiting for this clown ass nigga to tell me this

bitch's name. Say it, nigga. Say it. Monique. Come on, fuck nigga. I'm ready.

"It was...It was Neicy."

"NEICY?!?!?"

"Yeah...Neicy..."

My eyes exploded with shock. "My fucking sister, nigga?!?!?"

# CHAPTER THIRTY-FOUR

"My fucking sister, nigga?!?!?"

Feeling caught, I had no other choice to admit to what I did. Yeah, it was kind of fucked up. But if I was gonna earn Trish's trust, I had to confess that I was a dog ass nigga. Yeah, I fucked Neicy. It was a long ass time ago and it was when Trish and I first started dating.

I hope this new revelation wouldn't suddenly make Trish apprehensive of trying to help me. 'Cuz God knows I really needed to see if she could help me out right now.

"But look, Trish. That shit was years ago when you and I first started dating. Shit, Neicy and I was drunk as hell."

"Nigga! You fucked my sister! I should kill you and that fat ass bitch! You two are both pieces of shit! But why the fuck did Monique just call me and tell me you two fucked as well?!?!?"

My head dropped and I closed my eyes, shaking my head out of shame. Damn. Once again I got caught the fuck up. Yeah, so I fucked Monique, too. That was some years ago, too.

"Damn...How the fuck did you know?" I asked.

"'Cuz the bitch called me and told me that she found out I was sleeping with Chadwick. And Chadwick told her all about the fling we had and what not!"

"Wait! Wait one mothafuckin' minute!?!? So, you was cheating on me with that nigga? That square ass muhfucka? A northside nigga at that?!?! Man, you was really on some other shit!" I angrily spat.

This back-and-forth we had was starting to get really intense and I just knew this wasn't going to end well. Ughhh! I was getting mad that this was even happening right now because this wasn't supposed to be the reason for me communicating with her.

"Man, bruh, so you was just fuckin' my friends and family. Un-fucking-believable. But it's cool though. I'm glad I got to do all the shit I got to do. Yup! Just like how I fucked Myron. Bet you didn't know that either, huh?" Trish confessed.

My eyes suddenly widened in shock and rage. "You fucked who?" I had to hear her say that nigga's name one more time.

"Yeah! You heard me right! I fucked Myron, too! And his dick was so good. Better than that trash ass dick you walking around with, nigga!"

Scrunching my face in disgust and surprise, I smacked my teeth and said, "Bitch, fuck you! You lying! You just dropping names now!"

"Oh! You don't believe me? You want me to put us all on three-way so you can hear him beg for him to get a taste of my pussy?"

Hearing Trish go off like this was bizarre as fuck because the last time I saw this rank ass bitch, her ass was acting like a Jehovah's Witness and shit. Now this bitch was back to her old damn self, dropping all types curse words and expletives in the most ignorant ass fashion. But the more I thought about it, the more I realized this bitch was telling me the whole ass truth. She fucked Myron. My own muhfuckin' nigga fucked my bitch. Well, my ex-bitch. This shit was really blowing the fuck out of me right now. But it didn't surprise me, to be honest with you. At this point, I really didn't even care anymore. Everybody had pretty much fucked everybody.

"Trish…Listen to me for a sec. I fucked up. You fucked up. We all fucked up."

"Yeah! That's what the fuck it sounds like, mothafucka!"

"Look, bruh! Just calm down for a second. I'm trying to reason with you because I want us to squash this shit for the sake Ariyanna. I mean, even though you out here got me believing she ain't my daughter, I still wanna just dead this shit. I don't wanna involve no courts or nothin' like that."

"Dre…I wanna believe you so bad, but I just feel like you want something out of me. What is it? Just tell me," Trish said.

"I don't want shit from you. I just want you to not take my daughter away from me."

"But how you know she's even your daughter?"

"Look, bruh. We can go back and forth with that shit but any and everybody can tell Ariyanna is me and I am Ariyanna."

"Yeah, okay, well, you may be right. But you want something from me. What the fuck you want, Dre? Just be honest. Why you calling me all of a sudden?"

This is where I was gonna have to man the fuck up and tell her everything that was going on. "Trish, all bullshit aside, do you think I'm a rapist?"

"What? Nigga, what?"

"Bruh, for real. Although we had our problems, do you think I'm the type of nigga that is capable of raping someone?"

Trish was silent for a moment and then she answered, "No. I don't think so. But shit, you never know. What the fuck, Dre? What the fuck you got going on?"

"Man, listen. Don't judge me but the other night I fucked around and messed with this white bitch I met at the bar. Make a long story short, me and the white bitch fucked. I thought she was cool and I wanted to see if she wanted to kick it with me later on this week and whatnot. But then the white bitch gon' tell me she don't date niggas. Ain't that some shit for you?"

"Uh-huh. What else..."

"Well, later on that day, I went to go handle some business. By the time I came back to my crib, twelve was at my door telling me some detectives wanted to interview me because the white bitch is claiming I raped her..."

"Nigggga...Like what the fuck, Dre?!? You raped her?!?! Nah, you're fucked up! I gotta go!"

"NOO! I ain't rape that white bitch, man! That's what the fuck I'm tryna say!"

"So what the fuck you want me to do?!?!?"

"Bruh! Please, listen, I need you to help me and say you were a witness."

"Dre! How in the fuck can I even do that if I am all the way out here at this damn halfway house!?!? How can I even come up with a believable alibi? Man, you fucking tweaking right now, fa real! And then you want me to lie to some cops of your bullshit?!? Boy, you got me fucked up. Goodbye!"

"Trish! Please, I'm for real. I wouldn't dare do this shit to no female. I swear on my grandmama's grave I wouldn't do some foul shit like that. And you know me!"

"Yeah, yeah, yeah! Good luck, Dre! You know...Between you fucking Monique and Neicy and now this shit, you just gave me every fucking good ass reason why I really need to get my daughter back. Guilty or innocent, I ain't helping you with shit! Goodbye!"

Suddenly Trish hung up the phone.

"FUCK!" I shouted and then threw my phone across the

living floor! I was so pissed right now. My entire plan back-fired like a mothafucka! Now I knew for sure I was going straight to jail.

Since I couldn't take this anxiety anymore, I needed to go get drunk as fuck. "Man, fuck this shit! I'mma kill my fucking self!" I screamed as reached down at the coffee table, grabbed my wallet and keys and then stormed over to my phone lying on the floor. I grabbed it and saw that Trish was calling me back. "Please, bruh!" I quickly answered.

"Man, calm the fuck down. If you want my help, then you gotta help me!" she said.

"Okay! Anything!"

"Anything?"

"Yeah! Whatever you need, I got you!"

"Oh okay! Well, I need a place to stay until I get back on my feet."

"What?!? Nah!" I replied, smacking my teeth.

"You said you need my help, right?!?!?"

"Yeah!"

"Well, I need a place to stay and I need $2,000 to get this apartment. You do that for me and I'll help you out in this situation. Oh, and I want you to give me split-custody over Ariyanna. We trade weeks."

I had to think about this shit for a moment. Man, her crazy ass wanted to stay at my place and give her $2,000?!?! The only thing I couldn't wrap my head around was her then trying to get split-custody over Ariyanna. I didn't feel comfortable with that shit at all and she knew it. What the fuck?!? But seeing as how I was pretty much between a rock and a hard place, I gave in. "Fine…We'll work out a deal. When can you get here?"

"Pick me up tonight…I'll be ready," she said.

"Bet. Text me your address and I'll be there…"

## CHAPTER THIRTY-FIVE

"You got a nice ass place, Dre," I commented as I walked out of his shower fully naked.

"Man, put some fucking clothes on," he groaned from his bed. He was laying down watching television when I stumbled out of the bathroom with no clothes on.

"What? You act like you ain't never seen me naked before," I said.

"Yeah, but we're not together and—"

"And what?" I interrupted. "I know my body isn't what it used to be. But I have no shame. I'm just thankful to be alive. So fuck your feelings. Besides, I asked you to leave but you didn't want me to. So, bam, take that."

Dre was acting so paranoid, he didn't want to leave the room. Guess he thought I was going to go through his shit while he wasn't watching. It was like 2 AM in the morning and after Dre picked me up from Hope, we went straight back to his place. Ironically, it didn't take me long to pack because I didn't have much stuff. Don't even know why Pastor Shirley gave me until Sunday to get the fuck out. But whatever. I was gone now Buh-bye, bitch!

"Yeah, well, still, we not together," he said. "So, let's go ahead and talk about this plan."

"So, wait. We didn't have much time to talk about in the car but you need to recap to me what exactly fucking happened. 'Cuz I don't know. I still feel a bit iffy about all of this, Dre. I mean, how can I really trust that you aren't lying?"

Dre smacked his teeth and rolled his eyes. "Damn, girl. Like, what's the point of you even being here right now if you are gonna doubt everything I'm telling you? Like for real, I didn't do shit to that woman. I swear to God," he said.

"Okay, well, I believe you, damn. I'm just saying though. I'd feel a certain type of way if you got me lying for you knowing damn well you really did that shit."

Dre produced this nasty gawk at me and said, "Look at me. Do I really look like the type that needs to rape a bitch, let alone a white bitch, just to get some ass? Truth be told, I went damn near two years without fucking."

"What?" I exclaimed. "Nigga, you lying! Two years?!?"

Now Dre knew he was a goddamn lie if he was gonna lay there and run me that bullshit. Knowing this nigga, he couldn't go three days without pussy.

"Dead ass serious. Except for the other night, of course," he replied.

"WOOW! So you and I both was some celibate ass muhfuckas, huh?" I laughed.

"I guess so," he said, producing a slight smile. Damn. That was a side I kind of missed about Dre. He was looking so tired and vulnerable right now, but he still had a certain degree of cuteness to him that from time to time I missed. He was such a sweetheart early on our relationship when we were together. Oh well. Fuck him still though.

"Well, like I said, I believe you. And on that note, when you gon' run me my money? 'Cuz I can't help you until you send me my coins," I demanded.

"Damn. Shit. Fine. What's your CashApp?" he asked as he reached over to his nightstand and grabbed his phone of its charger.

"Dollar sign-TRISH4CHRIST," I replied.

"So, what's up that by the way?" Dre asked.

"What's up with what?"

"You really saved and shit?"

I didn't know what to say because I was still on the damn fence myself. I wanted to keep believing but now I truly didn't care anymore. "Well, yes and no. I mean, I was cool up until recently. A lot of shit will make you start questioning things. Anyways, I don't wanna talk about that right now. We need to talk about this story we need to run the police. So, what ideas you got?"

"Shit...I think you can say you were here visiting me and we got into an altercation and you saw Melissa and shit. And she definitely wasn't acting like a rape victim and whatnot," Dre explained. "I think the police will kind of buy that."

"Nah, I don't know about that," I replied shaking my head. "I mean, think Dre. You supposed to be the college grad and all. How is that proof you still ain't raped that white girl?"

"Okay, well, what do you recommend?" he asked. The slight annoyance in his voice made me know he thought he had this shit all figured out but he obviously didn't. Dude was such a know-it-all but didn't know shit. This nigga was definitely destined for jail if I didn't come to his rescue.

"Well, I'm glad you asked...But give me a moment, let me put my shit on," I said.

"Okay," he replied.

I spent the next five minutes putting on a quick outfit and then threw a bonnet over my head and made my way into the actual bedroom. "I need a drink. You ain't got no Henny here?" I asked.

Dre smacked his teeth and said, "Girl, it's almost 3 AM in the morning and you wanna drink right now?"

"Please? I ain't have a drink in years. I need something just to loosen me up and make me think of some more ideas and whatnot."

"I guess...I got some weed, too...," he replied with a raised brow. "You wanna smoke? 'Cuz I'd rather get high."

I stood there and thought for a second. Suddenly my conscience kicked in and was begging me not to succumb to the THC-temptation. But damn, fuck all that. I wanted to get high and drunk. It was time to live life a little. If I got drug tested, I'd just take some niacin pills.

"Sure," I replied.

"Cool, I got vape pen," Dre said as leaned over and rummaged through his nightstand and pulled out a vape pen. He took a few tokes and then passed it to me. I ain't never smoked out of one of those before but I guess I was willing to try. "What in the hell is this? You get high off this?"

"Hell yeah. Just try it. It's Pineapple Express. Good ass strain," he said.

"Okay," I replied reluctantly as I grabbed the vape pen out of his hand and wedged it between my lips. I cautiously took a few tokes, taking in the sweet, tangy aroma. "Damn, this taste good as hell. Where you get this from?"

"One of my guys on the job. I used to get them from Tanisha but you know..."

"Yeah...I'm sorry about that, too," I said as I began to lightly cough. "Damn, this hit kind of strong, too."

"Yeah. Be careful with that," he said. "Shit gon have you on a different planet in a few."

"Shit, I need to be."

"How's everything with your health?" he asked.

I took a deep breath and closed my eyes. "Fine," I smiled lightly. "Just managing. The doctor told me my cancer might be slowing down. So, I'm supposed to be trying this new therapy soon to see if it helps."

"Good to hear, I guess."

"Yeah...Anyways, enough about that. Where's the henny?"

"Haha, well, let's go in the living room," Dre said as he proceeded to get up from the bed and then march to his bedroom door. I got up and then followed him.

As we walked through the hallway, I was still so amazed that Dre was able to get this expensive ass townhouse in Hyde Park all by himself. I must say that although Dre had his doggish ass ways, he was definitely doing so good for himself. It was obvious he was serious about life and taking care of his shit, especially Ariyanna. And that I admired a lot about him.

Now back into the living room, I crashed on the couch while he went into his kitchen and came back out with a bottle of Henny and two red cups. The weed he gave me moments ago was starting to kick in and I was beginning to feel so nauseous. But in a good way.

"Damn, this shit is starting to hit me hard," I said, feeling my head getting lighter and lighter as each second passed.

"Yeah, I told you that shit was strong," he said with this slight, devilish smile. "You'll be straight though."

"Yeah...," I replied, rubbing the side of my head.

Dre sat the two cups onto the coffee table in front of the couch and poured a hefty serving into each. He then handed me a cup. "You gon be good?" he asked.

"Yeah, I'm straight," I said, feeling even hazier, but in a good ass way. This weed was definitely making me feel so relaxed.

"This shit is good as hell," I said. "Damn..."

"Yeah. Well, don't pass out just yet 'cuz we still gotta talk about this plan."

"I know," I responded. "So, I think you gotta say we did a threesome."

Yeah. I know. That idea sounded crazy as hell but it was the only thing that made sense to me at the moment. Dre needed to be willing to hear me out so he could see why my idea would make sense, too.

"WHAT?!?" Dre responded. "What is you talkin' about? A threesome?"

"Listen...Just hear me out. I knew you were gonna have that response but it's the only thing that's gonna make sense to a Detective. Just listen..."

"Okay. I'm listening," Dre responded doubtfully.

"Well, if I say I was there with ya'll and having sex with ya'll, I can be the third witness. I mean, it's your word versus hers. But if I said I was there, then I can contradict everything she said."

"Damn...I guess..."

## CHAPTER THIRTY-SIX

Trish was crazy as fuck for making this suggestion. Threesome? Really? This bitch was off her rockers but the more I thought about it, the more I realized she may have been onto something. It would make perfect sense for her to claim the three of us were doing some sort of threesome. The white bitch then couldn't dispute anything that Trish said happened that night.

But there was just one simple problem with Trish's idea. How in the fuck can she even prove I had sex with her?

"Well, the idea sounds like it could work. But the dilemma is how am I gonna prove that you and I were doing something together? Shit still sounds a bit shady, don't you think?"

"Yeah, that's true. I mean, they may ask me to take a test or something to see if I got your sperm in me, I guess," Trish said as she took a sip from her drink.

"Yeah, see, no, this shit ain't gon work. How the fuck is that gonna even happen?"

Trish chuckled. "Let me see that vape pen again," she said.

"Man, bruh, you tweakin' right now. You starting to get too high and drunk as fuck right now," I said. Man, I knew I should've never gave her silly ass that vape pen. "And aren't you on probation? Should you even be smoking?"

"Boy, bye! I sat up here and gave you the best idea in the world. Let me get that pen!"

"Fine!" I said as I pulled it out of my pocket and handed it to me. "But you still ain't answer my question! How the fuck am I gonna prove I got sperm inside of you unless we fuck or something??!"

"You just answered your own damn question," Trish responded as she took some pulls from the vape pen and blew vapor in my face.

I smacked my teeth. "See, now you on some other shit."

"Well, Dre, I don't know what else to tell you. The only way maybe is for you to go beat ya dick and then bust in a napkin and then I could put it inside of me."

"Man, nah! You on bullshit for real right now. I don't even know why my stupid ass even came up with this idea of trying to use you!"

Suddenly Trish got mad and said, "Fuck you. Yeah, your stupid ass needed my help alright! But Dre, you ain't got no other solutions to this shit. I'm trying to reason with your lame ass!"

"Man, give me my money back! I don't wanna do this shit no more." Trish was on bullshit and I didn't even know why I succumbed and had her up on my shit now. See, this is exactly what happens when you get too desperate.

"No. I ain't going nowhere. And I ain't giving you MY money back. We had an agreement. Now go beat ya dick and bring it back to me in a napkin."

"But, Trish, you're gonna get pregnant! Fuck you talm'bout with yo super-fertile ass."

"Really, Dre? Nigga, I have cervical cancer. I cannot have children, dummy."

I suddenly got quiet and realized I may have fucked up

and said some foul shit. Trish suddenly scrunched her face and looked the other way.

"Damn. I'm sorry. I didn't know."

"Yeah, yeah, yeah…Be sorry. That's why it's fucked up you wanted to take Ariyanna away from me," she cried. "I can't have children anymore, Dre. She's all I got," she sobbed as tears ran down her face. "Anyways, look, just do what you gotta do. I'mma be in the other bedroom, okay?" she said as she sat her red cup down on the coffee table and immediately got up from the couch.

"I'm sorry, Trish."

"Yeah, whatever. Like I said, it's the only thing I think is gonna work," she replied as she made her way down the hallway and into the guest bedroom.

Feeling kind of bad, I downed the rest of the Henny in my cup. I looked at the Henny bottle, which still had about a good fifth left, and grabbed it. I downed the rest of the bottle in one swig. This shit was getting crazier by the minute.

*Threesome. Threesome. Beat off in a napkin.* My thoughts kept running wild as the alcohol began to loosen me up a bit. "Fuck it," I said as I got up from the couch and made my way into the guest bathroom in the main hallway. Once inside, I sat down on the toilet, whipped my dick out and then grabbed my phone to look at some porn. As dumb as fuck I thought Trish was, she was actually somewhat a genius for this idea because it was the only thing that made sense at the moment. I guess all of that ratchetness was cloaking some hidden intelligence.

Once I pulled up PornHub, I quickly searched for some BBW porn. Once I settled on a particular clip, I played it, and then placed my phone on the edge of my bathroom's radiator. My dick getting hard, I began to stroke myself hoping I could get this shit over in a few minutes.

But, ughh...This porn wasn't doing shit. My dick could barely get erect. I just wasn't feeling this idea. Or maybe I had too much to drink.

"Fuck it," I said as I stood up and quickly pulled my pants up. If this idea is gonna work, I'mma do shit the right way.

# CHAPTER THIRTY-SEVEN

Although I knew it was a crazy ass idea, I knew it was going to be only logical thing to help Dre get out of his bind. But I be damned if he was gonna sit there and belittle me like that, especially given I couldn't get pregnant.

The more I thought about it though, the more I no longer felt comfortable even helping Dre out anymore. Telling this big ass lie to cover for him still just didn't sit right with me. Besides, I still didn't know if this nigga was lying about this entire rape situation. *Fuck him. This is a bad ass idea*, I thought to myself as I laid in the bed.

Truth be told, I should just get up and leave. I should just give him his money back and just head over to Neicy's place. I needed to talk to that hoe anyways to see if it was even true that she fucked Dre. But at this point, I didn't even care about that shit. That was years ago. Right now, I was just trying to get my life settled. All I wanted to do now was find a secure place to stay, get a good job, go back to school and try to rebuild some relationship with Ariyanna. That was all I cared about at the moment. Honestly, I felt like Dre kind of exploited me and the more I thought about it, the more I just wanted to run back into the room and fight him.

I shot up from the bed and dashed over to the door but soon as I got to the door I heard two knocks. "Trish," Dre muttered.

"What you want Dre?!?"

"I'm sorry. Just open the door," he said.

"The fuck for what? You got the napkin with your sperm in it?" I definitely wasn't going to do that shit so let me go ahead and tell his ass right now I wasn't down. "Dre, I don't wanna do this no more," I said.

"Just open the door, Trish."

"Fine!" I flicked the room light on and then opened the door. My eyes widened with shock when I saw Dre standing there with no clothes on except his boxers.

Suddenly confused, I scanned him up and down, taking in his body. I couldn't lie though. Dre definitely still had a nice body but why in the fuck was he naked?!?

"Dre??! What the hell?!?"

"Look. I can't beat my meat. Let's just fuck and get it over with," he said.

"Nigga is you crazy?!?! I'm not fucking you!"

"Trish, it's the only option. You were right. Besides, I can't get my shit up. Help me."

"DRE! You have lost your mothafuck—"

Without hesitation, Dre leaned in, grabbed me and started planting kisses all up and down my face and neck. "Boy, get off me! NO!" I protested, almost wanting to fight him off.

"It will be quick," he said in between the kisses he kept landing all up and down my neck.

"DRE!" I continued yelling but those kisses felt so good. Honestly, I hadn't had someone hold me and make love to me like this in a hot ass minute. "Dre...," I groaned again, but this time I was so turned on, probably because of that Henny and weed, that I was ready to do whatever.

Fuck it.

"Shit, that feels good," I moaned as Dre pushed up against the wall and began to slowly grind on me. Feeling his thick ass dick slide up and down my pussy was already sending me into a frenzy.

"Oh my god, Oh My GOD! I'm cumming! OH MY GOD!"

"Really?!?" Dre said as he looked at me somewhat surprised.

"Yes! I ain't fucked in a minute! Fuck it! I need some dick!" Not caring anymore, I grabbed his face and returned a basket of kisses, licking his face, ears, and side of his neck. The two of us were moaning together and he continued to grind on me.

"FUCK!" I screamed as pushed him off me and then switched sides, pushing him against the wall. I suddenly dropped to my knees and pulled his boxers down. His dick flung out rock hard. I grabbed his shaft and began to suck on it, going up down his veiny dick, giving him the wettest head I knew how to give. Yeah, I used to talk so much shit about Dre's dick but truth be told, he, too, had a pretty ass big ass dick. One that I desperately needed up in me right now.

"Fuck! Keep sucking that shit!" Dre groaned as he pushed my head up and down. Slobbering the tip of his dick, I circled around it with my tongue. I could feel his precum already oozing.

I couldn't take it anymore. I stood up and then as we made out, he pushed me toward the bed then laid me down. He quickly ripped my clothes off and then took his boxers off. Once he got my panties off, he spread my legs and dived right in between me, instantly devouring my insides.

"FUCKKKKKK! OH MY GOD!" I screamed as I felt

him wrap his lips around my clit and suck on it like a lollipop. "FUCK, I'm CUMMING!" I screamed, and next thing you know I was squirting all over the place.

"You want this dick? You ready for it?" Dre asked seductively.

"Hell yeah! Give it to me!"

He quickly stood up, pulled me closer to him and then spread my legs. My pussy already soaking wet, he slid right in and began to stroke my walls. My pussy tightened around his dick and we went at it for the next two hours, fucking like the world was about to end in a few hours.

## CHAPTER THIRTY-EIGHT

The following morning, I woke up and saw Trish snuggled up next to me. Wiping the cold out of my eye and rubbing the side of my head, I couldn't believe I ended up sleeping with this woman. My fucking baby mama. My cancer-stricken, crazy ass baby mama at that.

Oh well...It is what it is.

Hey, don't judge me but I had to do what I had to do. This entire idea sounded wild and stupid as fuck, but at this point, I had to be preemptive. I'd be damned if I was gonna end up like some nigga you'd see on the news who got his life fucked up all over some white pussy. White pussy that wasn't even that good at that. Fuck that. Ya'll got me fucked up if you thought I was gonna be up in some prison, letting some nigga think he gon fuck me in the ass. Hell no.

I glanced down at Trish. She slowly opened her eyes and looked at me. Suddenly a look of surprise came over her. "Oh my God! What did we do?!?!" she asked as she let me go. Quickly pulling the sheets back over her body, she moved to the corner of the bed. "Did we...Did we fuck?" she asked.

"Yeah," I said.

"Oh my mothafuckin' goodness.... I cain't...I fuckin't can't!"

"Yeah, I know right. I guess we had a little bit too much to drunk. Oh well. We still down for the plan, right?"

"Yeah...I guess....," Trish responded, looking at me with doubt laced in her face. "Dre...Did you cum in me?"

"Yeah...Pussy was too good, I guess," I confessed, somewhat smiling.

"Damn...Welp. I cannot believe we did this. Like, I feel like I'm in some alternative universe or some shit."

"I know right. But hey, it is what is, right?"

"I guess...

"Well, I guess we better get ready to head down to the police station," I said as I got out of the bed and then made my way into the bathroom. Now that I was sober and had a good look at Trish, I was still floored that I would do this. I mean, she wasn't ugly but she definitely wasn't the same. She was a good twenty pounds lighter, semi-frail and had a pall to her. I guess all those cancer treatments had some side effects on her skin. She looked like she aged a good ten years.

Honestly, I felt kind of bad for her because she would've probably been in a different situation if I wasn't so hard on her. There was a part of me that felt like I had some responsibility for her going to jail in the first place. But hell, that was water under the bridge. And I couldn't fault myself for her bad decisions. I made bad decisions, too, but I had to take full ownership of my shit. She needed to do the same. But now that she and I were willing to come to a compromise and help each other out, especially fo Ariyanna's sake, I think I had to do everything in my power to make sure she was good.

As millions of hot beads hammered my head, I let go of our fucked up past. I let the hot water drown away all of the bad blood she and I had. It was time to move on. The first thing I was gonna do when I got back to work was talk to my job's HR department and see if I could help Trish get a job. Shit, everyone deserved a second chance. I was also gonna talk to one of my guys, Garrett, who was into real estate. He rented section 8 units. Hopefully, I could see if he could cut Trish a deal and get her a better place so she and I could be closer once she got back on her own two feet. And then I could co-sign on a car for her so she could get a whip as soon as possible. Yeah, I just gave her two stacks so she could get her own place, but I had plenty of money in the bank. She could keep that money and use it to buy furniture and whatever else she needed. See, my whole thing was, I wanted to prove to her that although we still had a lot of issues to hammer out, we could make this co-parenting shit work. I had to let go of all of my past grudges and try my best to make sure the mother of my child had her shit together. I knew mama was gonna be thirty-eight hot with me, too, when she found out I was helping Trish get back on her feet. But oh well, Mama could be mad all she wanted, but this was my life. She made bad decisions when it came to laying up with my rotten ass, absentee father, so she had no right to criticize me if I was trying to help a woman in need.

*Damn...Was I sounding like a sucker right now?* I wondered to myself as I turned off the shower. Nah...This was the right thing to do. I had a lot of growing up to do. Even though Trish and I were about to do some stupid shit and possibly get in trouble for lying to the police, once I got out of this jam, I was determined to walk a straight line for the rest of my life. That meant no more messing around with random women. No more lying. No more manipulation. No more dog ass shit. The next woman I got with, I was going to do everything in my power to do right by her.

Soon as I popped in the shower, it completely slipped my mind that I needed to call up Shelly so we could arrange a time for Ariyanna and me to come over and hang out with her. Although I was still somewhat upset at the shit she said to me, I guess she had a point. So, it was every intention of mine to call her and apologize. I didn't want any bad blood between her and I and at this point it was just time to be a fucking adult all the way around. I didn't want to keep having these fucked up relationships with all the women in my life. Shit, truth be told, maybe it was God who put me in this crazy situation that made me realize why I needed to have Trish back in my life. Although it was too early to tell at the moment, I hoped she truly was going to start to make better decisions about her shit. And no, don't get it twisted. We just fucked. I didn't want any relationship with her at this moment. We could co-parent.

After I took a shower and hopped in an outfit, I made my way back into the bedroom. From the sound of it, it sounded like Trish was in the other guest bedroom taking a shower. I hopped in my bed for a sec just to cool off when I saw my phone buzzing away. I grabbed it and saw a 773 number calling me. Not knowing who it was, I grew nervous. Shit, this could've been that fucking detective. I quickly answered. "Hello?"

"Mr. Williams?" I heard a male voice answer on the other end. Sounded just like that Detective Wright muhfucka.

"Yes. Detective Wright?"

"Yes, this is him. How are you doing today, sir?"

"I'm...um...I'm doing fine. I was just about to run down to the police station to talk to you about what happened that night."

"Don't waste your time. The investigation has been closed."

"Huh? What happened?" I replied, my brow raised out of curiosity.

"Well, you're an innocent man, Mr. Williams. Turns out Ms. Melissa's boyfriend is the actual person who physically and sexually assaulted her. She came in early this morning and confessed that she made up the entire thing in trying to defend her boyfriend. I really apologize that you got caught up in all of this," he said.

My eyes widened with shock, I cupped my mouth, almost ready to pass the fuck out. "Yoooo! You've got to be fucking kidding me!"

"I'm not kidding. She and the boyfriend are currently under arrest. She's being charged with falsifying a police report and obstruction of justice. The boyfriend is being charged with rape."

"Wooooooooooooooow!" I damn near wanted to cry as I felt millions of butterflies invade the pits of my stomach.

"Mr. Williams...Word of caution. Just be careful who you meet. Sex ain't that good to end up in jail," he said. "You take care of yourself and good luck with everything. Have a good day."

"You do the same, sir. Thank you," I replied and hung up the phone.

Soon as I hung up the phone, I popped up from the bed, ran out of my bedroom and into the hallway screaming, "TRISH! TRISH! YOU WON'T BELIEVE WHAT THE FUCK HAPPENED!!!!"

When I cut the corner and made my way to the bathroom, I saw that the door was wide open and the shower was running. Curiously looking around, I then made my way back into the guest room where she had her shit at and saw everything was gone. "The fuck?!?!?"

With my phone still in my hand, I glanced down, pulled up her contact in my phone and dialed her but the phone went straight to voicemail. "What the fuck?!?! Did this bitch take off?!?! What the hell!?!?"

Instantaneously, extreme rage filled my core and every muscle fiber in my body was ready to hop in my Charger and go hunt that bitch down. Bitch thought she was slick! I didn't even know why I the fuck I trusted her ass in the first place! Something kept telling me this bitch was going to finesse the fuck out of me!

"You're fucking retarded, Dre! You stupid ass! You knew what the fuck this bitch was capable of!" I screamed to myself as I rapidly paced the hallway floor trying to figure out what I was gonna do next. I can't believe I just let this bitch spend the night, drink my liquor, hit my vape pen and then gave her some dick. Worst of all, I JUST GAVE THIS BITCH TWO STACKS.

*Let it go, Dre. Let it go. Karma's a bigger bitch than she is*, I heard a voice suddenly say.

"AHHHH! FUCK!" I growled shaking my head as I made my way into the living room and collapsed onto my couch. In total disbelief, I felt robbed. I felt exposed. I felt exploited. But you know what, like that voice just told me, karma's a bitch. Yeah, I just lost two stacks but whatever. Like I said, I had plenty of money in the bank. In the end, maybe this was another sign that perhaps Trish was far from redemption. That bitch is a loser and she was gonna regret pulling that fast one over on me.

After I managed to calm my anxiety, I suddenly let out a big laugh. Wow! The universe had to have been looking out for me because maybe had I ran down to the police station with Trish's ass and ran Detective Wright that story, I could've been in some serious ass trouble. I didn't even know why I would even succumb and think of such a stupid ass idea in the first place.

Buzz. Buzz. Buzz.

My phone started vibrating. "This probably this crazy bitch right here," I said as I quickly glanced down at my phone and saw that it was Shelly. I quickly answered and said, "Damn, I was just meaning to call you."

"Oh, were you?"

"Yeah. Look, I just wanted to apologize for my behavior the other night. That was totally uncalled for. You were right. I have a lot to learn and I wanna make sure you and I are on the same page when it comes to raising our son."

"No need to apologize, Dre. Actually, that was why I was calling you. I wanted to apologize. I think I was being a bit too judgmental and harsh. I think sometimes I can get a bit carried away, but it's cool though. I'm just glad you and I are on the same page," she said.

"True. Well, I appreciate that. I wanted to swing by later today with Ariyanna. You still got an open schedule?"

"Yeah. I do…I wanna meet that little cutie pie of yours!"

I smiled. "True. How's Junior doing?"

"He's good. I just took him to go get a haircut. He's starting to look more and more like you, I swear," she said.

"Hahah, wow. Ok, well, I'm about to get ready and head out."

"Okay, cool. I'll see you later. And thank you for apologizing. We're gonna be fine. We got this," she said.

"Thanks, Shelly. I'll see you soon," I said and then hung up.

It hadn't even been a second after I hung up that I immediately got a text from Trish. At first, I wanted to immediately delete the message but then I went ahead and read it.

"Nigga you got me all the way fucked up if you think I'm gonna lie 4 u. Thank you for the dick though. And don't even try to get your money back from CashApp. Fuck with me and I'll fuck with you. I'll run down to the police and tell them everything that happened. And we still goin' to court, pussy nigga."

"Wow. Whatever," I said to myself as I quickly deleted the message. She could have the money. I didn't care but as far as Ariyanna was concerned, she could forget about that shit. If this was the game she wanted to play then we can play it alright. Loser ass hoe. Then again, could I blame her for taking off? Nah, not really. I mean, I was kind of putting her in a bind by trying to lie for me. But damn, she could've at least been woman enough to tell me she wasn't down for the game. Truth be told, I probably would've just told her to keep the money and go on about her merry way. But like I said, it is what it is.

I trekked toward my kitchen, wanting to make something quick to eat before I swung over to my mama's place to pick up Ariyanna. As I slid past the dining room table, I saw a mound of mail piling up. It seemed like I hadn't opened any of my shit in some days. I picked up the mound of mail and went through each, sorting through bills and junk. Hell, eighty-percent of this shit was junk anyways. Once I got to the last letter, I saw an envelope from "American Life Mutual Company". The envelope looked legit as hell but I didn't know if this was some marketing material or a real letter from a life insurance company. "What in the hell is this?" I groaned to myself as I opened up the envelope. Quickly scanning the letter, my eyes widened in surprise. Tanisha listed me as a beneficiary on her life insurance policy, according to the letter. And after a thorough review, they were paying out $150,000 to me. "OH SHIT! WHAT THE FUCK?!?!?!?!"

## CHAPTER THIRTY-NINE

**AN HOUR EARLIER...**

"You crazy as fuck if you go and help that nigga," Myron angrily spat at me as I sat on the toilet inside of Dre's guest bathroom. As the shower ran, I started to second-guess once again whether or not I should help Dre out with this shit.

I had to weigh my options and I needed a voice of reason to help me see through this situation. That was why I called Myron to get his quick input. I knew he'd look out for me.

"I know. It sounds crazy as hell, but what am I gonna say, Myron?!? I mean, he even gave me $2,000 and I need the money."

"Man, fuck him and his money! Look, stop being so simple and realize what the fuck you getting yourself into. If you run down to the police station and help that nigga like, you will be an accomplice to obstruction of justice. Niggas get in trouble all the time for this. You interfering with an active police investigation, Trish!"

Thinking more and more about it, obviously, Myron was

right. Shit, I knew this all along. I didn't even know why I even let Dre suck me into this shit. And then he had the audacity to seduce me with weed, Henny and sex. He knew exactly what the fuck he was doing.

"Ughh! I can't believe this. And then we ended up fucking..."

"WHAT?!?!?" Myron screamed. "Are you fucking kidding me right now?!?"

*Shit.* I paused for a moment, biting my lip. *Damn it, Trish! Why did you let that slip out?!?!?* I quickly thought to myself. I knew that would tick Myron the fuck off.

"Ughhh! He seduced me though! He got me high and drunk as fuck and I just gave in. It was supposed to be a part of the plan!"

"OH MY GOD! You two are the dumbest mothafuckas I know on the PLANET! Why would you two even think that shit would be a good ass idea?!? I mean, I get why Dre did it but if you needed the money, why didn't you just fucking call me?!?!? I could've just put the damn fucking apartment deposit on my credit card!"

Damn, Myron was so damn right. "Myron, I was just afraid to call and ask. I didn't want to take money on your house and your kids! And then what if Quisha would've found out?!?"

"Yeah, but still. Fuck Quisha. And fuck them kids. You already know how I feel about you. Look, enough of this shit. Quisha is out and about with the kids with her mama'nem. Meet me at Oak Brook mall in like an hour. I'll pick you up, put you in a hotel and then we'll figure out something then, okay?"

"Okay," I replied as I quickly shot up from the toilet seat with the shower still running. I could hear Dre was still taking a shower in his room, so I quickly made my way back into the guest room, packed the small duffle bag I had with all of my shit and quickly made my way outside of his townhouse.

Although I felt kind of bad, the more I thought about it, the more I realized I needed to keep his money. Yeah, fuck him. That shit was mine now. Why? Well, I considered that shit a tax. For all the bullshit shit that nigga put me through over the years, the least thing he could do was give me two stacks to help me get back on my feet. Besides, I still couldn't fathom that this nigga would try to recruit me to help him lie to the police. Especially over a rape that I now know he probably did...This nigga thought he was so slick but I'd be damned if I was gonna be his fucking accomplice. He had me all the way fucked up.

Once I got a block away from Dre's townhouse, I took shelter at a bus stop, pulled out my phone and quickly ordered an Uber out to Oak Brook. From Hyde Park, it was gonna take me at least an hour to get out that way. Just in time to meet up with my real boo, Myron.

With $2,000 loaded on my card, I knew I didn't have to worry about money anymore. Myron was also gonna front me some cash. God was really looking out for me. Dre was the fucking devil. "Thank you, Jesus," I mumbled to myself when I saw that my Uber was now a minute away.

Some moments later, a gray Toyota Camry with a big ass Uber sign in the windshield pulled up to the bus stop. I stood up from the bench and quickly dashed in the car. Once inside, I pulled my phone out and shot Myron and text letting him know I was making my way out to Oak Brook Mall. Then I pulled up Dre's phone number and blocked him. Fuck him. That nigga was such a dirty, dumb ass, lying piece of shit. Yeah, that $2,000 was mine! And if he tried to threaten me to get it back, I was going to blackmail his ass with proof that he tried to get me to lie. And then I'd lie and tell the police he raped me. Let that fuck nigga try me and it was on.

※

About fifty minutes later, my Uber driver pulled into the vast, damn-near filled parking lot of Oak Brook Mall. It was a big ass mall all the way out in the west suburbs of Chicago. I hadn't been out here in years. Before I ended up in jail, I'd usually went shopping at River Oaks in the South Suburbs or North Riverside, which wasn't too far away from here. Oak Brook was kind of a ritzy ditzy mall. I wondered why Myron chose this place for us to meet up.

Before we hopped off the expressway, I kept wrangling back and forth whether or not I should turn around and make my way back to Dre's place. A part of me still felt so guilty for taking off the way I did. Dre probably did have good intentions. I mean, truth be told, he didn't have to give me the money. And then he let me stay with him. Nigga didn't even really put a protest when I demanded two stacks. Either he was super-guilty for raping that white girl and he couldn't just be real with me and tell me or...he was kind of low-key looking out for me.

But see, I knew niggas like Dre. That nigga was a fraud at the end of the day. All of his shit was a front. Yeah, he may have had a good ass job. A car. A nice ass townhouse. He had a lot going for him, but that nigga was a liar and a dog. Yeah, I made my fair share of mistakes. I definitely wasn't no saint. But Dre? That nigga fucked my best friend AND my sister. What kind of nigga does that? A bum ass, dirty ass, fuck ass clown! That's who! The more I thought about it, the more I realized all along I was being played. As much Dre presented himself as a nice guy, at the end of the day, he was a straight-up pathological liar and a sociopath. That nigga used any and everyone to get his way. Hell, he was even using my daughter to get back at me. The one thing that I couldn't stand the most about him, too, was his mama. That baldheaded bitch always defended her son at every step she could. Bitch never got my side of the story on shit. She always stuck up for him, even when she knew he was dead wrong with all the fucked up things he put me through.

Anyways...

With all of these thoughts about Dre running through my head, I had to send him one last text just to let him know how I really felt. "Nigga you got me all the way fucked up if you think I'm gonna lie 4 u. Thank you for the dick though. And don't even try to get your money back from CashApp. Fuck with me and I'll fuck with you. I'll run down to the police and tell them everything that happened. And we still goin' to court, pussy nigga," is what I wrote to his bitch ass. That'll put the fear of God in his weak ass.

"Which department store are you going to, ma'am?" my Uber driver asked me. Damn, this dude kind of reminded me of Olu. These African niggas were sexy as fuck, I swear!

"Oh, you can drop me off at the front of Macy's," I replied as the driver got deeper into the parking lot. Within a few minutes, we were at the front entrance of Macy's. "Thank you, sir. Have a good day," I said with a big smile as I hopped out of the car and dashed into Macy's.

I quickly pulled out my phone and shot Myron a text. A minute later, he started calling me. "Hey, baby! I'm here!" I said.

"Bitch! Who the fuck are you?!?!?"

My eyes exploded open. This was Quisha. *FUCK!*

"Umm...This is Myron's friend..."

"Wait. This voice sound real familiar," she said.

"Bruh, just give me my phone back!" I heard Myron scream in the background.

Not wanting to get any deeper into what the fuck Myron and Quisha had going on, I quickly hung up. My phone kept vibrating though. Myron, or probably Quisha, was calling me back. I wasn't going to answer.

Standing in the middle of the first level of the store, I closed my eyes and shook my head. This plan was already turning out to be a fucking nightmare. I didn't even know why I let Myron convince me to meet up with him! Ughh! Never again will I fuck with a nigga who already had a bitch.

"I should've known this shit was gonna happen! UGHH!" I groaned to myself, shaking my head. "Fuck it."

My stomach started to grumble. I wanted to get something to eat. Some moments later, I ended up in the food court and was debating what I wanted to grab to eat before I'd head back to the city. I hadn't called Neicy yet to let her know what my plans were gonna be but once I found something to eat, I was gonna give her a ring and tell her I left Hope early. Then again, I grew kind of curious why she hadn't called me all this morning. It was damn near one PM now you would've thought she would've called to check up on me by now. Hrrrrm...I wondered if Dre texted her.

Anyways, scanning my options in the food court, I decided I wanted to get some Sbarro's. I loved their pizza, especially their meatballs. So, after I ordered and ate two slices, some garlic knots and a side of meatballs, I ordered an Uber and headed back to the city. What a fucking waste of thirty dollars though. Shit, I was gonna text Myron and tell him he needed to reimburse me for making a waste of a trip. He was a clown ass nigga, too, truth be told. Nigga couldn't even get a handle over that fat ass Quisha bitch. Gosh, she was so fat, nasty and disgusting. I mean, I knew I didn't look my best at the moment, but damn, that bitch was just so sloppy. I didn't understand why Myron was letting that bitch have so much control over him.

Once I got back onto the South Side, I called Neicy and told her I was on my way. She told me she had been meaning to call me, but she got caught up with her job and didn't have time to hit me up to see how I was doing. She told me she'd be home in about an hour, so I would've needed to waste some time elsewhere before she got back.

So, with about a good thirty minutes to spare, I had to the Uber driver drop me off at the Beauty Mart, which was right around the corner of Neicy's crib. Once he pulled up to the entrance of the store, I hopped out and walked inside. Shit, I hadn't been here in a long ass time. Before getting locked up, I was in this place at least three times a week buying all types of shit.

The wigs I currently had were starting to look a damn mess, and now that I had me some extra coins to spare, thanks to Dre's wack ass, I was gonna buy me a bomb ass lacefront. I could probably get someone to put in on the low. I wondered if my chick, Janyla, was still doing hair. She lived right around the corner from Neicy and she'd only charge me $30 to do my shit.

I walked in the store and was immediately greeted by this older Asian lady. "Good afta-nun," she said in her thick accent.

"Hey, how ya'll doin'?" I replied with a little fake smile.

She didn't respond as I kept walking down the first aisle where all the lacefronts were at. Now that I was about to get back onto my bad bitch shit, my eyes quickly flew to this fly ass, body wavy Brazilian Remy. My real hair was starting to grow back, thanks to this tea tree oil and vitamin e pills I was taking, so there should've been no problems with getting this shit stitched into my head. I looked at the price tag and my mouth dropped. It was on sale for $100! Usually, a 24-inch lacefront went for $400 at the minimum! I grabbed the package and then made my way back up to the front counter.

No one was virtually in the store other than some other lady and her kids.

"Excuse me, ma'am. I wanna go ahead and get this."

"Okay. No problem," she said as she snatched the hair out of my hand and rung it up. "Three-huned and ninety-five dolla you pay," she said.

"Excuse me? How much?"

"Three-huned and ninety-five dolla…"

Suddenly I scrunched my face and said, "But the price back on the rack said $100. Why you charging me $400 all of a sudden?"

"Look, that was special we had last week. Now the price is three-huned and ninety-five dolla. You not want, you go somewhere else. We don't want no problem."

"Well, damn, I don't want problems either, but that's false advertising. If the price changed, ya'll should've changed it back."

"Okay, you just leave ma'am. Leave the store."

Confused, I stood there wondering why all of a sudden this lady was getting flip with me. When I used to come here years ago, the owner, some older man who used to work the counter was so nice to me. I wondered what happened to him. But this bitch right here! Her little nasty ass attitude was starting to bring out the worse in me. I almost had to contain myself from cursing her the fuck out but I'd be damned if she was gonna stand here and belittle me. All because I simply asked a question.

"Ma'am, you don't have to get rude. I just wanted to know why the sudden price difference, but if that's how you feel, I can gladly go and spend my money elsewhere."

"Okay, fine! You want for one-hunned dolla! You have! Just buy and leave!"

"Okay, well, damn!" I replied as I pulled out my wallet and handed her my CashApp debit card. The bitch may have been rude but I wasn't gonna walk away without that weave. She snatched the card out of my hand and then ran it through her credit card machine. That shit right there just made me even more upset but I had to keep telling myself to calm down and that this shit would be over in a few seconds once I got my shit.

"It no go through..."

"What do you mean it didn't go through?"

"IT NO HAVE MONEY! Credit card declined!"

"Naw! You need to run that card again, baby. And you need to lower your voice."

"Okay! You no have money, you need to leave now! Get out!"

Suddenly I flipped out. "Bitch! I don't know who the fuck you talkin' to like that but I will come across that damn counter and choke the fuck out of you, lil hoe! Watch who the fuck you talkin' to, bitch! You up in our neighborhoods selling yo cheap ass shit and trying to price gouge. I should report you mothafuckas!"

"MA'AM! YOU LEAVE NOW! GET OUT!" I heard a male Asian voice from behind me. I turned around, a man, looking no older than fifty was standing there with a wooden baseball bat in his hand. "What you gon do with that? Beat me to death?!?!" I said as I scanned him up down, determined not to go anywhere. I'd be damned if these Chinese muhfuckas were gonna stand there and openly disrespect me.

"Sista girl, it ain't worth it. Just leave," one of the customers, an older black lady, said as she made her way out the door.

"Naw! Fuck that! And mind ya business, bitch!"

"Goodbye!" she said rolling her eyes, making her way out the door.

"I ain't going nowhere until you run my card one more time! I know I got money on it!" I protested but my gut feeling was telling me perhaps Dre quickly contacted his bank and got his money back. If he did that shit, I was definitely running my ass down to the police station to snitch on his stupid ass. Nigga better not fucked me over!

"I'm callin' the muhfuckin' police! Ya'll wrong as fuck!" I said as I grabbed my phone out of my purse. I glanced down and saw Dre sent me a text message.

"Trish...I was really rooting for you but I see you still on the same fuckery. I contacted my bank and quickly got my money back. And FYI, the police called and said that they are dropping the investigation. The white girl lied. FYI – if you think you're gonna get custody or visitation rights over Ariyanna, think again. I'm already lawyered the fuck up. See you in court. Good luck with everything."

My eyes widened with rage, I was ready to explode. "FUCK!" I screamed, stomping my feet on the floor. Suddenly, pain from my hip shot up to my back. "AHHH!"

"LEAVE MY STORE!" the man yelled as he raised the bat at me.

"Man, fuck you!" I glanced over at the lace front sitting on the counter, grabbed it and then tried to dash out the store.

"COME BACK HERE!" the man yelled as he chased after me. But with my hip hurting, I couldn't get that far. Suddenly, the Chinese man ran up behind me, got the bat around my neck and started choking me out.

"GET. OFF. ME!" I cried in midst of choking, trying to pull the back off my neck. But the man just squeezed tighter until we both fell to the floor. Kicking and screaming, I was struggling to breathe as I tried to fight this dude off me.

"YOU STEAL! CALL THE COPS! SHE STEAL!" the man cried.

"YO! GET OFF HER! YOU HURTING HER!" I heard another customer inside the store scream. "HE'S GONNA KILL HER!"

"SHE STEAL! SHE THIEF! SHE NO PAY!" the Chinese woman screamed.

But as the man continued to squeeze the bat around my neck, I could feel my body weaken and my lungs began to squeeze tight, running out of air.

"YOU NO PAY!" the man screamed.

Fighting for my life, I just knew I was gonna die. I still tried to kick and scream, but all of my energy began to quickly dither away. This is it. This is it! You're gonna die! Then I felt my eyes close and all I could see was the depth of eternal darkness.

# CHAPTER FORTY

**TWO YEARS LATER...**

"HAPPY BIRTHDAY TO YOU! Happy birthday to you! Happy birthday, dear Shawn! Happy Birthday to you!"

Cheerfully singing out hearts out, a bunch of us were circled around my one-year-old son, Shawn. Sitting in his high chair, he had his big doe eyes glued to the cake in front of him. He didn't give a damn about anything other than that cake obviously.

"Daddy! Look! Shawn is about to stuff his hand in the cake," Junior yelled as he pointed at Shawn. "Leave him alone, Junior. He's hungry!" Ariyanna chimed in.

It was about thirty of us gathered at this clubhouse at the Kenwood Park District, not too far away from my townhouse. Mama and some of her friends, my kids, friends and family members were watching Shawn dive his tiny hand into the small cake in front of him.

You might be wondering who in the hell I got pregnant this time. Well, Shelly and I fell in love with one another. Shit happened pretty quickly, too. Weeks after we started "co-parenting", one thing led to another and she and I were glued to each other. Next thing you, she was pregnant once again. But this time it wasn't an accident. We had this planned. We wanted to have a bigger family.

As crazy as it may sound, Shelly was truly God-sent. Without her, I would've never made so many remarkable changes in my life. She really forced me to look in the mirror and recognize that I had a lot to learn about women. Granted, she made some crazy ass mistakes herself, which she gladly recognized, but she made me become a better man. She pushed me to finish undergrad and eventually coached me into how to prepare for the LSAT and get into law school. And because of her, I was now in my first year of law school at DePaul. Although I was missing my cousin, Tanisha, every day, I was forever thankful that I was listed as a beneficiary on her life insurance policies. Before that unexpected cash, I didn't even know how I was going to pay for law school. And speaking of Tanisha, it was truly tragic that a year after she got killed by the police, lo and mothafuckin' behold, Candreka's trifling ass did indeed get pregnant by some nigga. And that nigga ended up being a big-time credit card finesser that she was doing dirt with. The two of them got caught up in some shit and up in federal prison for bank fraud. Now her ass was locked up for a decade. I felt so sorry for her kid but that shit was kind of karma for fucking around on cousin.

Oh, and speaking of karma...As I looked at Ariyanna, I kept thinking about Trish. It was so fucked up what happened to her. So fucked up, I didn't even want to think about that shit at the moment. All I knew was that I was thankful that her true intentions came out that day. She showed me that no matter how much you try to help someone, sometimes they have it in them to fuck you over. Granted, I was still wrong for putting her in a bind to help me to potentially lie to the police. However, it was obvious she still had so much resentment for me that she was willing to forgo the possibility of us starting fresh and being good friends and co-parents for our daughter.

Oh well. Life moves on...

I glanced over at Shelly as she stood to my right and said, "Damn, Shawn finne tear that whole cake up!"

"Yeah, I know. He's gonna get diabetes!" she laughed.

I leaned in and planted a kiss on her cheek. "I love you," I said in her ear. "You mean so much to me."

"I love you, too, bae," she replied.

Some moments later after we watched and laughed at Shawn devour his cake, Shelly threw her glance toward the other kids surrounding us. "Okay, kiddies! Do you all wanna go see the magician?"

"YESSS!" the crowd of kids cheered.

"Okay, follow me!" Shelly replied as she led about ten kids over to another part of the clubhouse where a magician was about to put on a show for them.

Mama, a few feet away from us, was talking to one of her friends. I walked over and she looked at me with a grin. "My grandson gon be kind of chubby, I see," she laughed.

"Hahaha, we'll see. I don't know where he got that sweet tooth from 'cuz I don't even like cake like that," I replied.

"You did when you were around that age," Mama said.

"For real? You lying," I grinned back.

"Nah, I ain't. Anyways, Dre, I need to talk to you for a sec," Mama said.

"Damn, I was just about to say I wanted to talk to you as well."

"What about?"

"Just follow me," I said as I gently grabbed her by the wrist and led her over to a corner of the clubhouse where we could have some privacy.

"What's going on, Dre?"

I took a deep breath and then exhaled. "Well, I know I kind of put the cart before the horse. But I'm ready..."

"Ready for what?"

"Marriage. I'm about to propose to Shelly."

Mama suddenly clasped her mouth with her hands, her gaze widened with surprise.

"I know, mama," I said as I began to grow nervous as fuck. My core filled with anxiety. Yeah, I was ready to do this. I had to. Shelly meant so much to me now. Now that we had another child together and we were now living together, it was time to make that move. Truth be told, I should've did this a long time ago, but I wanted to make sure her and I both were in the right space and state of mind. I was ready to spend the rest of my life with her. I pulled out the black ring box from my back pocket, opened it up and showed Mama the big ass diamond ring I bought for bae.

"Dre...I'm so happy for you!" Mama exclaimed as she glanced down at the ring. A tear trickled out of her right eye. "I'm so proud, son! Oh My God! But...Damn...Fuck!"

"What?" I was somewhat confused by her last statement.

"Dre...I should've told you this but I felt soooo bad...I..."

"You what?"

"I invited Trish to the party."

Suddenly my eyes exploded with anger. "Mama! What the fuck?!?" I growled, but low enough so no one else could hear us. Obviously, I didn't want to make a scene. And I definitely didn't want Shelly to see the ring in my hand.

"Why wouldn't you tell me that?!?!?"

"I know, Dre, but listen."

"Mama, this is the same shit you pulled last time! Like, what the hell?!?!?"

Mama closed her eyes and exhaled. "Dre, just listen to me. I know she made a lot of bad mistakes. I mean, really bad mistakes. But she came to my church last weekend and I felt so bad for her. She is so tore up now. When was the last time you even saw her?"

"Shit, the last time I saw her was when she was tried to walk away with my money. Luckily, I quickly called my bank and got my shit back!"

"Damn…Okay…Well, she really ain't doing too well, Dre."

"She said that shit the last time! Now the bitch is healed from cancer. What the fuck she got now? Kidney failure?"

"Damn, how did you know?"

I huffed and rolled my eyes. "Mama, I didn't know. But damn. I can't keep doing this back and forth with Trish. Ariyanna doesn't even know who that woman is! I don't want her around my daughter….AT ALL!"

"Dre…I hear you but listen, Trish just needs a little upliftment right now. She's on dialysis. She needs a kidney transplant. She's already had three strokes. She barely can get around. She just looks so bad now."

"Whatever, mama. Fine. But I don't want her around Ariyanna. Period. Keep her ass at a distance. And I mean that shit. Shelly is Ariyanna's mother now."

"Understandable, Dre. Look, I get it. But trust me, son. When you see Trish, you are gonna be in a world of surprise. It's gonna make you really think about some shit. Trust me…"

"Well…Whatever. I guess…"

"I'm so proud of you though, Dre. And hey, think of it this way. When Trish comes and sees that you're now engaged and about to get married, think of it as karma giving her a glimpse of what could've been possible between you two," Mama said. "Anyways, when are you planning on popping the question?"

"After the magician's show," I replied nonchalantly.

"Okay, cool. Well, I'll get out of your way now," Mama said. "Thank you for everything, Dre." Mama leaned in and gave me a tight hug. "I love you," she mumbled and then walked off.

Although seconds earlier I was fuming with rage, I was now even angrier given that at any moment Trish was going to bumble her ass in here. If that woman tried as much to even give eye contact to my daughter, I swear I was going to let go and go crazy.

Fuck Trish. Yeah, I knew I was an asshole for thinking that but she deserved everything that happened to her. She was the byproduct of her own fucked up decisions. That bitch was a straight-up loser. So, yeah, fuck her.

※

"Alright, this is it! You ready?" the PACE bus driver glanced back in his rearview mirror and asked me.

"Yeah, I'm read," I replied in a mumble. My eyes hazy, I was staring out of the window of the van, ready for the driver to help me out. Since I was now virtually confined to a wheelchair, any time I had to get around the city, I had to have the assistance of a PACE paratransit van.

My life drastically changed that day I tried to run out of that hair store. I swore I thought I was gonna die but God spared my life. Unfortunately, due to the brain damage I suffered from being almost choked to death, half my body was paralyzed. I also suffered extensive kidney damage which led to me having three strokes back to back some months after the altercation.

Although the owners of that hair store were arrested and the store was forced to close down, I didn't escape punishment. Once I was released from the hospital, I was required to spend another six months in jail for violating my probation. Once I got out, ironically, I found myself right back at Hope with Pastor Shirley. At that point, I had no other choice. Monique and I definitely weren't friends anymore. Neicy was done with me. Myron eventually got married to Quisha and then they moved to North Carolina.

I lost everything.

Every single thing. And all because I was impulsive and made one bad, impulsive decision. Luckily, the only thing I didn't lose was my church and the forgiveness of Pastor Shirley. Although she and I had it out that night, she still saw beyond my flaws and allowed me to come back to Hope, no questions asked. I guess she felt so bad for me when she saw my physical condition.

Don't get it twisted though. Now that I was back living at Hope, Pastor Shirley had some serious demands I had to fulfill if I stayed there and worked for her. And one of those demands was that I had to do twenty hours of community service a week. Ironically, that was how I ended up reconnecting with Dre's mama. She saw me at a food bank drive her church was hosting. At first, I didn't think she was going to speak to me when she saw me but she eventually made her way over and we talked. She told me all about Dre, his children, his new girlfriend and how he was now in law school. A part of me wanted to get so mad at her but then I had to check myself and realize Dre was doing him. He was living his life to the best of his abilities, pushing forward with his goals. I, on the other hand, was living out the consequences of my reckless and ratchet behavior. Just as much Dre deserved all the blessings he had coming in his life, I deserved all the hell coming my way.

Once the bus driver wheeled me off the lift of the van, I pulled out my phone and sent Dre's mama a text message letting her know I was at the entrance of the clubhouse. Some moments later, she sauntered outside and then approached me. "Hey, Trish. I'm glad you can make it."

"Hey, Ms. Williams. Thank you for inviting me," I

mumbled. Because of the strokes, my speech was very jumbled.

"Well, let me go ahead and help you in," she said as she walked behind me and began to push my wheelchair. "Thank you," I replied.

We made it inside the foyer and just before we were about to enter through the double doors of the main room of the clubhouse, Dre's mama stopped and looked down at me. "So, I did tell Dre I invited you."

"Okay," I responded.

"So, just to let you know, he's not too thrilled that I invited you but he's okay with it."

"Okay," I replied. "Can..Can I tal—"

"No. Don't even think about it. Dre doesn't want you around Ariyanna. I'm sorry it had to be this way but Dre is very serious. And he means it."

I lowered my head, almost ready to cry. I couldn't even see my own damn child. Hell, I didn't even know what was the exact purpose of me even coming.

"I un-understand," I stuttered. "One day, I hope."

Ms. Williams pursed her lips and didn't respond. "Well, let's go inside. I'mma just wheel you over near the food and you can fix you a plate. We got some ribs, hot dogs, hamburgers, 'tata salad and chips."

"Okay," I responded.

Ms. Williams rolled me in and before we could make it to the food table, Dre ran into us. We all froze out of fear and shock. Well, I froze out of fear. Dre probably was shocked. Shocked that I looked wretched. I had on a hand-me-down purple polka dot dress I got donated to me from the Salvation Army. A blonde wig crookedly adorned the top of my head. This morning when I got ready, I tried my best to adjust the wig, but to no avail, I ended up looking like ET when he was wearing that wig.

"Hey, Trish," Dre muttered.

"Hey, Dre," I replied.

The two of us just kept looking at each other until Dre leaned down and said, "Don't talk to Ariyanna at all or I will ask that you leave. Understand?"

"Okay," I replied. "I ju-just nee-ne-needed to get out of the house," I replied. Fighting back tears, I glanced away and then said to Ms. Williams, "I guess I'mma fix me a hot dog."

"Okay," she replied as she rolled me away. Dre walked off.

After Ms. Williams helped me fix a plate for myself, she rolled me over to a corner by myself. "I'll be back in a few to check up on you," she said. "Okay," I replied. I then glanced down at my plate and began to break apart the hot dog. I slowly lifted my hand and put a piece of it in my mouth. I had to take my time since half my mouth could barely move.

As I ate, from afar, I could see Ariyanna playing with who looked like a few of her friends. She was getting so big. Wow, I felt so disgusted with myself seeing my daughter growing so fast before my very own eyes. I wasn't even there in most of her life to see her get bigger. Seeing her talk and carry on, I could see bits and pieces of myself in her. Eventually, she along with the group of friends trekked closer to me.

"I wanna get something to drink," one of the little girls said. She looked no older than six and had a head full of red hair. As Ariyanna got closer and closer, a part of me was so tempted to call her over and talk to her but I knew if I did, I would be kicked out. So, I kept my calm and kept my gaze latched onto baby girl.

"Who is that over there?" I heard one of the girls say as she looked over at me.

Ariyanna looked over and froze for a second. Oh My God. Oh My God. She was recognizing me. Did she know it was me? I wondered to myself. Damn near shaking in my wheelchair, anxiety bubbled within me. I didn't know what I was going to say or do if she managed to come over and talk to me.

"I don't know. She looks so old. Probably someone's granny," Ariyanna said. "And she has that ugly wig on."

"HAHAHAHAH!" All the girls exploded into laughter as they grabbed sodas out of a cooler and ran back over to another side of the room.

Suddenly I wanted to break down and cry. Someone's granny. Damn, I was so unrecognizable to the point where truth be told, at times I didn't even recognize myself. What was I even doing here? What was the point? This was torture, I kept thinking to myself. I had enough at this point. I was thankful Ms. Williams felt sorry for me and invited me over but this was too much. My own damn daughter thought I was someone's old ass grandmother.

Just before I was about to put my plate down and quietly attempt to roll myself away so I could leave, I saw Dre walk up to the DJ at the far end of the room. He grabbed a microphone. "Attention everyone, I have a very important announcement to make. Shelly, can you come up here with me. Ariyanna and Junior, you come here as well," Dre said. "It's very important."

The chatter coming from adults inside the room came to a halt. Parents instructed their children to quiet down and come huddle next to them. I still remained off in the corner, watching everything from afar. Dre's mama told me about Shelly but this was the first time I'd seen her upfront and in person. Well, not necessarily upfront since I was several feet away by myself, feeling like a complete stranger.

Shelly was holding who I presumed was Dre's one-year-old son, Shawn. She walked up next to Dre. Ariyanna and Dre's other son followed suit. Dre then looked at Shelly and said, "Look at my big family. This is amazing. Who would've thought this would be my life a year ago."

Suddenly everyone in the room began laughing. Seeing that a few of Dre's homeboys (except Myron) was here, I guess they laughed because they knew Dre had a past.

"Anyways, first, I'd like to thank everyone for coming out this afternoon for Shawn's birthday party. Although some people think birthday parties for one-year-olds are pointless, this is also another opportunity I wanted to have to celebrate an important milestone in my life and in Shelly's life." Dre then turned to Shelly and said, "Shelly…You know we started our situation a bit rough. You came out of nowhere unexpectedly and I didn't know what to think of it. But, as time went on, you proved to me that I was capable of being a better man. And for that, I'm forever thankful. And Ariyanna is thankful, too!"

All of a sudden, I could see Dre pull out from his back black box. He got down to one knee and the entire room filled with unexpected gasps. He opened the box and even from several feet away I could see the glimmering of the diamond ring.

Shelly, caught off by surprise, clasped her mouth with one hand as she held Shawn with the other.

"GO 'HEAD, BOY! DO YOUR THANG!" someone from the crowd of parents shouted.

"Shelly, I love you with all of my heart. I want to be with you for the rest of my life. Will you marry me?"

"YES! YES, I WILL!" Shelly cried as Dre rose and then slipped the engagement ring onto Shelly's hand.

I couldn't take it anymore. I had to leave. I felt like this was all one big set-up. Ms. Williams knew good and goddamn well what she was doing by inviting me out here and I felt punked! That bitch knew Dre was gonna propose to this bitch and that was why she invited me out here!

Suddenly, I mustered up so much energy, I wanted to stand up and scream and curse everyone the fuck out. But when I tried to stand up, my right leg just simply couldn't move. It was like I was fighting against gravity. A tear streamed down my face. Fuck it. Using what energy I had, I just looked away and rolled away and out into the hallway of the clubhouse. I was so enraged and nervous, I had to use the bathroom but I had absolutely no idea where it was. So, I just shitted and peed on myself. Luckily, I was wearing some depends. Thank God I had an extra diaper in my purse.

Once I managed to find the women's bathroom, which was all the way down the hallway, I strolled inside and instantly released tears. I rolled into the handicap stall and just sat inside there for twenty minutes, crying my heart out. That could've been me getting proposed to. I could've been Shelly. But I messed up my life. Now look at me. A loser.

A minute later, I heard the bathroom door fly open and then few women stumble inside. I instantly grew quiet since I didn't want anyone to know I had been in here crying my heart out.

"EWW! It smells like shit, ass, piss and fish up in here! What in the FUCK?!?! Good GAWHDT!" one of the women growled. "Anyways, girl. You saw the bitch that was all the way in the corner in the wheelchair?"

"Yeah, girl! Who was that?!? I was so confused on who that was? Who was that, someone's grandma?"

"Naw! Girl, that was Dre's first baby mama! You don't remember that LaTrisha hoe?"

"WHAT!?!?!? Hoe, I know you fuckin' lyin'! Why she looked like that?!? And why the fuck was she even here? Girl, that bitch looked a hot ass mess! What happened to her?"

"CHILE! Where the fuck do I even begin?!?"

## ABOUT THE AUTHOR

QUAN MILLZ is a prolific and profound urban fiction writer known for writing some of the most salacious and scandalous urban fiction thrillers in the contemporary urban fiction space.

Follow Quan Millz on Facebook Instagram for the latest updates on book releases and upcoming film projects!